THE PURPLE DON

AN ILLUMINATI NOVEL

SLMN

SUNDAY, NEW YEAR'S EVE 1989

The wind whipped through the streets of West Chelsea, and the snow felt like confetti as if it were nature's own celebration of the New Year.

It was bitterly cold, but the bright lights of the big city held it at bay, at least for the people waiting in line to get into Pulse, the newest nightclub in Manhattan. The line was a dragon breathing smoke in the freezing air. All colors, all fabrics. Expectant faces hoping to get inside, and more importantly, be seen. Stockbrokers in Italian loafers and leggy models in miniskirts braved both the elements and slight humiliation of waiting with the commoners. All they wanted was in because Pulse was the type of club where mere money couldn't grant you access. You had to be somebody *with* money. So Pulse was the city's litmus test, and the crowd waited eagerly to pass.

Several limos ejected their content: a ball player, an actor, a rock star; but none elicited more than a curious glance, a stretched neck or two, or the crisp pop of the paparazzi.

Until *he* arrived.

The milky white limousine slid to a smooth stop, its back door perfectly aligned with the red carpet that led to the front door of the club. The first to get out was a no-neck Italian behemoth in a black suit and mirrored shades, looking like the underworld version of the secret service. He scanned the crowd quickly and expertly, and—once satisfied—reached back and opened the limousine door. A pair of fishnet stockings and pumps stepped out attached to a curvaceous brunette with hair down to her full, rounded ass. Behind her was her body double in blond, followed by Seth Goldstein, a childhood friend of the main attraction, and a man he called his "Meyer Lansky."

...and then

"That's Joey Diamonds!"

"I love you, Joey!" called several men and women, each of them meaning it.

Joey emerged from the limo in a tailored silk suit designed by Giorgio Armani. His fashion statement was punctuated by his large four-carat diamond pinkie ring, his diamond-encrusted Rolex watch, and a bottle of Dom Pérignon in his hand for good measure. Many men in the crowd wore similar outfits, but it simply looked better on Joey's 6'2" toned frame. Everything looked better on Joey because he had the type of beauty Italian sculptors immortalized in the ancient days. His long feminine eyelashes were offset by a pair of cold yet sparkling grey eyes (from which he got his nickname), a square jawline and a dimpled chin, that looked so perfect it may well have been designed rather than created by God. Androgynous in his appeal, yet worn in a rugged New York City sort of way. He reminded many of a young Travolta.

Joey moved as if he were in a movie scene and all eyes were on him, or as if he were in a book and his every action was detailed in poetic prose. Fluidly, smoothly, with economy of effort. He made it look easy.

"Hey Mikey, how you doin', eh?" Joey greeted the linebacker-built Black bouncer. "Happy New Year, from me to you," he added, handing him the bottle of Dom.

Mikey took the bottle, nodded appreciatively at the label and smiled.

"Thanks a lot, Joey, and Happy New Year to you too."

Someone in the line thought a push would get him further to the door, making the crowd inch too closely to Mikey.

"Back the fuck up! I'm not tellin' you again!" Mikey bassed.

Before disappearing inside with his entourage, Joey turned back and cracked, "And don't hit nobody with that bottle. It'll make me an accessory." Then he winked and hit Mikey with the smile that made even straight men question their sexuality.

Inside, actors partied with rock stars, moguls and models, but it was those in the underworld in attendance that were the stars' stars, because—as the saying goes—everybody loves a gangster. They represent the best and the worst of American success stories. They are who most men want to be and most women want to be *with*, but the awe of the law plus the lack of raw nerve keep them from achieving that goal. Partying with them had this voyeuristic appeal. It was like walking amongst panthers, and Joey had the jungle cat on full display.

At 24, he was becoming the best-known underworld figure in New York, partly because he was the only son of Vincenzo Diamanti, Don of the Diamanti crime family—the most powerful of the five New York families. To the streets, he was a true Diamanti: a cold-blooded killer that committed his first murder before he was old enough to drink. But to the world, he was that *too beautiful to be real* kid with the million dollar smile and diamond eyes. The kid that had an illegal fireworks display on the Fourth of July every year in Brooklyn and regularly brought gifts to the neighborhood old folks home.

He was a true gangster and a gentleman.

The girls headed for the dance floor, while Joey and the rest headed for the dark booth in the back, so they could see without necessarily being seen.

"Joey!"

He heard a female squeal his name like she was sneezing it. He turned around to see a redhead with a pageboy haircut quickly approaching. She gave him a hug and a kiss on the lips.

"Thank you, Joey! I got the part!"

Joey's eyes crinkled and he looked confused.

"The commercial," she reminded him, bubbling with excitement. "Remember, you called the guy who owed you a favor and he—"

Joey chuckled at the recognition.

"Okay, right, the commercial!" he said, still only slightly remembering her. "Congratulations, sweetheart. I know you'll knock 'em dead."

"Deader than dead," she snickered.

"Okay, just when you're a star, don't forget us little people, eh?" he smirked.

She palmed his dick, gave it a squeeze, and whispered in his ear, "There's nothing little about you, Joey. Call me so I can thank you properly, huh?"

"I'll do that," he replied in a soulful whisper.

She sashayed away, looking over her shoulder, doing her best Monroe imitation.

As they slid into the table, Seth remarked snidely, "Six months and she'll be a fuckin' fluffer in a porno."

Joe chuckled.

"Jealous?"

"Should I be?" Seth shot back.

Before Joey could respond, the waitress arrived with a bucket of Dom Pérignon and four glasses. Joey smirked at the irony.

"Courtesy of the guy over there," she said, nodding toward a table with three super cool Italians. They all raised their glasses. Joey raised his.

"Friends of yours?" Seth suspiciously questioned.

"Friends of the *family*. Coupla foot soldiers of the

4

Genoveses," Joey replied as he popped the Dom. He looked up at his bodyguard, Rocco.

"Rocco, do me a favor. When nobody's looking, bring me a real drink, eh? Who the fuck drinks this stuff?" Joey poured himself and Seth a flute full, but set it on the table, untouched.

Seth looked at him, and he knew he wanted an answer to his earlier quip. Instead, Joey changed the subject.

"So tell me about the Russians..."

Seth knew what he was doing, but let it go and replied, "They're in Brighton Beach."

"Of course."

"Of course, but the brunt of the operation is in Israel. They call it ecstasy, or X for short."

"Sounds sexy," Joey snickered as Rocco slid over to the bar.

"It's 'sposed to do just that. Designer drug. It's been out on the West Coast for a while, but now they wanna bring it back East and work the clubs," Seth explained.

Joey listened as Rocco brought him back a double vodka.

"They say they can manufacture it for twenty cents a pill and getting it out of Israel is no problem, but they need your connects at JFK to get it through customs—not to mention the blessing to operate in Manhattan."

"But the Gambinos control the clubs. Not us," Joey reminded him.

"The clubs, yes; Manhattan, no. Remember, these are Jews," Seth replied. "They cross their T's and dot their I's. They know nothing moves through the City without the Diamanti approval. They know how it works, and that's why they're offering it to you."

Joey nodded and sipped his drink.

"Whaddya think about this X? Will it move?"

"People on the Coast swear by it. They say it makes you wanna fuck all night," Seth answered, eyeing the nearby men like he wanted to test it out *right now*.

"Yeah? Maybe we oughta try it," Joey cracked with a wink.

"Don't try to appease me," Seth shot back with a straight face but a glint of a smile in his eye.

"What?" Joey asked, playing dumb.

"Anyway," Seth began, ignoring the feint. "I think we can get a three, maybe even a five-year run before the cops will even put it on their radar. It's harmless; not like crack and the Blacks."

"Okay, I'll run it by the old man. If he gives the nod, set up a meeting," Joey told him.

Seth nodded, downed his flute, then refilled it.

"So now, you wanna test me? What's eatin' you?"

Before Seth could answer, Joey's beeper went off. Joey reached down to look at it.

"Irony," Seth replied sarcastically.

"Huh?" Joey asked, listening with only one ear.

"Nothing." Seth said, draining his drink.

"Naw, it's the old man," Joey informed him, with slight confusion in his tone.

"It's fuckin' three in the morning... I'll be right back."

Joey slid out of the booth and headed for the bathroom hallway. As he approached, a short bull of an Italian guy came staggering out of the bathroom and bumped Joey hard. Joey waited half a beat for an apology, but the guy had already turned to walk off.

"Hey," Joey chuckled with his palms up and a shrug. "What, am I invisible?"

"Naw, just in the fuckin' way," the drunken bull spat.

Joey chuckled again, but this time it sounded more like boiling water. The bull was too drunk to detect the difference. Joey took one step closer.

"Okay, fair enough. So I'll apologize. Everybody's happy," the bull snorted.

"Yeah? I got a better idea. Why don't you suck—"?

6

That was all he got out, because the punch Joey threw knocked the other half of the sentence right back down his throat. The punch dazzled the bull, but didn't drop him.

He charged at Joey with a drunken bellow, but Joey easily sidestepped him, grabbed him by the back of his hair and slamming his face into the wall, breaking his nose on contact. After seeing blood, Joey went into a trance—slamming the guy's face into the wall three more times, until he slid down the wall, unconscious and leaving a trail of blood all the way down. The ever-vigilant Rocco was on his way before the first punch was thrown, but by the time he got there, the guy was already asleep at Joey's feet.

"What happened?" Rocco asked.

Joey shrugged with a smirk. "I was in the way."

"Who is he?"

"A fuckin' nobody. A piss ass Bonanno."

"You want me to take care of it?" Rocco asked, looking Joey in the eyes.

He knew exactly what Rocco meant.

Joey looked down on the guy with the power of life and death. Wondering if it was the same feeling Caesar had when he stood above the vanquished gladiators in the colosseum, deciding which way to turn his thumb. Joey adjusted his cuffs, chuckled and replied, "Eh, it's New Year's Eve. Let em' wake up so he can tell his friends how he got knocked on his ass by Joey Diamonds."

They laughed and walked away.

Joey gathered up the entourage to leave and found that instead of two girls, there were now six. He made a joke about the Pied Piper and made everyone laugh as they stepped out into the frigid early morning air. As they approached the limo, a black tinted Lincoln pulled up and the passenger side window went down. It was one of his father's men.

"Ay Joey, the old man wants to see you."

Joey thought about it, but stopped short of climbing into the limo.

"Yeah, I know. I was just about to go somewhere and call him," Joey replied.

"No, he says he wants to see you now," the man emphasized.

Joey glanced at Rocco, then Seth, who looked away. Joey raised his eyebrows as if to say, "How should I know?" Then he turned to the Lincoln and said, "Yeah, okay; let's go."

The back door was opened from the inside. Joey disappeared inside, closing the door as the Lincoln pulled off.

Vincenzo Diamanti stood at the window of his study, looking over the Diamanti Estate in Staten Island. From his window, he could see the waters of the Upper Bay, and it made him think of simpler times. He was 68 years old, yet he looked 48, with a craggy type of handsomeness one might expect to find amongst longshoremen and dockworkers.

Vincenzo had massive hands and had actually made his bones in the Brooklyn Naval Yards, running the union rackets, when the Diamanti family was the weakest of the five New York families. Under his father, Anthony Diamanti or "Pizza Tony," the Diamantis were basically confined to Brooklyn and the petty rackets. But during the Mafia wars of the late '60s and early '70s, Vincenzo came into his own and proved himself a modern-day Caesar when it came to strategizing the demise of his adversaries. When finally the smoke cleared, the Diamantis sat atop the five-family hierarchy and Vincenzo ruled with an iron fist, minus the velvet glove. He was a man who fully understood the power of violence, which made even his allies fear him. Old age arguably mellowed him, as his plethora of accomplishments left him nothing else to prove. Now he spent his time with his beloved wife of 48 years and groomed his son to take over the family. That is until...

———————

Nothing about this situation sat right with Joey. The abruptness of their arrival, the brusqueness of their demand, the terse silence as they rode. In that instant, on that long trip in the dark of night, Joey imagined how it would be when the end came. Stone-faced, hidden in passing shadows. A silent death. His only question was, would his own father be the one to give the nod?

They pulled the Lincoln into the circular driveway that wrapped around an exquisite marble fountain of Poseidon. A pristine replica of the one in Italy. The house sat above the Todt Hill section of Staten Island—one of the five highest points in New York, and it was built to look like it owned the entire view.

When he went to knock, the front door was opened by Vito, his father's trusted doer and bodyguard of the past twelve years. Whenever Joey saw Vito, it always made him smile because Vito was the spitting image of Yogi Berra. Joey stepped inside, gave Vito a tight hug and hit him with a Yogi-like line that he always did. "It's like déjà vu all over again. How you doin', Uncle Vito?"

"How are ya, kid?" Vito returned, reciprocating the hug warmly.

"You tell me," Joey probed. Whenever he got in trouble as a kid, he could count on Vito to gauge the old man's mood for him.

Vito shrugged.

"I don't know nothin'. The old man says to bring you directly in."

Joey smirked.

"Good ol' Uncle Vito. Never learned to whistle 'cause he kept his mouth shut, huh?"

Joey punctuated the crack with a snicker, but it was only to cover his nervousness.

Something wasn't right.

Vito walked Joey to the study, where Vincenzo stood at the window, looking out onto simpler times. When he didn't acknowledge their presence, Vito announced, "Boss, Joey's here."

"I'm old, Vito, not blind," Vincenzo replied in his gravelly voice, finally turning to look at his son Joey. "Vito, you can go."

"Okay, boss. See you in the mornin'," Vito replied, closing the door behind him as he left.

Vincenzo stared at his son, which to Joey felt like an eternity. It was like Vincenzo was weighing Joey's soul. It made Joey uncomfortable to be scrutinized so intently, yet still not able to read his father's poker face.

"What's wrong, Pop?" Joey questioned with genuine concern.

"What's wrong?" Vincenzo answered, picking up a manila envelope from his desk. He slowly rounded it and approached Joey. "This is what's wrong."

He extended the envelope to his son. Joey looked at it, and a stinging premonition told him what was inside. He felt sick to his stomach. Joey could feel his fingers starting to tremble, but he was damned if he was going to give the old man the satisfaction of seeing that, so with supreme effort, he controlled the tremor by looking directly at his father as he held out his hand.

"Take it," Vincenzo told him with quiet authority.

Joey took it. He unclasped the envelope as his father watched him intently. He opened it and let the contents slide out into his hands. They were black and white glossy photos, the kind a private detective would take. They were of Joey and Seth locked in a naked embrace. Another was of them, entangled on the bed. Another and another followed, but Joey already stopped looking. He had never felt more ashamed in his life. He wished he didn't have to look into his father's eyes, the eyes of the man he loved and idolized; the man he wanted to be. But at the same time, he had to look into his father's eyes *because* he loved and idolized him. But when he looked up, all he saw was unmasked disgust. Where there had once been pride when he looked at his son, there was only contempt. Cold pure contempt.

"Pop, I'm so—"

Joey began, but that was all he got out.

He saw the backhand coming, and if he wanted, he could have easily dodged it, but he took the harsh blow—powerful enough to stagger him and draw blood from his mouth, yet not impactful enough to hurt him. His father's disappointment had already done that.

In spades.

"My own flesh and blood," Vincenzo boomed, his voice trembling with rage. "My own flesh and blood, a fuckin' frocio!" His father repeated: "Frocio!"

Just hearing the word thunder from his father's mouth hit him like a second blow.

His father repeated: "Frocio!"

It was the word he and his friends used to call guys who were too sissy to play football, and instead wanted to jump rope. The guys who threw a ball like a girl and took Home Ec. instead of Shop. *They* were as his father repeated "frocios," not him. But hearing the word come out of his father's mouth made him question his whole premise.

"Pop, let me explain," he began in Sicilian, but his father cut him off and bassed, "No! Speak to me in *their* tongue, speak to me as a stranger!" Vincenzo raged back in Sicilian.

Language became an unbridgeable chasm between father and son.

"Who told you?" Joey questioned in English.

"Does it matter?" Vincenzo shot back in Sicilian. "All that matters is what you are and what you were."

Joey braced himself. "And what's that, Pop?"

"What you are is this!" Vincenzo barked with cold venom as he motioned toward Joey, then added with a catch in his throat, "What you were...was my son."

Although his demeanor did not change, Joey could see his father struggling to maintain his composure for the subtle squeezing of his right fist.

"You...are no longer welcome...in my home. Your mother doesn't know. When you want to see her, you will tell me in advance. Arrangements will be made. As for...the family...your crew...do they know about you?"

"No." Joey said, almost a broken whisper now.

"They loyal to you?"

"To a man," Joey replied, finding at least a tiny amount of pride amongst the shame. But they would become words he would regret.

Vincenzo simply nodded pensively, then added ominously in Sicilian, "The affairs of this family are now closed."

Joey knew exactly what his father was saying: that he would never become a Made Man. It all felt like an excommunication.

"Pop, I'm sorry," Joey blurted out, not knowing what else to say.

To the naked eye, Vincenzo did not respond to the anguish in his son's voice. "And now...I'm gonna turn my back. Don't be there when I turn around."

The hardwood floor subtly creaked as Vincenzo shifted his weight and turned his back to his son.

Joey stood there, glued to the spot. Every fiber in his body wanted to fall to his knees, grasp his father's leg and beg his forgiveness. Something told him deep down that his father would relent, but he would never respect him. The only thing that could earn his father's respect was what he did next...

With tears streaming down his cheeks, he turned and walked out.

Vincenzo listened to the receding steps with an equally heavy heart. His glance fell on the pictures. He glanced at the blazing fireplace to his left. He tossed the pictures into the fire, then quietly watched his son burn.

SATURDAY, JANUARY 4TH 1990

"You want to talk about it?" Joey asked.

"No."

"You sure?"

The only answer Seth received was the steady percussion of the speed bag as Joey worked it over. Seth knew he had a lot on his mind, because he always worked out harder on mornings when something was up.

They were in Joey's studio apartment in the DUMBO section of Brooklyn. His floor to ceiling windows looked out onto a panoramic view of the Brooklyn Bridge.

"You can always take it out on me." Seth joked. "Haven't you heard? The battered look is in for the '90s"

Joey couldn't help but smile. Seth always knew what to say to make him laugh, in spite of himself.

"So what are you going to do? Bottle it up inside and just let it eat its way out? You think you're the only one to have their family turn their backs on them? My mother *and* father read the *k'vod hamet* for me, the Jewish way of honoring the dead."

Joey, shaking his head, went from the speed bag to the weight bench, then took off his shirt and tossed it aside as he sat down. He listened to Seth's every word, but didn't respond. Part of him wholly blamed Seth and the other part felt guilty because he did.

"I'm good," Joey replied with a grunt as he lifted the 225-pound barbell and began doing vigorous reps.

Seth smirked and shook his head.

"You're not a rock, Joey," he remarked, watching him work out, and admiring the flex of his chest and the way his six-pack tightened with each rep. "You may look like one, but you're not."

Joey put the barbell back in the rack with an exasperated sigh.

"Look, I said I'm fine, okay? What's done is done. I just...I don't...I don't know what I'm gonna do now."

Seth sat down on him, straddling his lap.

"What do you mean, what are you going to do? You're Joey Diamonds; you can do whatever you want!" Seth smiled, trying to lure Joey's ego out of its funk. "Maybe you could try out for the Yankees. They'd love a switch hitter."

Joey instantly got the joke and laughed.

"And that face," Seth added, leaning down and framing Joey's face with his hands, then kissing him hard on the lips, with a flirtatious flick of the tongue. "On Broadway? Forget about it; you'd be the toast of the town! Believe me, there's a million people that would love to hire Joey Diamonds."

"Hire?" Joey echoed with disgust. "Work a job like the crumbs? I'd rather be dead first."

"What's wrong with being average?"

"Being average—" Joey shot back, then moved to get up.

Seth stood up and Joey went to the kitchen counter to get his bottle of water. He took a sip and said, "Remember that *Superman* movie when he gave up his power to be a regular guy?"

"Vaguely," Seth replied, nonplussed.

"Yeah, well he did. He gave it all up for Lois Lane. I remember thinking, 'This guy's an asshole!' He gave up the ability to leap tall buildings in a single bound for a *broad*! But *in the end*, he came to his senses. Of course, they made it seem like he had to come back and save the world, but that was bullshit, because the bottom line is, *nobody* wants to be a regular guy. Not even a regular guy," Joey concluded.

Seth approached him.

"Then let's get out of the city. Get out of your father's shadow and plant your own flag," Seth suggested.

Joey looked at him curiously.

"We? You love New York. You said you could never live anywhere else."

"Hey Paisano," Seth cracked, doing his best De Niro, "We're in this together. You're the Don and I'm your consigliore. We'll remake the *Godfather*, so instead of Sonny buffing the bride's maid, he'll be buffing Tam!"

Seth could tell that Joey was touched by his profession of solidarity, but he didn't let it show. His father had instilled in him to never let anyone get close to you, especially your enemies.

Instead of words, Joey answered him with a kiss that Seth readily devoured. When they broke the kiss, Seth looked deep into the other man's eyes and said, "I love you, Joey."

Joey winked and replied, "I know you do."

It used to bother Seth that Joey never said "I love you" back, but he had come to accept the fact that he wasn't ready to say it, even though he knew he felt it.

"I'll call you."

"Where you goin'?"

"To feed Mitzy. I haven't been home in two days; I'm probably a cat murderer by now," Seth joked as he put on his coat. "But think about what I said, okay? This could be a good thing."

Joey frowned. "A good thing? How about that!"

Seth gave him a forlorn look, mustered a smile then shrugged, "Wishful thinking."

Seth walked from the room, closing the door behind him, leaving Joey contemplating his fate...

Leave New York? Plant the flag? Get out of his father's shadow? The last thought made him shake his head. How could he get out of his father's shadow, when the old man's tentacles expanded like a compass in all directions? The five families of New York were the epicenter of the Mafia, controlling families as far away as California and Canada, and the Diamanti family was at the epicenter of the five families. Not since Carlo Gambini had one boss been closer to being the Boss of Bosses like Vincenzo Diamanti. It was often said that if the old man stood up and spread his arms, his shadow would cover half the country. Getting out of his father's shadow couldn't be done geographically; it had to be done willfully. At the moment, Joey didn't have the will. All his life, he had idolized his father; wanted to be his father. He wasn't only in his father's shadow; his father's shadow was in him.

He grabbed the remote and turned on the TV. The news popped on. He went to the refrigerator, only half listening, until he heard:

"Yes, Carol, I'm here in Brooklyn, where the New Year has come in with a bang. Three, actually. I'm in Sheep's Head Bay, the scene where the third gangland style hit has taken place."

Joey's ears perked up, as he turned to the TV. Bob Weather of Channel 4 News was standing in front of Smiley's, a bar that Joey knew very well.

"Police are tight-lipped, but we know that one Thomas Maselli was gunned down outside of this bar. His murder happened only minutes after James Braza and an unidentified woman were murdered execution-style in a Queens motel. The third man, yet to be identified, was shot at a stoplight on

Avenue U. Sources close to the police say that too is believed to be mob-related..."

Joey couldn't believe his ears. He stared at the screen. Maselli and Braza were a part of his crew, and if the third man —yet to be identified was killed on Avenue U—his gut told him it was Fat Nicky Boselli, another member of his crew. The first words to pop into his head were his father's:

"They loyal to you?"

"To a man."

With those three words, he had signaled their death warrant. His father always believed in a scorched Earth approach. Vincenzo didn't believe in leaving bad blood to rot. If Joey's men were loyal to him, with him gone, it would leave a seed in their hearts that any ambitious Capo could exploit against the Boss, and Vincenzo brooked no dissention. Not to mention the fact that the crew may have known his son's dirty secret, and that would've embarrassed the Don. Joey read his father's train of thought like a musical composition, the logical harmony forming the melody of murder. Joey knew that since three of his men were dead, the other two were as well; they just hadn't been found yet. And if his crew was dead, then...

Without hesitation, Joey grabbed his keys and his gun and shot out of the door, wearing nothing but sweatpants and sneakers. He flew down the stairs, three at a time, and then burst out into the freezing New York morning. His breath visible as he ran, jumping into his black Cadillac Eldorado and lurching into traffic. The blanketing snow and ice sloshed under his wheels as he sped along the street, heading for Atlantic Avenue, the route he knew Seth would take home, and the route he knew the killer would take...waiting for Seth. He thought about the photos and the type of surveillance it would have taken to get them. They had been watching, so if they could shoot pictures, they could shoot bullets. The inevitability of his thought made him mash the gas, making illegal turns on right, and bursting through red lights, the angry blare of cut off drivers' horns left in the wake of the intersections.

He was just in time to be too late.

As he turned onto the street, he saw Seth's red Saab 9000 at the light, beside a brown work van with its roll door wide open and the sounds of multiple guns exploding simultaneously. The barrage of bullets rained with such force that the Saab was rocking on its axle, while Seth's body danced in the passenger seat as if he was being juiced with live electricity.

"Nooo!" Joey roared furtively, as he sped down the block. By the time he was in range, the van was skidding off. He pointed his pistol out of the window and let off shot after shot, skipping to a halt behind the Saab and continuing his assault as he climbed out of the car. He managed to bust out the van's back window as it disappeared around the corner. His gun sat back on its haunches, empty and smoking. He watched the van disappear around a second corner when he turned back to Seth. He knew at first sight that he was gone.

"Fuck!" Joey grumbled at the heavens. "Fuck!"

He looked through the shattered windshield at what was left of Seth's face. He staggered, dropped his gun and grabbed his head with both hands. The world seemed to spin, faster and faster, making everything around him seem out of focus. He opened the car door and Seth's body leaned out. Joey caught him in his arms.

"I'm sorry...I'm so sorry," he stressed, cradling his dead lover in his arms. In the distance, he heard sirens. His mind told him to go, but his heart told him to never leave. Reluctantly, he obeyed his mind. He gently laid Seth's lifeless body on the cold ground. He kissed the top of his head.

"I...I," he mumbled, but hearing the sirens come closer, he didn't attempt to finish his statement.

He started for the car, remembered the gun, went back to

get it. Then he jumped in the car and sped off, heading straight for his father's social club.

———————

The Italian American Social Club was on Pleasant Avenue in Harlem, in the heart of the Italian enclave. His father ran his empire from a modest office in the back of the spacious building. Made Men and their associates came in to play cards, drink coffee, and wreak havoc on the rest of society.

Joey skidded up, double-parked, and left the door open as he stalked across the street—blood covering his neck, chest, and sweatpants. Standing outside was Frank D'Amato, who was called Frankie Shots, and four of his goons. Frankie had just become the underboss of the Diamanti family after his father's trusted underboss, Teddy Ruggiero, had died. At 38, Frankie was one of the most feared gangsters in New York. He had risen quickly through the ranks, from street thug to button man to Capo, and then he was underboss to the most powerful family in New York.

He and Joey hated one another.

On Joey's part, it was because Vincenzo treated Frankie like a second son, and wanted Joey to look at Frankie as an older brother. Vincenzo wanted Frankie to take Joey under his wing. They both resisted, because—on Frankie's part—he knew he was being asked to groom the next Don of the family, but Frankie had too much ambition for that. So he relished in his current role as he watched Joey cross the street.

Joey stepped on the curb and one of the goons got in his path. Joey shoved him out of the way.

"Get the fuck outta my way," Joey spat, as the other three goons closed rank.

"Hey hey, Joey, calm down, okay? Calm down," Frankie told him from the third step of the club.

"Then get the fuck outta the way, Frankie! I'm here to see the old man," Joey seethed.

Frankie stepped down and approached Joey. Flatfooted, Frankie was barely 5'5", but he was built like a bull.

"I can't let you in, Joey. The old man says he doesn't want to see you, okay? So why don't you go home, clean up, eh?" Frankie advised him.

"How'd he know I was coming, Frankie, huh? How'd he know I had a reason to come?" Joey surmised, then made another attempt to go in. One of the goons put his hand on Joey and he pushed it away. Out of fear and reflex, the goon reached inside his coat.

"Oh, you gonna shoot me, Liuni? Huh?" Joey growled, getting in Liuni's face. "You fuckin' cock sucker, I'll make you eat that gun!"

"Hey Joey, you're way outta line here," Frankie warned, but kept his tone friendly. "We're just doing what the old man said, okay? Just following orders. It ain't our fault."

Joey looked at Frankie, and the glint of a smile in his eyes told Joey all he needed to know.

It was Frankie.

It made perfect sense, and he cursed himself for not seeing it sooner. But one thing still eluded him. How did Frankie know?

Now that Joey's eyes burned with recognition, Frankie let his shine with acknowledgement. The two men eyed each other intently until Frankie—like the winner he felt he was—bowed out gracefully.

"Go home, kid." This weather...could be the death of ya."

Joey smirked coldly at the implication, and then replied, "Whatever you say...Boss," turning and walking away.

TUESDAY, JANUARY 16TH 1990

Joey surveyed the scene from behind his mirror-tinted sunglasses. Seth had a large turnout for his funeral, but it was the absence of his parents that rang an ominous tone in Joey's mind. Their shame of who he was overshadowed the natural love of parent to child, making Joey wonder: would the same be true of his father? Once the tables were turned, would Vincenzo do the same? Joey mingled politely with the crowd. Faces blurred together, voices droned, merged and murmured around him. Nothing could pull him from his cocoon.

Until he saw her...

She could have been Italian, Latin, Black, Egyptian, or Asian. Her smooth exotic skin tone was every ethnic fantasy. But in reality, she was half Sicilian and half Brazilian, mingling the best genes of the races, passionate in love and blood. They constrained and complemented each other, creating a woman irresistible to forget after one glance. Although she wore a leather trench and moved demurely because of the setting, Joey could tell by her stride that she had never been tamed, and something primal swelled and made him determined to do just that. As she approached, her eyes never left his, her gaze seemingly reading his mind and challenging him to try, uttering "I dare you," with her eyes.

I dare you.

When she got close, he cracked a dimple and said, "Te Amo."

She smiled brightly, then enveloped him in a warm hug.

"You remembered me," she said, with appropriate surprise.

"How could I forget?" Joey retorted.

They broke the hug and Joey stepped back so he could look at her.

"Well, for starters...the last time you saw me I was a dirty little tomboy, twelve years old, playing football and fighting boys," she giggled.

"And as I remember, you had a pretty good left hook," he chuckled, and they shared a laugh. "But it's the eyes...they never change."

"No, they don't," she agreed, taking off his shades and putting them on to conceal the glint in her green eyes. "Joey Diamond Eyes."

Joey smiled.

"That was a long time ago. Now, they just call me Joey Diamonds."

There was an awkward pause as the realization set in that they had both momentarily forgotten why they were there, being overwhelmed with their reunion.

"It was devastating to hear what happened to Seth," Te Amo said, shaking her head and taking off Joey's sunglasses.

"Yeah," Joey responded. "He uhh, he didn't deserve this."

"I know what you mean," she replied, understanding the context completely.

"Were you...there?"

Joey looked at her without saying a word, but she comprehended his silence.

"Well listen, I'll umm, I'll be in town for a couple of days," she began, going in her purse, pulling out a pen and giving him her number. "I would really like to get together while I'm here."

"Yeah, I'd like that too," he replied.

"Yeah," she chirped, flashing a smile to rival his. "Then I'll look forward to your call. Nice seein' you again...Diamond Eyes," she said with a wink and walked away.

He watched her disappear into the crowd, then turned his attention back to Seth's rose-laden coffin, as the cemetery workers prepared to lower it. It was in that moment when he realized that Seth was truly gone. He thought about the nature of funerals and realized they weren't for the deceased; they were for the living to give them closure, and it made him smile. It made him see that the part of Seth that was dead was the part he could never possess, but the part he had, no one could ever take away.

The memories.

Joey remembered when he first met Seth. He was 22 and Seth was 20, working at the Sam Goody in Joey's area. The manager was into Joey for a few thousand, so he had stopped by to see him. Watching the cashier as he waited for the manager to make a phone call, he noticed a steady stream of people, mostly teens, come up and make transactions without any merchandise changing hands.

"What's with the kid? The cashier?" Joey inquired.

"He's a good kid, why?"

Joey could tell, whatever was going on, the manager didn't know about it. So he waited until he was about to leave and approached Seth.

"Maybe you don't know, but any rackets 'round here, I get a piece too," Joey said smoothly with a smirk.

"I don't know what you're talking about," Seth replied, playing dumb.

"No?" Joey smiled. "Then maybe I'll take it up with your boss and straighten it all out."

That got Seth's attention.

"Or maybe me and you, we can work it out, eh? So what you got? Pills? Pop Rockers?"

"Tickets," Seth reluctantly admitted.

"Tickets?" Joey echoed.

Seth sighed, exasperated with Joey's lack of understanding.

"Concert tickets! You know, shows?"

"You must have half the tickets stashed back there, huh? How about two tickets for Springsteen."

"Three hundred bucks."

Joey whistled.

"That's pretty steep. How about no charge? Ask around about me and I'll...I'll see you tomorrow," Joey told him and stepped off.

The next day, he returned.

"So how about those Springsteens?"

"I asked around and nobody seems to know who Joey Diamond Eyes is. Three hundred bucks," Seth replied, suppressing a smirk.

Joey found the crack hilarious.

Joey got the tickets (for a negotiated $150) and learned that Seth had found a way to bootleg concert tickets. As an early adherent to computers, Seth proved himself a wiz, and for the next 18 months, the two of them made close to seventy grand bootlegging concert tickets, Broadway tickets, and Yankees tickets.

Joey would find out that the ticket scam was just the tip of the iceberg, because Seth had a helluva financial mind. Joey started to keep him around more and more, and the two of them grew closer. Joey found out that Seth was gay when he tried to set him up with a girl.

"Whaddya mean, no? Didn't you see her? The broad looks like fuckin' Madonna! I'm talkin' the Holy Mother herself! She's heavenly! Fuck you mean, no?"

"I don't like girls, Joey," Seth answered, watching his reaction.

"Don't like girls? What, you're a fuckin' frocio?"

"I prefer the word *gay*, but if you want to be an Italian asshole, then yeah. I'm a frocio!"

Joey was driving at the time when he told him. He got to a light and kind of looked at Seth curiously. It wasn't like Seth wore his sexuality on his sleeve like he was flaming, but it would've been obvious had Joey really paid attention. The fact that he hadn't paid attention both cheered and upset Seth at the same time. Cheered because Joey had simply accepted him, no questions asked. It was upsetting because he wanted Joey to see him for him, since Seth was beginning to fall in love with Joey. After a few moments that seemed like forever to Seth, Joey simply shrugged and said, "Okay...fuck it. I'll boff the broad," and accelerated on the green.

Several weeks later, their relationship blossomed.

They were in Seth's apartment, counting money from the night's take of the ticket scam. Seth sat on the couch and Joey sat on the love seat, the money all over the coffee table between them. Seth had been thinking about it since he first laid eyes on Joey, but he felt emboldened by the fact that Joey hadn't treated him differently since he found out he was gay. He had even joked with Seth once while they were playing pool. Joey was bent over the pool table when he looked back over his shoulder at Seth and said, "Hey, don't stand behind me with that stick. Makes me nervous."

Seth's heart told him Joey knew how he felt. He had to know. The way he looked at Joey, Joey had to know the vibe he was sending. He had to feel it. But his head told him it was just Joey being his self-centered self. He didn't see any of Seth's advances because he didn't see Seth. He was just a pawn in Joey's world, a moneymaking pawn that had no separate existence from his assigned function.

But Seth had to know. He was tired of guessing, of assuming, of fantasizing. He had to know, even if Joey cursed him out or worse. And make no mistake, it could be worse. He knew Joey was a cold-blooded killer. What if his advances were taken as disrespect to his Italian manhood? What if he broke some Sicilian code of honor between friends?

At that time, eyeing Joey across the coffee table, desire trumped reason and discretion, as Seth blurted out, "I wish I was a girl."

Joey, without looking up or losing count replied, "What are you talkin' about?"

Committed to his course of action, Seth swallowed a dry lump and answered, "So you'd like me...like how you like them."

Joey looked up and flashed the smile that always made Seth want to strip and said, "I like you just the way you are, eh? Now, pass me that bag."

"No," Seth said firmly, standing up. "I'm serious, Joey, I'm not playing around, okay? I don't want you to like me; I want you to want me like I want you. I want you to do to me what you do to them."

Joey sat back in the love seat, the large stack of money still in his right hand.

"Wow...Seth, umm, listen... You're a good friend. Really. But I don't know what to say. I'm not...like that."

"No?" Seth smirked, the energy in the room telling him not to let up or let go. He slowly rounded the coffee table, encouraged by every step he took and that Joey didn't halt. "You're sure? You're sure you've never thought about me the way I think about you? Never? You're not curious?"

Joey smirked and replied, "Seth, look who you're talking to. I fuck a different broad damn near every night. What's to be curious about?"

By the time Joey had finished his comment, Seth was

standing between Joey's legs as he sat back, masculine and reclined.

"Power," Seth purred. "To see if the power you have over a woman you have over men, too. That's the power only gods have, Joey. Who wouldn't want that?" Seth asked rhetorically, as he sank to his knees, making sure to never lose eye contact with Joey. It was like he was a snake charmer and Joey's was the snake. One false move and he knew he'd be devoured. Seth uttered the one word that spoke directly to Joey's ego. Power. Truth be told, he hadn't looked at Seth like that. He'd never looked at Seth, period. Like everything else in his life, Seth was simply a means to an end, but seeing him for the first time and seeing him eye level with his crouch was intoxicating and an undeniable turn on.

"Yeah, you're right," Joey answered, licking his lips. "Who wouldn't want that?"

Seth unzipped his jeans and freed his nine-inch rod that was stretching the fabric to get out. He slid his dick in his mouth and curved Joey's toes in his shoes.

"Fuck," Joey groaned, seizing a fistful of Seth's hair and began thrusting his hips and fucking his mouth.

Unprepared for all nine inches, Seth gagged until he relaxed this throat to accommodate Joey's length. Seth sucked and bobbed furiously, eager to feel Joey's load coat his throat, but Joey pulled out and gruffly demanded Seth to "turn around and bend over."

Seth eagerly complied, dropping his pants around his ankles and gripping the arm of the couch. Joey spread the pucker of his asshole with his thumbs, then thrust his hard, thick dick deep inside. Seth's knees weakened with delicious pleasure as he began to thrust back, meeting Joey, thrust for thrust.

"Yes, Joey, yes!" Seth gasped, taking every inch.

"You're beautiful," Joey grunted, pumping furiously.

"Tell me again!"

"You're beautiful."

"Ohhh, I love you, Joey."

"I know you do."

It would be the first of many times, many lust-filled secret nights—or so Joey thought, until his lust could cost Seth his life.

"Joey!"

He heard his name being called, and his mind told him it wasn't the first time. He snapped out of his thoughts and turned to see Te Amo standing beside him. They were the only two in the cemetery, as the sun was partially submerged on the horizon, giving the sky a curious purple haze.

He had lost track of time.

"You okay?" she inquired with obvious concern.

"I thought you left."

"I was leaving, but something told me I should stay. I'm glad I did, because you look like you could use someone to talk to."

Joey grinned warmly.

"I know a place. You want a drink?"

"Sure."

"To Seth," Te Amo toasted, holding her glass aloft.

"To Seth," Joey nodded and clinked glasses.

They were at a bar called Seven in the Financial District, a trendy spot favored by brokers from Wall Street. The place was only half packed. Joey and Te Amo occupied the back corner booth while the sounds of George Michael's "Careless Whisper" played on the jukebox in the corner.

"So tell me...if you would've given Seth's eulogy, what would you have said?" Te Amo probed.

Joey shrugged, toyed with his glass and replied, "I don't

know, I'm not so good with words, you know so…maybe, a great guy and an even better friend. The brains of the operation," he joked.

"The brains?" Te Amo echoed, her tone urging Joey to elaborate.

"The guy was a wiz. When I met him, he was bootleggin' concert tickets. Made a fuckin' fortune."

They shared a laugh.

"The thing I'll remember most is his sense of humor. You know, his wit. He was so witty. He could always make me laugh," Te Amo said.

"Yeah, he was a funny guy. Were you close?"

Te Amo waffled her hand.

"Kinda sorta. I haven't been back to the City since I left, but we spoke from time to time."

"I wonder why he never mentioned you," Joey remarked, sipping his drink.

"He probably thought you wouldn't remember me," she replied.

"You keep saying that but listen, I definitely remember you, 'cause you were a doll. The feisty Spanish doll with the name that meant *I love you*. Definitely stuck out in my mind," Joey flirtatiously assured her.

"Well, if I was such a doll, how come you never said nothin'?"

"Come on, you were a kid," Joey waved her off.

"I'm only three years younger than you. Besides, that didn't stop you from doin' Maria Piazza," she teased.

Joey chuckled.

"That don't count."

"Why?"

"She was a slut."

They laughed.

"I had the biggest crush on you, Joey. All the girls did… and some of the boys," she quipped.

Joey subtly shifted in his seat.

"So, like I'm not tryin' to pry, but...are you like *just* gay, or..." Te Amo let her voice trail off, to let Joey fill in the blanks.

He downed his drink, then replied, "Well I'm not *just* anything. The thing with Seth was such a thing, you know? Forget about it. I love women," Joey assured her.

Te Amo could tell he wasn't comfortable with the subject, so she changed it.

"I know maybe you don't want to talk about it, but what happened with Seth, you said he didn't deserve it. Did you mean, it was meant for someone...else?" she asked. He knew the someone else she was referring to was him.

"No, but...it's complicated."

"I'm sure, but just so you know, Miami's beautiful this time of year and my family would make sure you're taken care of," Te Amo offered.

"Who's your family?"

"Reyes."

"No disrespect, but I've never heard of 'em."

She smiled, knowingly.

"Believe me, you will when you get to Miami."

Joey smiled, shrugged casually and answered, "Eh, you never know. Maybe one day, but no time soon."

"Not even if I say 'please' and bat my eyes?" she asked, playfully batting her eyes.

"Couldn't hurt," Joey cracked, and they shared a laugh. He added, "I appreciate what you're doing, really, and just as soon as I straighten things out, I'm on the next thing smoking,"

"I'ma hold you to that," she said, a look of determined femininity coloring her expression.

"I'm sure you are."

As their gaze lingered, there was no question as to where the night would take them. The spark had been lit on first glance. Both felt it, but there was something else, something neither could name. So it made them much more curious.

Joey paid the bill and they headed out. It had begun to snow, already coating the ground with a thin white layer, broken only by the passing footprints. Joey turned his head to say something to Te Amo, but something caught his attention in the corner of his eye.

"Joey look out!" Te Amo bellowed, but Joey had already seen it.

Three men in long coats and Russian mink hats across the street, all holding semi-automatic weapons. They definitely had the drop on Joey, but they waited half a beat too long as he grabbed Te Amo around the waist with one hand, pulling her to the ground with him, and lifting his pistol from his waist with the other. As he fell, he let off a series of shots, but at the same time he heard another series of shots fired from close to him. He turned to see Te Amo, pistol in hand, firing on the would-be assassins. The few pedestrians on the street screamed and ducked, as the windows of parked cars and storefronts shattered all around them.

A van skidded up, and the three men jumped inside, barely escaping with their own lives as Joey and Te Amo came up from cover—firing and peppering the rear of the van with shots that sent sparks flying off the bumper as it drove away.

Adrenaline pumping, chests heaving, Joey and Te Amo looked at one another. She could see in his eyes that he was seeing her in a new light, a light he didn't understand, and therefore didn't trust.

"We gotta get out of here," he announced, and without hesitation they did just that.

For the first couple of blocks, they drove in silence—a silence she wanted to fill with some sort of explanation, but didn't know where to begin. At the next light Joey turned to her and said, "Just tell me you're not a cop."

She blurted out a nervous giggle, less out of humor and more because of relief in seeing which way his thoughts were flowing.

"No, I'm definitely not a cop," she assured him.

Poker faced, he assessed her.

"Hold out your hand," he instructed her.

She held it out, palm down. It was totally steady. The light greened, and they pulled off.

"Okay," he said and she lowered her hand. "My uncle Vito taught me that," he said. "Undercovers are usually high strung on the inside, a bundle of nerves. They just have good poker faces. But the hand...you can't fake a steady hand, you know? It means the person is of the life," he surmised, adding under his breath, "or," but she didn't catch it.

"I told you...my family."

"The Reyes Family," he replied.

Te Amo nodded, gauging his reaction.

Joey drove in silence a few more blocks, keeping his eye in the rear view mirror, and his gun in his lap, finger on the trigger.

"So...about this offer of Miami."

ONE YEAR LATER: WEDNESDAY, FEBRUARY 19TH 1991

The driver of the black tinted Lincoln Town Car cut through the city streets like a true New Yorker. He dipped in and out of lanes, zipping through yellow lights and taking curves with aggression and finesse. But any casual observer would think he was lost, the way he squared blocks by making a series of right turns, until he was right back where he started. Or the way he would abruptly U-turn in the intersection, or suddenly pull to the side of the road on the Cross Bronx Expressway. But every maneuver was part of the plan to make sure they weren't being tailed, and stretching a 20-minute ride from Manhattan to the Bronx into a two-hour adventure. But the evasion was well worth it. The man in the back would not stand for being tailed to a meeting as important as this. He didn't even allow his people to say his name in idle conversation. They were to say "that guy" or "him," or simply point their pinkie finger to signify the expensive pinkie rings he was known to wear. Any mention of his name was a death sentence. No reprieves. He was determined not to go down because his name was mentioned, so the driver knew what would happen if the Feds followed him to the meeting. He hated to think about it.

He pulled up to a small house in the Hunts Point section of the Bronx. A couple of other Lincolns and Mercedes were already parked.

"We're here, Boss."

"Everything clear, Jimmy?"

"Yes, sir."

"You sure?"

"Yes, sir." Jimmy affirmed, knowing he had to show 100% confidence in his own abilities.

"Okay...Is it rainin'? I can't tell through the fuckin' tint."

"No, Boss, it ain't rainin'."

"Eh, bring the umbrella anyway. You never know."

Jimmy knew he wasn't talking about rain. It was a last precaution, just in case any of the other Bosses were less careful than he was. Jimmy rounded the car, umbrella in hand. When he opened the car door, he opened the umbrella, thereby shielding the Boss from prying eyes.

The Boss, Salvatore Romano—or "Bill Sally," his nickname since his bruiser days—rose to his full height of 6'4". Even at 66, he still had the build of a linebacker, though good eating had given him a considerable paunch. Health-minded, he tried to watch what he ate and worked out three times a week. He wanted to be on top of his game in every way, because he said, "Everybody wants to be the Boss, but me...I just wanna be the best."

And it showed. The Romano family was the second most powerful family in the country; second only to the Diamantis aka the Romanos hated archrivals. Before the Mafia war of the '70s, Vincenzo Diamanti and Salvatore Romano had been close. But greed, envy, and deception put them at each other's throats. The only thing that kept the fragile truce was the fact that they both loved money more than they hated each other. So the peace held on...

Until now, which was why the meeting had been called. As he walked the driveway, the 5'4" Jimmy struggled to keep the umbrella over Salvatore's towering figure.

"Hey, Jimmy. Maybe if I carried ya, it'll be easier, huh?"

"Sorry for not being taller, Boss."

"You being a wise guy, Jimmy?"

"No, Boss."

"Too bad," Sal chuckled. "I like wise guys."

By the time they got to the side door, a short, pudgy man with a receding hairline opened it and stepped aside.

"Nicky Four Eyes, c'mere. How you doin', huh?" Sal greeted, as he stepped aside, giving Nicky a hug and a kiss on each cheek. "It's been too long."

"Hi ya, Sal. How are ya?" Nicky returned. "Everybody's waiting for ya in the basement. Whatcha drinkin'?"

"Whatever you got," Sal replied, as he descended the stairs.

Jimmy went upstairs to wait with the other soldiers, because they weren't allowed in the basement during the meeting between the Bosses.

The basement was sparse yet neat. The floor was covered with an old, plain blue carpet. In a semicircle, several armchairs had been arranged. It was obvious that the chairs had to have been brought in to appease the ego of the Bosses. Each would be given a similar chair. Had an inferior chair been substituted and offered to one of them, that alone could be taken as a snub that could snowball disastrously.

Waiting for Sal was Joe "Joe Pro" Provenzano, the acting Boss of the Casini family, who stood for Sal when he came in a crossed the room to greet him.

"Big Sal, good to see you," he gruffed in his trademark gravel toned voice.

Six feet and rail thin, it looked like Sal could wrap his arms around Joe Pro twice.

"Joe Pro, whaddya know, huh? It's good to be seen," Sal chuckled good-naturedly, then he looked to the man who didn't stand to greet him.

Vincenzo Diamanti.

The two men sized each other up coldly.

"Vinnie," Sal said in greeting with a slight nod.

"Sal," Vincenzo begrudgingly returned, his jaw muscles clenching and unclenching subtly.

"Have a seat will ya, Sal, so we can get started!" Joe Pro requested, and Sal obliged. Joe Pro slid to the edge of his seat and said, looking from one to the other. "I wanna thank you both for agreeing to this sit down. I called it because it pains my heart to see what's going on. I'm almost 80 years old, almost older than the two of youse put together. I remember when both your fathers sat where you sit now. God bless their souls. I remember, 'cause I've seen it all. Me and the Boss. The Boss is the last of the original Bosses. Luciano, Bonanno, we seen 'em all. So I see where this thing is headed, and I wanna know what can we do to stop it...please."

Sal leaned forward to take his drink from Nicky Four Eyes, who then headed back upstairs. He took a sip and said, "Uncle Joe, you know there's nothing I wouldn't do for you and Don Braza, but I did not start this...situation. This in an internal affair of the Diamantis, which I as a man of honor have become compelled to mediate for reasons already known. Now, blood has been spilled on both sides. But I'm a reasonable man. All I ask is that it be approved by the Commission for me to open the books to a man I've opened my home to. A solution, incidentally that would solve both Vincenzo's and my problem," Sal concluded.

Joe Pro nodded, then turned to Vincenzo.

"Vincenzo," Joe Pro began, "I know the situation, and

speaking on behalf of my Borgata, I have no objection to the Romano book being opened. But how do you feel about your son becoming a—"

Vincenzo cut him off.

"I...have...no...son," he seethed.

Joe Pro dropped his head and raised his hands. "I meant no disrespect. But the fact still remains."

Vincenzo tented his hands in front of himself and said, "It pains me to think such treachery would be condoned by a body as honorable as yours. An attempt was made on my *life*; a Boss, an act that demands the swiftest of justice. But not only are the culprits not pursued, but the only man to whom all fingers point is to be rewarded by my approval?"

Sal looked at Vincenzo and addressed him directly.

"Vincenzo, we have had our difficulties in the past, but I swear on my grandchildren that I had nothing to do with that. You must remember, that this man too—in the company of my own daughter—barely escaped an attempt on his life as well."

"Vincenzo, as a member of the Romano family, Joey will be the responsibility of Salvatore. If anything were to happen, we will hold Sal responsible," Joe Pro said to Vincenzo, then gave Sal a warning look that Sal accepted with a nod.

Vincenzo sat silently, then said, "If this man in question should become a problem...I will hold you *both* responsible."

Joe Pro breathed a sigh of relief.

"So be it...now...can we renew the truce?"

Vincenzo slowly rose from his chair, followed by Sal. The two men stepped tentatively forward, then embraced and kissed each other on both cheeks. When they broke the embrace, Sal thought he saw a smirk on Vincenzo's face, a smirk he knew all too well. It was the smirk Vincenzo wore whenever he had won. But Sal looked again, and it was gone.

Sal thought about it again as he got in the car a few minutes later. He prided himself on being astute, on picking up on the things others missed. But after assessing the situation, he shook it off.

"Hey, Jimmy. Stop at the phone booth will ya? Call Miami."

"And say what, Boss?"

"Tell him...congratulations."

Ten minutes later, Joey's mobile phone rang. He was out on the patio of a high-rise condo overlooking Miami Beach. Several girls sat around the pool topless. When the phone rang, Joey's boyfriend Enrico answered.

"Yeah," Enrico said, nodded, then hung up. "He said, 'congratulations.'"

Joey smiled and caressed his cheek. "C'mere and say 'hello' to the next Don."

Joey pulled Enrico closely and kissed him sensually, causing Enrico to tingle all over. He hated that Joey could do that to him so easily.

Joey smiled at him, like he could read his mind, and he wore the smirk like a taunt.

"Everything is going according to plan," Joey winked, then smacked Enrico on the ass and walked away.

Enrico watched him with a hate only love could muster. He had a plan, too—one Joey wasn't planning for—and he contemplated it with a taunting smirk of his own. As he picked up the mobile phone, he thought about the chain of events that brought him there...

JANUARY 1990: MIAMI

The gull wing of the Lambo door flew up and Enrico Valdez stepped one ostrich shoe out onto the pavement in front of Maxia, the hottest club in South Beach. He stepped out fully, giving the crowd a taste of his radiant, boyish good looks: clean shaven, long wavy hair in a ponytail, and an arrogant swagger.

As he passed the valet and tossed him the keys, he whispered coldly, "You scratch it, you die."

The valet took extra precaution, as if he were parking an egg.

Inside, the club was huge—at least five thousand square feet, and every inch of it was covered with party people. Enrico wasn't well known in Miami, but his delicious looks and air of wealth were a global familiarity. Women flirted and he flirted back, cutting through the massive crowds. The women were all over him, but he had only one in mind.

And then he saw her...

And him.

They were ensconced in a booth in the back in the dark. They were laughing. He was drinking, she was sniffing coke.

The music pounded in Enrico's ears, as he squinted his eyes to see who the guy was, but couldn't quite see his face.

Enrico made his way through the crowd, never taking his eyes off them. The guy whispered in her ear; she kissed him, offered him the coke, but he turned his face away. Enrico quickened his pace, because he wanted to know who the guy with her was. When he got there, the guy was kissing on her neck and she was pawing his prick through the silk pants, a rather large prick he inadvertently observed.

"Te Amo," Enrico said, suavely caressing each syllable of her name, "and I thought you loved *me*."

"No querido," she giggled drunkenly, "that's only my name."

"May I?" Enrico inquired.

"No," Te Amo answered dismissively, but Joey smoothed it out with, "Of course, my friend."

Enrico chuckled and slid into the booth.

"Oh, I'm much more than a friend, my friend."

"Yeah? Well, I'm much less, so you get no argument from me," Joey shot back smoothly.

"Glad to hear it," Enrico retorted, then said to Te Amo in Spanish: "You go to New York and you come back with strays?"

Before she could answer, Joey replied in Spanish: "In new York, we call them mutts. They like to tag along."

The two men eyeballed each other steadily. Despite later developments, their first encounter was a testosterone-filled encounter. Te Amo sensing it, threw her arms around both their necks and said, "Boys, boys, what are you doing? Don't you know girls just want to have fun? I so love the world right now," she squealed, then began dancing sensually in her seat.

Enrico took one look at her and surmised her state with one syllable: "X."

"No ecstasy," she corrected him, running her tongue slowly over her lips.

Joey perked up. He had seen her take a couple of pills, but

he thought they were just Quaaludes. Now, remembering the name, he filed the info away for later retrieval.

"Who needs a pill to give you ecstasy, when you have me?" Enrico crooned as he caressed her cheek, making her close her eyes and enjoy the sensation. Enrico took her by the hand and said, "Come on, dance with me."

"Noooo..." she intoned, like a spoiled little girl, slipping out of his grasp. "I'm already dancing...with Joey."

She turned to Joey and threw her leg over him. Her already short skirt hiked up, and it was plain to see that she wasn't wearing any panties.

"You wanna dance with me, Joey?" Te Amo whispered seductively in his ear, sucking the lobe then running her tongue along his neck.

"Why not?" Joey replied.

"No," Te Amo said, looking into his eyes as she straddled his lap. "I mean...dance...right here."

"I want *this*..." Joey smirked, sliding his hands along her inner thighs and finding it wet and creamy.

Red-faced and rejected, Enrico got up and stormed away. But he didn't go far. He couldn't resist turning around and watching as Te Amo unfastened Joey's jeans, as his already hard dick popped up. Te Amo let out a lustful gasp.

"Joey's a big boy!"

She lifted up her skirt and impaled herself on his long, hard dick, getting it only halfway in before she creamed all over it— her sensuality magnified by the effects of the X pill.

"Oh fuck!" She gasped. "Fuck, Joey, I've been wanting to do this for so long."

"It's all yours, sexy. Show me what you can do with it," he replied, gripping her hips and forcing her to take the full length.

He took her by the back of her neck and pulled her down so he could whisper in her ear, "Everybody's watching."

"I want them to," she growled, riding him harder and grinding him deeper.

Joey stroked her to the rhythm of "French Kiss," a song by Lil' Louie, known to hypnotize dancers with its incessant bass line and shifting tempo. He was in tune with Te Amo, loving the reckless abandon she displayed for life. It was an energy that matched his. It was so delicious, it felt forbidden.

Enrico couldn't pull his eyes away from the spectacle. He was repulsed, he was attracted. He was repulsed by that to which he was attracted. He was engrossed, but it wasn't just the sex, which he wouldn't realize until later. The energy spread like electricity around the club. In small pockets across the club, dirty dancing became sex on the dance floor. Not everyone, but enough to act like a conduit to the next pocket, until the smell of sex began to drive the crowd into a frenzy. The camera was turned on Joey and Te Amo, unbeknownst to them. Although the table blocked the view of Te Amo's juicy ass bouncing with every stroke, it was clear what they were doing, as she rode him—faster and faster, harder and harder.

"I'm ready, baby," she cried, "Oh God, I'm about to—" she tried to say, but ended the sentence in a squeal so sensual, it made Joey lose his grip and explode in her hot, wet pussy.

Heart racing, she pushed her hair out of her face, smiled, and said, "Welcome to Miami," then kissed him passionately.

For the next week and a half, Joey soaked up all the sun and fun Miami had to offer. Being a Brooklyn boy, things like water skiing and deep-sea fishing were new experiences for him, and he enjoyed every minute. Te Amo was his guide and constant companion, showing him everything, including how to dress Miami-style.

"What's wrong with how I dress?" Joey questioned, arms extended to punctuate the question.

She took one look at his snazzy outfit that would've worked in Manhattan and said, "Everything you wear is so New York," with a Brooklyn accent, making Joey chuckle.

She took him to Lincoln Road, a major shopping center in Miami, and outfitted him with soft pastels, linens, and Cuban-style shirts.

"Thanks a lot, now I look like Crockett from *Miami Vice*," he quipped.

Every day was a new adventure and every night was another party, until Joey woke Te Amo up and announced, "Okay, head's clear, vacation over. Time to get to work."

Te Amo rolled over on her stomach.

"Later."

Joey pulled the sheet off of her and playfully, but firmly slapped her bare ass.

"Get up!"

She jumped and, out of instinct kicked at him. He grabbed her ankle and used it to drag her to him.

"Come on. I gotta put something together before I go back to New York."

She sat up and looked at him.

"New York? You're going back?" she asked, incredulously.

Joey chuckled.

"Of course! What did you think, I was gonna hide out here forever? No fuckin' way! Father or no father, either I wet my beak in New York or we all die with dry lips."

Te Amo looked at him with a subtle smirk playing across her lips.

"What are you gonna do? Take your father to war?"

The smile disappeared from Joey's face and his eyes turned a cold wolf-like shade of grey.

"If I have to," he replied, then got up from the bed.

Te Amo got up after him.

"Joey, that's crazy and you know it! Why push your luck? Miami's an open city. There's plenty of money to be made.

He looked at her.

"Sweetheart, do me a favor, okay? Shut up and get dressed; we got people to see."

"Like who?"

"You're taking me to see your boyfriend, Enrico," he replied, then leaped out of the bed.

Enrico lived in a high-rise condo on South Beach. His fifteenth floor view was panoramic, and seemed to take in the entire Atlantic Ocean. Te Amo pushed the powder blue drop top Ferrari down Ocean Drive, further filling Joey in on Enrico during the drive. She had already told him that he was an expert smuggler that worked for her family, getting drugs in and large sums of money out.

"Cuban?" Joey inquired.

"Honduran."

"How long has he worked for your family?"

She shrugged as she turned into the ramp of the underground parking level under the condo.

"About a year, give or take."

"Before that?"

He ran guns in and out of Nicaragua for the Sandinistas."

"And before that?" he delved.

She looked at him as she parked.

"He's good, Joey. Believe me, we checked."

"Okay," Joey shrugged, "but you can never be too careful."

They took the elevator up to Enrico's floor. By the time they got to the door, he was already opening it for them.

"You have ten minutes," Enrico said as he walked away from the door.

"Querido," Te Amo playfully simpered, "I thought you always had time for me."

"I do," Enrico replied, then added with emphasis, "For *you*. Seat?"

Joey sat down, surveying his surroundings. Enrico had very minimalist taste. His hardwood floors were so polished that they looked wet, reflecting every step. The floor-to-ceiling windows covered the South side of the condo and led out onto a patio with a pool. Twelve feet away, an ivory white piano sat alone in the middle of the room. The 50-inch TV displayed highlights from the Heat-Knicks game and held Enrico's attention, until the sportscaster announced that the Heat had won, 104 to 98.

"Fuckin' New York trash," Enrico chuckled, then looked at Joey, making his last statement seem ambiguous.

Joey smiled, enjoying Enrico's futile attempts to engage him. It would happen, but on Joey's watch.

"Yeah, I never liked the Knicks either," Joey began. "Now, the Yankees, that's a different story."

"Nine minutes," Enrico replied.

Te Amo spoke up.

"Joey has a proposition for you."

"Yeah? Well first, I want to know more about Joey. Who is he? How long have you known him?" Enrico probed.

Te Amo looked him in the eyes and said, "Never question me, Enrico. If I bring him, he's good."

Enrico could see Te Amo's mother in her eyes, so he relented.

"Lo siento, pero you know I'm a cautious man, Te Amo. You can..." Enrico began, but Joey finished the sentence.

"...never be too careful. I agree. Listen, maybe we got off on the wrong foot, but I assure you, you have my utmost respect and consideration," Joey intoned diplomatically.

Enrico nodded, tented his hands and responded, "Please continue."

"I know a guy who knows a guy, who wants to get a package out of Israel."

"X?" Enrico surmised.

"Exactly," Joey confirmed with a nod.

"How much are we talking about?"

"Seventy-five grand."

"Seventy-five grand?" Enrico echoed, with a slight chuckle, then looked at Te Amo. "Is he serious?" he asked while still laughing.

It was at that moment when Joey decided he would break him. But Enrico didn't sense the rage in Joey. Te Amo did, because she saw his jaw muscles subtly flex.

"We gotta start somewhere," Joey remarked, doing well to keep his composure.

"Not there!" Enrico laughed again, resisting the opportunity to throw Joey's arrogance back in his face. "Listen, for seventy-five grand, you don't need a smuggler; you need UPS! I mean, it's not worth it. Miami's flooded..."

"I'm not thinkin' about Miami. I'm moving it in New York," Joey corrected him.

"That's even worse! The clubs are owned by the fuckin' mob. The Gambinos, not to mention the Diamanti factor in Manhattan."

"Enrico, you're talking to a Diamanti. Joey Diamanti."

Instantly, the laughter subsided. Enrico looked at Te Amo, then at Joey. Joey could tell that Enrico's mental wheels were turning, but he gave him credit for a good poker face.

"So what do you need me for?"

Joey subtly smirked.

"Me and the old man ain't seeing eye to eye."

"I'm definitely not trying to get in the middle of a family beef."

"You won't be," Joey assured him.

Enrico looked at Te Amo.

"Have you spoken to your mother about this?"

"That's our next step," she answered.

"And my first concern. I work for her, so before we go any further, I need to know where she is on this," Enrico remarked.

"Then I guess our business here is done," Joey said, standing up. Then Enrico and Te Amo followed suit. "Besides," Joey added, "by my watch, we only have a minute left on those ten."

Joey extended his hand. Enrico accepted it, firmly.

"And for the record, seventy-five is peanuts to me, too. But, you do this with me, and you'll see more money than you've ever seen in your life. Think about it," Joey told him, then walked out the door.

Te Amo kissed Enrico on the cheek.

Enrico watched her walk out. He disregarded Joey's words because his mind was too busy screaming, "Jackpot!"

Enrico went back to the bedroom, threw himself on the bed and howled with laughter.

Jackpot indeed.

They called her Reina Coco, the Queen of Cocaine. Her name was Sophia Reyes, but she was born Sophia Sandoval in an impoverished section of Brazil where even the police feared to go.

Her dark Brazilian hue and long, jet-black hair made her

the target of men's abusive affection at a very young age. One of those men was her uncle, who raped her when she was eleven years old.

"If you tell," he hissed in her face—his rotten, drunken breath searing her senses. "I'll kill you."

The next night, she went to him.

"I want...to do it again," she mumbled, head down, seemingly in shame.

He laughed.

"A whore, just like your mother," He chuckled, thinking of the days when he raped her mother, his sister.

He took her behind an abandoned building and threw her on the ground. As he lay to enter her—his savage features exaggerated by lust and illuminated by the light of the full moon—she watched as his expression abruptly changed from pleasure to indescribable pain.

She had inserted a razor inside of her pussy. When he penetrated her, he impaled himself on the excessively sharp edge, splitting the head of his dick in half.

As he howled, she pulled the blade she had concealed in her sleeve and silenced him forever by slitting his throat.

"You should've killed me," she hissed in his dying ear.

Sophia rolled him over on his back as he gargled his own blood. Then she went into a zone, slicing him over and over and over, until his body was covered with blood and her heart was covered with coldness.

When she got home, her mother took one look at her blood-soaked daughter and cried, "Mi Dios!"

"There is no God," Sophia replied with a maniacal look in her eye. "I killed him."

It took her mother two days to realize that wasn't one sentence; it was two, and the "him" was her uncle. Being that her uncle was a known gangster, her mother feared for her life. She sent Sophia to America and wouldn't see her for twenty years, until she returned for Carnival, and met the man that would make her a queen.

Antonio Reyes.

Reyes was the head of the only Colombian cartel big enough to rival Pablo Escobar's. He was a cold-blooded killer, but he had a weakness for beautiful women, and Sophia was the most beautiful woman he had ever seen. She cast the spell of Carnival on his heart and, two months later, they were married—Antonio to her beauty and Sophia to his money. The marriage was destined to end badly, yet Sophia willed it to end in death. She conspired with Antonio's chief lieutenant to ambush him, thereby giving control to the lieutenant. But before he could even warm the throne, she murdered him herself in her marriage bed and—with the backing of Escobar —took over the cartel. She kept Antonio's name simply because she had a sense of humor.

She stood at the prow of her hundred-foot yacht named Jade. At 47, she could easily pass for 27. Her dark Brazilian tone was still flawless, because she rarely wore makeup. She didn't need it. She felt the presence of the ocean on her face, blowing open her kimono, to reveal her svelte yet shapely figure in a green, two-piece bathing suit. They were far out in the Atlantic, out in International waters—a place where she liked to conduct business meetings because no country had jurisdiction.

She liked to keep her enemies off balance.

One of her bodyguards approached her.

"Señora Reyes, your daughter is here," he informed her.

"Gracias," she replied, and he walked off.

Reluctantly, she tore herself from her thoughts to go see her only child.

Joey and Te Amo had flown out to the yacht in a helicopter. They landed on the helipad onto the top deck of the yacht, then headed below. By the time they got to the yacht's living room, Sophia was waiting for them, seated with drink in hand.

"Cómo está, Mama," Te Amo greeted her mother as she crossed the room. Then she bent down and kissed her mother on the lips.

"I'm fine, Baby Girl," Sophia smiled, "and pleasantly surprised that you would come all the way out here to see your poor mother."

"Mama, you are a lot of things, but poor isn't one of them," Te Amo remarked, making Sophia chuckle. Then she turned to Joey and added, "She likes to exaggerate; it lets her play the victim."

Sophia looked at Joey, subtly assessing him.

"And I assume you are Joey Diamanti."

Joey approached her and kissed her hand, saying in Sicilian: "Rose of the Ocean, you are even more beautiful than I imagined."

They weren't just empty words. Sophia had that type of effect on men. It wasn't just her beauty, but the ethereal quality of her sensuality that cast a spell.

"My Sicilian is rusty, so you either said I'm beautiful or you're looking forward to dinner."

Joey chuckled.

"The former."

Then I thank you or...*grazie*," Sophia replied.

Te Amo understood every word, which sent a jolt of jealousy through her senses, but she let it go.

"So tell me, to what do I owe this honor?" Sophia inquired.

"Joey had a prob—"

"Joey's a big boy now; he can speak for himself, Te Amo!" she chided her daughter, then turned to Joey. "Now, come sit. Talk to me."

Joey set down next to Sophia, and she adjusted her position to give him her full attention.

"Basically, I had a problem...with my father," Joey admitted.

"So I've heard."

"And I feel like the attempt on my life was...his call," Joey concluded with a clenched jaw. It was still hard for him to fathom his father hated him so much that he wanted him dead.

"I see," Sophia nodded. "And the problem you speak of, what happened?"

Joey glanced at Te Amo, who nodded. He took a deep breath and answered, "It was uh, because of a relationship that I had with a...a relationship with a man."

"Oh," Sophia remarked, her brow slightly raised. She hadn't expected that. "And for this you feel your father would want you dead?"

"My father is a product of the old country. Besides, no one would've made a move like that without him. So it would seem—"

"Things...are rarely as they seem," Sophia scolded him, with a Sphinx-like smile.

Joey nodded his *touché*.

"Still, what walks like a duck, you know?" he continued. "Anyway, I'm goin' back to New York and carving myself a niche. But to do that, I need a little help," he explained.

"What about the problems if we go along with...this niche?" Sophia probed.

"I'll handle them as they come."

"But then, your problems become my problems," she surmised.

"I can handle my own problems, Señora Reyes."

"But can you assure me that they won't become mine?"

Te Amo, sensing her mother's reluctance, couldn't hold her tongue any longer.

"But Mama, what Joey has in mind can be huge. Besides, we are Reyes; problems are our middle name, no?"

Sophia eyed her daughter coldly, then turned back to Joey.

"Joey, I need you to go upstairs while I speak to my niña for a moment," Sophia requested.

"No problem," Joey answered, standing. He turned to her and kissed her hand once more. "Despite the circumstances, it was an honor to meet you, and if I have my way, we will meet again," he assured her with the brunt of his arrogance.

"And I bet you're used to having your way, aren't you?" she returned, toying him with flirtatiousness.

Joey let his smile speak for him, then turned and left, closing the door behind him.

When she was sure he was out of earshot, Sophia stood and faced Te Amo.

"I don't like this. I don't like this at all. If I didn't know any better I'd think your father was working an angle on me to get back at me. Has he got anything to do with this? Anything at all?"

"Nothing." Te Amo said, squeezing her mother's hand.

Sophia studied her daughter's face.

"Nothing, I swear Mama. He's a friend of a friend, and I think he's worth the trouble," Te Amo explained.

"He's a Diamanti."

"I know."

Sophia stood, eyeing Te Amo with a steady gaze, until she looked away. She could never hold her mother's gaze.

"So you expect me to believe that your father has nothing to do with this, and he's just a friend you want to go into business with?" Sophia chuckled lightly.

"It may not seem like it, Mama, but like you just told Joey, things are rarely what they seem." Te Amo smirked.

"I have spoiled you, child," Sophia mused ruefully as she turned to the bar and refreshed her drink. "Sheltered you from the vulgarities of the real world."

She looked at her daughter through the mirror behind the bar. She was her spitting image, inside and out. She had the beauty and the swagger of a jaguar in the Brazilian jungle. Inside, she had the cold-heartedness and the cunningness. But she was young and naïve, and Sophia knew that in order for Te Amo to survive in their world, she would have to sacrifice her to it.

Sophia sipped her drink, then turned around and announced, "If you trust your judgment, so will I. But this is your responsibility. Enrico may get involved in what he chooses, but I will extend nothing more. No protection, no support. You...are on your own, Baby Girl."

"Thank you, Mama," Te Amo responded solemnly.

"We'll see," was Sophia's enigmatic reply.

She turned back to her own reflection and watched her daughter's in the mirror as Te Amo left the room.

PRESENT DAY, AUGUST 1997

The courtroom was filled to capacity for what the press was calling "The trial of the Purple Don." Besides the media, most of the people were Joey's supporters, including several well-known movie stars, athletes, and rock stars. Joey knew how to use the media to his advantage. He had come out of the closet at the right time. When the prosecution had least expected it, he used Diane Reynolds' *Night Talk* to announce to the world: "I'm gay."

His strategy was to put the Federal Prosecutor, Steven Rein, in the position of coming across as a gay-basher, to divert attention from his bloody rise to the top—from spoiled heir to the Diamanti throne, to a powerful Capo in the Romano family. But, it was inevitable that Joey's strategy ended up tying the Prosecutor's hands during jury selection, because he was forced to raise the question of sexuality and to disqualify anyone that had religious or personal prejudices against gay people. This put the defense and the prosecution on the same page, minimizing the defense's need to use preemptory challenges, and weighted the jury in Joey's favor. Even the legal analysis talking heads had to acknowledge the brilliance of the strategy.

"Diamanti's legal team has managed to do what no lawyer has done since the Star Council: get the prosecution to *help* bias the jury!"

With this in mind, the Prosecutor gave his opening statement. "Ladies and gentlemen of the jury, welcome. I want to personally thank each one of you. This may be called jury duty, but it is not only a duty; it is your *right*. It is your right to make your voice heard, to take an active part in ensuring that your community, my community, *our* community stays safe from those who would bring it harm," he began, slowly pacing in front of the jury box.

"Now I know you've heard a lot in the news and on TV about Mr. Diamanti. Let me say from the onset what this trial is *not* about. It is *not* about who Mr. Diamanti is as a human being; it is *not* about anyone's sexual orientation or inclination. That's what Mr. Diamanti wants you to believe, but I know that —as conscious Americans—you can see through the smoke and mirrors. Now, this is not about who Mr. Diamanti *is*, it's about what Mr. Diamanti has *done*—and that is murder, extort, rob, destroy, cheat, and steal. All this was done in the name of personal gain, of Mr. Diamanti's greed. Despite what he says, Mr. Diamanti isn't being prosecuted for his sexuality. In fact, up until his very public announcement, we weren't even aware of his...orientation. So put that out of your minds and get ready to focus on a man so cold-blooded, so ruthless, so...evil that Al Capone and John Gotti pale in comparison. *That* is why we are here, and in the end, I *know* you will see that all too clearly. Thank you."

The Federal Prosecutor concluded, dabbed his forehead with his handkerchief, and sat down. He wasn't known for giving rousing opening statements, so no one expected any fireworks. But he felt satisfied that he had gotten his point across.

"I'm gonna eat this guy's lunch," chuckled Ray Rollins, Joey's lead attorney.

He rose slowly, knowing all eyes were on him, and he was definitely an eyeful. He was only 55, but he already had a head full of grey hair, which those in the know knew was only dye, because he knew jurors—especially women—preferred Silver Fox lawyers. It made him look that much wiser. He complemented the distinguished gentleman look with an expensive flair for fashion. He was always immaculately attired in tailored, double-breasted suits, with shoes made at the finest shoemaker in Manhattan, and a diamond bejeweled TAG Heuer watch. He drove a white Ferrari and had his own private jet. Rollins was a highly successful lawyer, but many said he sold his soul, because he was known as "the mob lawyer." In his thirty-year career, he had represented some of the most infamous mobsters, drug lords, and corrupt politicians in America. But, as he always said, "It pays well, and somebody's got to do it."

A lot of people had questioned, if Joey was denying he was a mob boss, then why would he have hired "the mob lawyer"? They thought he was sending mixed messages, when in actuality he was sending subliminal ones...

Rollins buttoned his double-breasted Armani suit as he rounded the defense table and stepped in the middle of the courtroom, looking at the jury. The courtroom was silent, awaiting his first word, so he waited a few long moments to heighten the drama.

"Guilty!" he bellowed, just loud enough to fill the courtroom. "Guilty, Guilty, Guilty! What's the point of a trial? Because if our friendly neighborhood Prosecutor is right, where's the key, so we can throw it away?" Rollins began. Then with a chuckle, he approached the jury box, leaned on the rail, and added, "You ever notice...you ever notice how the Prosecutor gets up here and *paints*, and I mean that, paints the worst possible picture of a guy or gal? You ever notice that?"

He looked from face to face, and was encouraged by a few subtle nods.

"Now don't get me wrong. Sometimes the defense does it too. But the bottom line is that this is a trial, not an inquisition. So we are here to *find* the truth, not *create* it, you follow me?" Rollins asked then took a few steps away from the jury box.

"So today, we're gonna throw out the blueprint and focus on *finding* the truth. I won't play *his* game," he said, pointing to the Prosecutor. "And say what my client didn't do just to refute what he says my client *did* do. No. But since the government has already told you what this trial *isn't* about, I'll tell you what they'll try and *make* it about. They want to make it about Mr. Diamanti's illustrious name, a name the government wants you to think is linked to organized crime. But that's not the case. I think it was Shakespeare who once said something like, a rose by any other name would smell just as sweet. But a rose...is also the past tense of rise. My point? Words, names, they can be confusing. But I trust in your ability to see through any such confusion. Mr. Diamanti is a businessman, a movie star to some, and a helluva nice guy to most. But what he is not is a criminal. He is not the Gay Don, the Purple Don, and any kind of Don. And he *definitely* is *not* a murderer."

JANUARY 1990

J oey dreamt that Seth was riding his dick backwards, calling out his name in passionate anguish. When he awoke, he realized it wasn't a dream, but it wasn't Seth. It was Te Amo.

"You couldn't wait for me to wake up?" Joey asked, amused. He crossed his arms behind his head and watched Te Amo's perfect figure as she rode him like a wave.

"You didn't ha—" she began but was interrupted with a guttural moan, "—have anything to do with it."

"Can I watch?" he smirked.

"Wait, wait," Te Amo gasped, riding him harder and digging her nails into his stomach. She threw her head back, and with a shriek came all over his dick.

"Too late," she giggled, then leaned down and gave him a kiss. "You should make a mold of your dick. You'd make a fortune."

Te Amo got off him and headed to the bathroom.

"What about me?" he yelled after her.

"You're a big boy. You can take care of yourself."

She jumped in the shower. Joey chuckled, shaking his head

at her audacity. He got up and followed her into the bathroom. She was showering with the curtain open.

"Move over," he told her.

She handed him the soap and he lathered up her back.

"So what's the deal with the Russians?"

"All taken care of. They want to meet at three," she answered.

He massaged her as he lathered her up.

"Whaddya know about these guys?"

"Nothing. I thought you knew something about them."

"Seth set it up, but we never had a chance to meet."

"Think we need some extra bodies?" she questioned.

He thought about it for a moment, then answered.

"Naw. They don't have a reason to be less than friendly... yet," he smirked.

She glanced over her shoulder, with a lust in her eyes and a devilish grin on her face.

"Yet? What are you plotting in that mind of yours?"

He licked his lips, slid his hands along the small of her back and up to her shoulder.

"I can show you better than I can tell you," he said. And with that, bent her over and finished what she started.

———

They were in Little Havana, at a Cuban sandwich shop that Te Amo said served the best Cuban sandwiches in Miami. When they arrived, the Russians were already there. Joey glanced around casually, as he could see how the Russians had a couple of men strategically placed around the restaurant's outdoor-seating area. In the center of all the security sat a man not much older than Joey. He was dressed casually, in khakis and a Cuban-style shirt, but Joey could tell that the man carried weight. Joey took it as a good sign that they didn't send a lackey to meet with him.

As he and Te Amo approached, the man stood up to greet them.

"Joey Diamonds," he said with a strong Russian accent, hand extended. "It is good to meet you, yes?"

Joey shook his hand and found that he had a strong grip. Up close, Joey could see that he was a body builder.

"Same here, ah..." Joey returned, asking for his name without asking.

"Zev," he answered.

"Zev? Just Zev?"

"Just Zev," Zev assured him. A friendly smile was plastered on his face. He turned to Te Amo. "And it is even better to meet you."

When she extended her hand, he kissed it.

"Sit, sit," he urged them. "You drink vodka, yes? Drink vodka with me," Zev suggested, then snapped his fingers and the waiter brought over a bottle of vodka, three glasses, and some bread. Zev took the bottle and filled the three glasses.

"Whoa, I'm used to vodka in shots," Te Amo snickered.

"Ah, Americans," he playfully waved her off. "You nibble, nibble. In my country, you drink, you *drink*. And friends, we come together. We break bread, yes?"

Joey understood the importance of custom, so he didn't object. He lifted his glass as Zev toasted, "To health."

"Salud," Joey seconded.

Te Amo nodded as they all drank, downing a good portion of their drinks and taking bites of the brown bread.

"And...it is very sad what happened to Seth, eh?" Zev remarked.

Joey nodded solemnly.

"Yeah, I wish I could've stopped it, you know?"

"Those things happen, but it is upsetting when they happen so close to home."

"Close to home?" Joey echoed, because Zev's tone said he was speaking personally.

"Seth was my cousin. I was the one that asked him to speak to you."

"I see," Joey replied, subtly glancing around, mentally re-assessing the situation.

Sensing the air of tension, Zev remarked, "As I said, these things happen. I blame nobody but those who pulled the trigger, which is part of why I wanted to see you. Zev is with you against who is responsible."

The two men locked gazes, and Joey knew he had an ally. He grabbed the vodka bottle, refilled their glasses then toasted, "To Seth."

"Da," Zev seconded.

"Salud," Te Amo chimed in.

Then they drank and again broke bread.

"I appreciate your offer of assistance...truly. I can *promise* you, his death won't go unpunished, but I can't tell you when. Things are crazy in New York, but the sooner I can re-establish myself, the sooner I can straighten everything out. Which is why I wanted to see you," Joey explained.

Zev nodded, downed the rest of his vodka and replied, "Unfortunately, I'm going to have to decline your offer."

Joey was instantly disappointed, but concealed it well.

"Why so?"

Zev shrugged humbly.

"Because I'm not the Boss. My word, how you say, carries weight. But the deal I brought to you has already been taken."

"By who?"

"I think you already know the answer to that."

Joey nodded.

"I understand. But tell me, would it be possible if I spoke to the Boss?"

Zev eyed him curiously, popped a piece of bread into his mouth and replied, "I don't see why not, but I don't see why."

"Because I think I can make him a better deal," Joey answered. "Besides, I'm a confident man, and I can be pretty convincing when I have to be."

Zev filled his glass halfway, pondering.

"No disrespect, but the word in the City is that you have... fallen from grace. I don't see what you have to offer."

Joey shrugged, nonchalantly, downed his glass then responded, "Like I said, I can be pretty convincing. I mean, hey I convinced you, right?" Then he hit him with the pearly whites.

Zev chuckled.

"Let's just say, I'm curious."

Zev barked something in Russian, and a few seconds later, one of his goons came over and handed him a mobile phone. He dialed, spoke in Russian, listened, looked at Joey then said goodbye in Russian, hanging up. "Two days from today in New York."

Joey nodded, then stood up. Zev and Te Amo followed suit. The two men shook hands firmly. "Nice meeting you, Just Zev. I'll see you in New York."

Zev smirked.

As Joey and Te Amo walked away, he asked her, "Whaddya think?"

"I think if we're going to New York, we're gonna need a crew."

"You musta read my mind."

"You call this a crew?" Joey quipped, as he glanced around the dimly lit strip club that night.

Te Amo had just pointed out the team she had in mind. They were all women, nine total. Four were Spanish, three were Black, and two were White. They were all dancers and waitresses at a little out-of-the-way club in Liberty City, a rough part of Miami that no tourist would dare to tread.

"Believe me," Te Amo assured him, "looks can be deceiving."

Joey scrutinized them closer. He watched one of the Spanish girls work the pole like an exotic acrobat, wrapping herself around it with the graceful slither of a snake. They were all beautiful, but he still doubted their prowess.

He wouldn't for long.

"They're fuckin' strippers," he chuckled.

"You're expecting a bunch of no-neck guidos?" she cracked.

"I mean, a little testosterone wouldn't hurt."

"Look who's talking," she snickered.

"Fuck you," he replied, without malice.

He surveyed the girls again. He caught the eye of the Black waitress. She winked and blew him a kiss.

"You say they're good?"

"Not the best, but *very* good," she assured him.

"Let's find out how good."

Later that night, he met all of the girls back at Te Amo's condo. As they filed in, Joey looked them over, one by one. Looking each in the eye as they passed, he could see each had seen their own version of hell. Beautiful on the outside, but life had taken their beauty on the inside. It's much harder for a woman to mask true coldness, and from what Joey saw, he knew it would put a chill up anyone's spine.

Most took seats around the room, some chose to stand, but they all watched and assessed Joey just as he had done them.

"I appreciate all of you for coming. Te Amo, you wanna do the honors?" Joey requested.

"No problem," she replied, and then introduced each girl. She started with Maria, who resembled Rosie Perez so much that Joey had to do a double take. Next was Chi-Chi, so dark he thought she was Black until she opened her mouth and her accent came out Latin-flavored. The next girl was Black, jet-black: the color of midnight, had it been made out of silk. She was a Nigerian named Maliah, long-legged like a black widow and just as deadly.

Next were the two White girls: twins named Alicia and Amanda, both blond with blue eyes. They looked like America's dream, but in the trailer parks of Columbus, Georgia, they had lived America's nightmare. Standing beside them were two more Black girls: Bianca and Marilyn. They called her Marilyn because she was light enough to pass for White, and with her blond hair, she resembled Marilyn Monroe. Bianca was straight ghetto: gum-popping with a sassy Black attitude, but her smooth cinnamon complexion broke hearts, and the razor she often had in her mouth made many a kiss taste like death.

The last two girls looked Indian, but hey were Nicaraguan; the most exotic of the bunch and the most dangerous. Mianna and Anita looked like sisters, but were not related, except for the fact that they were both stone cold killers. After the introductions, Joey looked around and began.

"It's good to meet cha. All of youse. Now, Te Amo has vouched for every one of you, but I need you to vouch for yourselves. So what I mean is, what we're about to do could easily get us all killed, or...make us all very rich. But the bottom line, if the former ain't worth the risk of the latter then so be it, but I'ma hafta ask you to leave, because once I open this door, there's no turning back."

He paused to give anyone who wanted to leave time to go. Instead, Chi-Chi said, "Nobody's going anywhere. We're a team, and our loyalty is to Te Amo and the Reyes family."

Murmurs of agreement rippled across the room.

"'Til death do us part," Maria vowed.

Joey nodded, approvingly.

"Okay, I like that. So here we go. Do youse know who I am?"

A few nodded, and Marilyn remarked, "I sure wanna get to know you, cutie."

Joey smirked.

"And you will. I'm Joey Diamonds, from New York. I'm here because some people back home don't think I deserve what goes with that name. I'ma prove 'em wrong. But to do that...I need your help," he explained, pouring himself a drink. He took a sip and continued.

"Now Te Amo says you're pretty good. Well, the people we're goin' against are even better. Besides that, they've got the whole City under their thumb. Between the five families, they've got half of the NYPD on the take. Now, for anybody takin' score, they'll make the odds pretty long, huh? But an old-timer once told me, "Sometimes being underestimated has its own odds." I believe that, but now...we gotta prove it. If we can do that...*when* we do that, the City is ours."

For the moment, no one spoke, contemplating the words. Then Bianca said, "So let me get this straight. You want *us* to go in wit' *you* against the whole fuckin' Mafia?"

"If that's what it takes," he answered dead seriously.

Bianca laughed.

"Yo, Te Amo, who the fuck is this guido?! He's fuckin' crazy! But you know what, I fuckin' love crazy!" she snickered, flipping the razor with her tongue. "I'm in!"

Bianca's remark made everyone laugh, including Joey.

"Me too! I ain't never been to New York City," Amanda said, purposely exaggerating her Southern drawl.

Te Amo looked at Joey and smiled.

"Looks like you got your crew. So what do we do now?"

Joey smirked and replied, "We start with the Russians."

Mikhail "Mickey" Pavlov was one of the biggest Russian gangsters in the City. He had his hands in all of the Russian rackets and a few joint ventures with Mob families. He ran a crew out of Brighton Beach, made up of mostly Russian Jews from Moscow by way of Israel. He usually held court in a bar in Coney Island. He and Zev were there, waiting for Joey to arrive. The contrast between the two was stark. Up against Zev's smooth looking youthfulness, Mickey wore his age with rugged gruffness. Covered in tattoos, with wisps of grey hair haloing his head, he resembled a thuggish Boris Yeltsin. A former bodybuilder, at 60 he still had his size but he also had a huge beer gut to match. With his goons spread out around the room, he and Zev sat in his favorite back booth, enjoying their favorite pastime: drinking vodka.

"Man, pretty girls in here tonight, eh?" Mickey remarked, eying the women spread out around the bar—some talking to his goons, others talking to each other.

"It's a bar; they come for the two d's: drinks and dick," Zev said with a smirk.

Mickey roared with laughter.

"Very good, Zev, very good. I must remember that. Look at that one, Zev, the Black one. She is Black like Cuban, No? Have you ever fucked a Black bitch, my friend?"

Zev poured more vodka.

"Probably in Vegas."

"I fuck them all. I am like, Russian bull. Black bitches love it," Mickey chuckled.

Several moments later, Joey walked in. The goon by the

door got off his stool and approached him. Joey raised his arms as if he were ready to be frisked. Zev called out something in Russian and the goon looked at him. He waved the goon off and waved Joey over. Joey still opened his coat to reveal that he was unarmed, then walked over to their table. Zev stood up to receive him with a firm handshake.

"It's good to see you," Zev greeted.

"I appreciate the opportunity to be heard," Joey returned.

Mickey leaned back in his chair and gave Joey the once over, wearing a curious smirk.

"So this is Joey Diamonds, eh?"

"Sans the Diamonds," Joey quipped, adding with a shrug. "I'm currently unemployed."

Mickey chuckled and accepted Joey's outstretched hand. His glove-like hand swallowed Joey's, putting his hand in a Russian bear hug.

Joey sat down and Mickey waved the waitress over. She was a cute blond with a short skirt.

"Bring us another bottle of vodka, and a glass for my friend," Mickey ordered.

"Sho' thang," she replied with a wink and country drawl, as she sashayed away.

The three men watched her swaying ass.

"New waitress," Mickey remarked. "Never saw her before. When she says she come from Georgia, I get confused. I think she mean country of Georgia," Mickey chuckled.

Joey smiled.

"They come from all over to take a bite of the Big Apple; what can I tell you. God bless America, huh?"

She brought back the bottle and sat a glass in front of Joey. Again, Mickey watched her walk away. His mind already tasted her country flesh.

"So Mr. Pavlov," Joey began, but Mickey cut him off.

"Mickey. Call me Mickey. Any friend of Zev's is a friend of mine."

Joey nodded with subtle grace.

"Thank you. It's an honor to call a man such as yourself, a friend."

Mickey opened the new bottle, poured them all a glassful; he toasted to friendship, drank, then remarked, "I like you, Joey Diamonds, so I'm not going to waste your time...or mine. What you ask of me, I cannot do. I have a deal in place for the X, and I am a man of my word."

"I understand, but some of the men with which you deal are...less honorable. No disrespect to your judgment, but some of these guys ain't worth the air they breathe. Now this was my deal; you brought it to me first, but I got...cut out. So I'm cutting back in, and I'm askin' for this dance if I can clean the dance floor, you follow?" Joey proposed, keeping steady eye contact with Mickey.

Mickey smiled at the metaphor.

"My dance card is full. So please, I hate to tell a friend no. Embarrass me no longer."

His tone was polite, but Joey could tell he was firmly closing the door on further discussion of the matter. He had come prepared for that. Unfortunately, Mickey wasn't prepared for Joey.

"I understand," Joey nodded. "But hopefully, in the future, we can find common ground."

"To the future," Mickey toasted, downing his glass.

"Salud," Joey seconded then did the same. "But listen, I know you guys love vodka. But me, when I celebrate, I do it with champagne and a new friendship is definitely a cause for celebration," he added, waving the waitress over. When she got there, he said, "Listen sweetheart, you got any Dom back there? Whatever you got, bring me your best, will ya?"

Joey pulled out a wad of money, peeled off a couple of hundreds then handed them to her.

She eyed his bankroll and quipped, "For all that, you got it all..." she winked.

"I'll keep that in mind," Joey smirked as she walked off. He turned back to Mickey and Zev. "Now listen, I've got this thing. It's not official, but maybe we can work together."

"I'm all ears," Mickey responded.

The waitress returned, carrying a bottle of Dom and two champagne glasses by the stems. When she sat them down, she bent in front of Joey to put one of the glasses in front of Zev. Joey eyed her ass and thighs.

"You part thoroughbred or somethin', sweetheart? You're built like a stallion," Joey retorted. Lustfully and without hesitation, he slid his hand up the back of her skirt. She jumped slightly, then bit her bottom lip.

"You sure you know what to do with that?" she purred.

"Watch me."

He slid his hand out, but what was in it, Mickey never saw coming.

From the minute Joey walked in, he was set in murder mode. Looking around, he saw the girls spread out strategically around the room. He smiled to himself. When the goon approached him, he had expected to be frisked, which is why he didn't bring a gun. He knew the meeting would be informal, not a lot of security. There was no need for it...or so the Russians thought.

Amanda had just gotten the job the day before. The owner wasn't hiring, but it's hard to say no to a beautiful country girl with a killer head game. She sucked the job right out of him. She was the first one Joey saw when he walked in.

But he wanted to give Mickey a chance. Always give a man a chance. Mickey blew it once the champagne was ordered. That was the cue. Amanda slipped the .380-millimeter into the waistband of her panties, grabbed the Dom and two glasses.

Two glasses.

Zev was the only one to notice. She didn't bring three glasses; she only brought two. In the back of his mind, he asked why, but in the front of his mind—in the place where one's attention is located—it got caught up in the facial expression Amanda made when Joey slide his hand up her skirt.

The jump was real, because Joey deftly pulled her panties aside and ran a finger up the length of her pussy and grabbed the gun. Her bent body shielded Joey from Mickey. He was caught up in the moment, too. So once Joey said, "Watch me," and Amanda quickly pulled away, Mickey found himself fact to face with the abyss of a gun barrel.

Without hesitation, Joey pumped two slugs into Mickey's face at close to point blank range. The first shot entered his eye and exploded through it, leaving a gaping hole. The second hit him in the forehead, dead center. Then, as Joey stood up, he pumped three more into Mickey's head. He was dead before his body hit the floor. He didn't even twitch.

It happened so fast, that by the time Mickey's goons could react, the girls had their guns out ready to spark. One dude tried to go for his gun, but Maliah blew that thought all over the pool table with three shots from her 9mm. Seeing that, the rest cooperated, handing over their guns and laying on the floor.

After Joey lowered his gun, he looked at Zev. The two men eyed each other squarely. Joey put the gun down on the table, knowingly within Zev's reach, then picked up the bottle of Dom.

"We both know that had to happen. I gave him a chance. He just went the wrong way." Joey summed it up as he popped open the champagne. He poured Zev a flute full then himself a flute. "Now, you're the Boss. I'll be in touch."

Joey took his swig straight from the bottle then turned for the door, leaving the gun on the table. Zev watched him walk out.

He had forced Zev's hand and Zev knew it. He had used Zev to get a meeting with Mickey. Now that he lay dead on the floor, Zev was a part of it, whether he liked it or not. He had two options: go to war over Mickey or accept the crown on Joey's team. Joey figured Zev for the latter. For one, Seth was the common denominator, and Seth already pledged his support to Joey. To go against that would be to go against his word. Besides, everybody wants to rule the world, and Joey had given him the opportunity to rule his. With one deft move, Joey had eliminated an adversary and secured an ally.

Zev mumbled to himself as he contemplated the situation. He slowly raised the flute and drank the champagne.

At the same time in Manhattan, at a restaurant in Little Italy, Louis "Bananas" Bonanno was having dinner with two of his soldiers, Mike Rizzo and Tommy Lombardi. Louis Bananas was the Capo of the Crew that ran the clubs in West Chelsea for the Gambino family. He was a Made Man that wore his Mafioso ties on his sleeve, decking himself in open collar shirts, wrap-around sunglasses, and gold chains.

They were discussing business in Sicilian over linguini with clam sauce, when the waitress came over, carrying an expensive bottle of red wine.

"Excuse me, Mr. Bonanno, this is from the lady."

Louie took the bottle and looked around the restaurant.

"What lady?" he asked.

The waitress pointed at Alicia, across the room, sitting alone. She gave him a friendly, yet flirtatious finger wave.

"She says it'll be great with your meal," the waitress added, then walked away.

"Shit, I bet she'll go even better," Louie remarked, staring hard at the Southern belle. He waved her over.

Alicia playfully pointed to herself, as if she didn't know who he was talking to.

"Of course you," he called, "Come over here, huh? Join us."

She got up and crossed the room with a strut that commanded attention, especially from Louie and his soldiers. When she got to the table, Louie told Rizzo, "Hey, Rizz, what's the matter with you? Get the lady a chair!"

Rizzo grabbed a chair from an empty table and sat it next to Louie. Alicia sat down and giggled, "Thank you."

"No, thank *you*," Louie returned, turning on what little charm he had.

"You have good taste in the grapes."

"Well, actually it wasn't my suggestion," she admitted.

"No?" he said with a slight frown, "then whose?"

"Joey," she answered simply.

"Joey?" Louie echoed, his tone getting tense. He looked at his soldiers.

"Joey Diamanti. He says it's a peace offering for cancelling your deal with the Russians. He says there's been a misunderstanding, but he's willing to sit down, at your convenience." Alicia delivered the message, word for word.

"A sit down, huh?" Louie chuckled, a sure sign that he was boiling and ready to show her why they called him Bananas. "Listen, you fuckin' cunt, you tell that fuckin' cock suckin' faggot, he can suck my dick. Who the fuck does he think he is?" he barked, bringing attention to the table.

Rizzo reached to calm him down, but Louie already snapped. He grabbed Alicia by the hair and twisted it, pulling her out of the chair and to her knees. He leaned down and hissed in her face, "You're lucky we're in public. You tell Joey he's a fuckin' dead man and you...if I see your fuckin' face again, it'll be on a fuckin' milk carton."

He released her, flinging her to the ground. Unruffled, Alicia quickly gained her composure and stood up. The whole restaurant was riveted, especially Rizzo. He would never forget the look in her eyes—a look that told him they'd definitely see her again.

"Enjoy the wine," she said with a smile that didn't reach her eyes. Then she walked away.

"Fuck you and the fuckin' wine!" Louie growled, standing up and launching the bottle at her.

It barely missed her, but Alicia didn't look back or flinch as the bottle smashed against the exposed brick of the interior. She walked out, leaving only the tingle of the doorbell in her wake.

PRESENT DAY, AUGUST 1997

"And then what happened?" the Prosecutor questioned.

Rizzo shrugged and replied, "and then she just walked out. A coupla hours later, we found out that Joey had whacked Mickey the Russian."

Rollins shot to his feet.

"Objection, Your Honor. That is hearsay."

"Sustained," the Judge, Hendon Bartholomew, agreed. "The jury will disregard the last sentence."

"To rephrase, a couple of hours later you learned that Mikhail Pavlov had been killed by *somebody*," the Prosecutor reiterated.

"Yeah, somebody," Rizzo replied sarcastically, looking at Joey.

"Mr. Rizzo, could you tell us what the two meetings had in common, in your mind?"

"Certainly," Rizzo answered, adjusting his tie and leaning into the microphone.

Ever since becoming a Federal informant, Rizzo relished playing the role of mob historian-slash-expert in Federal trials.

"See, the Gambinos and the Russians had a deal. The Russians would be allowed to move the X."

"X being the designer drug, ecstasy, is that correct?" the Prosecutor clarified.

"Yeah, ecstasy. So yeah, we had a deal because nothing moves in Manhattan without our approval," he explained rather proudly, even though he was never more than a lowly soldier.

"Now with Mickey—I mean *Mikhail Pavlov*—being the sorta head of the Russians, our deal was with him. See, the Russians operate different from the Italians. They don't have families and like...Bosses. Everybody's pretty much independent, but guys get together and do scores. So, since Mickey had his hands in everything, he pretty much ran the Russian end of things."

"So how did his death affect relations between the Gambinos and the Russians?" the Prosecutor probed.

"It pretty much died with him. The new kid in town Zev took over, but he wouldn't deal with us, not without Joey Diamanti being a part of it," Rizzo answered.

"And then what happened?"

"Well, we had to deal with it, because we had other deals with Zev, especially the gas tax thing and that was bringing in millions for *all* the families. So we couldn't just, you know, whack 'em. Plus, you know, Russians...they ain't too smart; at least smart like us Italians. So if you go to whackin' the smart ones, the dumb ones could really become a monkey wrench. So we went to the Diamantis and complained. They said that Joey was no longer a part of that family, so we put a hit on Joey Diamanti."

"And what were the results of that...hit?" the Prosecutor probed.

Rizzo gave him his, "Come on, really?" look, glanced at Joey and shot back, "Well, obviously we missed."

The courtroom broke out in laughter. Even Joey chuckled.

Red-faced, and slightly flustered, the Prosecutor said, "I mean, what was the chain of events subsequent to the conversation with the Diamantis?"

"Pardon my French, Mr. Prosecutor, but that's when the shit really hit the fan!"

"Okay, here we go."

"Showtime."

"Smile for the camera, you greasy cock sucker."

The team of FBI Agents buzzed with sarcastic excitement as Frankie Shots pulled up to the Italian American Social Club, his base of operations. The FBI Agents were posted in a dirty faced apartment building directly across the street. The place smelled of cold pizza, corn chips, cigarettes, and determination —the last being the dominant odor because they were relentless in their pursuit. They all wanted the Diamantis so badly they could taste it.

As soon as Frankie Shots and his bodyguard Carmine got out of the Cadillac Seville, the cameras began to click incessantly, shuttering their every step into bite-sized pieces of intel.

Frankie knew they were there. They made no attempt to hide their surveillance, their talks, and their watchful eyes. Frankie looked up at their window and gave them the finger.

It had become such a regular occurrence that on the days Frankie was too occupied in his thoughts to remember to flip them the bird, he liked to think they were disappointed.

Frankie liked the idea of disappointing the feds.

"Fuck! Picture that!" Frankie spat. Then he turned and walked inside.

"I fucking hate that arrogant little prick," one of the FBI Agents hissed.

Inside, the rest of Frankie's crew was sitting around, drinking coffee, playing cards and talking. Three TVs blasted around the room in order to drown out the bugs that Frankie suspected were planted in the room. He went through the back door that led to the back steps of the tenement the club was under. He climbed the stairs to the third floor and headed down the hall to the end apartment. He knocked three times at the door. A few moments later, an old man bent with age answered.

"Frankie!" he tried to say, but his hoarse greeting was broken up by a fit of coughing. His eyes bulged like a frog and his chest heaved.

"Uncle Carlo, how are you?" Frankie greeted him with a hug. "You're lookin' good."

"Good? I'm ninety years old. Over here, just to wake up is great," Carlo replied as he shuffled alongside Frankie.

Frankie chuckled. "Knock on wood, eh?"

Frankie entered the bedroom, opened the closet door, pushing aside Carlo's clothes and the panel that was propped up to cover the hole in the back of the closet. It was tall enough for a man to walk through, and it led to the next apartment. It was the extra precaution they took in order to beat any bugs. Only the most important meetings and calls took place there.

Frankie picked up the phone and sat on the old bed as he dialed a number. The phone rang twice then Vito, Vincenzo's bodyguard, answered. "Yeah," Vito said.

"It's the kid," Frankie began, referring to Joey as *the kid*. "He did the Russian, now he's tryin' to muscle his way in on some of the action in the clubs. They feel like they got a pebble in their shoe, and they wanna know what you should do about it."

"Okay," was all Vito replied. Then he hung up.

Frankie hung up, tapped a cigarette from a packet and lit it. He pictured in his mind Vito relaying the message to Vincenzo, who was sitting right beside him. Vincenzo never spoke on the phone. The old man was smart, Frankie thought, but maybe not smart enough...

The phone rang. Frankie picked up.

"You tell them, they're free to handle their problem. Our hands are washed," Vito reported.

"Okay," Frankie answered, then hung up. He took a drag of his cigarette, savoring the smoke and the godlike power he had in his hands. Of course, it wasn't his power...not yet. But he knew it was all a matter of time.

He exhaled and dialed another number. The phone was picked up on the second ring.

"Yeah?"

"He just gave the Gambinos the green light."

"Okay, I'll make sure the word reaches the kid."

Frankie hung up, tapped his cigarette in the ashtray and took another long drag. There was nothing he'd like better than to let the Gambinos kill Joey, but he needed him alive just a little longer, to be the scapegoat.

It was all just a matter of time.

The last call was the shortest: two rings and two succinct words.

"Do it."

Then he hung up and went back in his hole.

———

Three nights later, Zev sped along the Cross Bronx Expressway in his midnight blue Porsche 940. He was on his way to see Joey, who had a safe house in the Bronx. He smoothly flipped lane to lane, dipping in and out of traffic as he sped toward his destination. He was going to tell Joey that the Gambino family had a hit on him. As he came off the exit, he thought about how he had come to find out.

Mickey had an arrangement with the Gambino family involving shipments of caviar coming from Russia. Their contact was a top-ranking soldier named Peter Amuso. When Mickey was killed, Zev inherited all of his connects. Zev already knew Peter because of Mickey's contact with the operation. He and Peter hadn't talked too much; it was always cut and dry, but Peter had taken him aside and said, "I guess congratulations are in order, huh?"

Zev just looked at him.

"What is it you are saying?" Zev asked, emotionlessly, even though he knew exactly what Peter was talking about.

Peter held up his hands and replied, "Hey, no disrespect. It's just, Brooklyn's a small place, and we run in similar circles, capice? But I understand, you know, we all gotta go sometime. Me? I got plans too, and I like you, so maybe we can help each other out one day."

"Maybe," said Zev.

"And maybe that day is today. You got that thing with Joey D?"

"Joey D?" Zev echoed, playing dumb.

Peter smiled conspiratorially.

"Joey D, you know...anyway Joey's a good kid; he's got a future, but things are about to get dark, *real* dark, if you know what I mean. Tell him to make sure he watches his mirrors. The family's got the green light," Peter explained cryptically.

Zev eyed him suspiciously.

"So why do you tell me?"

"Tell you what? I ain't told you nothin', and that's exactly what I'll say if it ever gets back to me. But you're a smart guy; I figure you'd know what to do with a gem like that, you know? We run in a tough crowd, so it's always good to have a favor or two. So keep it between us and nobody'll know you and Joey owe me, eh?" Peter concluded, then walked quickly away.

For a moment, Zev contemplated not telling Joey the information. He knew how conniving Italians could be, almost as conniving as Russians. So he knew Peter had an angle; he just couldn't see why you'd risk the wrath of your family just for a favor. Or were the Gambinos testing him to see how he would react? And lastly, why did he even care? Why get mixed up in all of their Italian bullshit? He could just let things play themselves out and make a deal with the last man standing.

Deep down, he knew that Joey would be the last man standing. He had seen more money in the last few months than he had in his whole criminal career, and he had Joey to thank. Sure, he used him to set up Mickey, thereby forcing his hand and making him a conspirator after the fact. But once the smoke cleared, he was now the Boss, a move that would've taken a war to pull off on his own. Besides, he did owe Joey a modicum of loyalty because of Seth. Russians are very sentimental...

Which is why he was pulling up to the building in which Joey was holed up. He parked the car and chirped the alarm. He smiled when he spotted the thin homeless woman in the alley, pushing the shopping cart piled with what anyone would assume were her only world possessions. When she saw Zev, she smiled back. It was Maria. The girls rotated, keeping the building under surveillance. All people saw was a crazy bag lady. She was crazy all right, but the kind of street sweeper she had in the cart would sweep more than trash. The building was a seedy, rundown tenement. It was a Black and Latino area, which Joey chose on purpose. That way, any White face would stick out.

Zev took the stairs to the third floor with gun in hand, off safety.

He got to the apartment and knocked. A few moments later he heard, "Who?"

"Me."

The door opened, and Te Amo was standing there with a Colt .45 in her hand. They both tucked their pistols in as he stepped through the door.

"Where's Joey?"

"In the salon," she quipped sarcastically.

"Huh?"

"Go look in the living room," she answered, heading for the kitchen in the opposite direction.

He walked the length of the dim hallway, toward the living room. Unlike the outside, the apartment was clean and well kept; the living room was adequately furnished. A big screen TV covered one wall, lit with the somber colors of *Batman*. Chi-Chi lay on the floor, watching it. When he looked to the right, he couldn't help but laugh despite the gravity of the situation. He understood what Te Amo meant by *the salon*. Joey was sitting in a leather recliner, reclined and wearing nothing but sweatpants, as Marilyn gave him a pedicure. Maliah was giving him a manicure and Anita was giving him a facial.

Joey looked up when he heard Zev's laughter, and shook his head. "This is what happens when you go to the mattresses with a bunch of broads."

"Shut the fuck up," Anita scolded him, "before you crack your mask."

"I'm like a Ken doll over here. Hey Zev, please get these cunts somebody to kill, will ya?"

Hearing the word "kill," Zev's mind returned to the current situation. "We need to talk."

Joey nodded, swung his legs to the floor and got up.

"Come on, while I get this shit off my face," he said.

They went to the bathroom and Zev talked while Joey wiped the cream off with a towel.

"The Gambinos have a price on your head."

Joey stopped and looked at him, studying him intently.

"Since when?"

"Recently. I don't know. I learned about it today."

"From who? Where? Tell me what you know," Joey demanded in rapid-fire fashion.

Zev started from the beginning and as he talked, Joey paced the floor like a caged jaguar in a zoo. When he finished, Joey growled, "Again, tell me again."

And Zev did. Joey listened intently, scrutinizing Zev's every word, stopping him several times, as if he were interrogating him or trying to catch him in a lie. He wanted to know, but the most painful part was to hear that the Gambinos had gotten the green light. That could mean only one thing.

His father had no only turned his back on him, but wanted him removed from the game completely.

When he survived the hit, he told himself that his father would've never okayed a hit on his own son. There had to be another explanation. But now, it was rock solid. He knew the Gambinos would never move without the green light and only his father could've given that green light.

"Who the fuck is this guy? What's his name?" Joey probed.

"That is no matter; the point is what will we do now," Zev replied, trying to keep a lid on Joey's anger and guide him to a better, clearer state of mind.

It didn't work.

"Fuck do you mean, it don't matter? You protecting this guy or something?" Joey barked. "This cock sucker tells you I'm marked and thinks he can play both sides? Who the fuck is he?"

Zev bristled, not at Joey's tone, but the implications. He

spoke calmly in a measured tone, but it was the measure of a cold heart growing frozen.

"I did not have to bring you this. That fact alone I urge you to remember."

The two eyed each other evenly. Tension filled the bathroom. Joey felt it and reluctantly relented, recognizing Zev's sincerity in his anger. "Zev...I'm not asking you to go against your word. You have *my* word that nothing will happen to this guy. I just need to know what I'm dealing with."

Zev thought for a moment, then his gaze softened. "Peter Amuso."

Joey nodded then pinched his lip, pensively, pacing as he talked. "Okay...this is what you tell him...tell him I freaked, that I pulled a gun, whatever, dress it up, make it sound good, follow me? And then you follow *him*. Have someone good pin a tail on him. I don't care if the fuckin' Feds are following the son of a bitch; you follow them *and* him. I wanna know who he goes out of his way to meet, and trust me, he'll do just that," Joey surmised.

Zev nodded. "And what will you do?"

"I'm going to a Yankee game; the Red Sox are in town," Joey replied, then walked out of the bathroom.

At Yankee Stadium, the Red Sox were in town and the Bronx was on its worst behavior. Scalpers peddled their wares openly, because it was as if the police looked the other way for Yankees/Red Sox tickets.

Louis "Bananas" Bonanno and his raven haired six-year-old son walked through the crowd. His son was dressed in Yankee pinstripes from head to toe, Don Mattingly's Number 23 worn proudly on his back. He carried a right-handed baseball glove because it was still too big for him to wear, but he had to have it.

Louie got into the spirit as well, wearing an identical glove as his son's and a Yankee cap on his head. They looked like the average American father and son, not the gangster and his kid. Louie looked forward to this first time with his son, because it reminded him of the times with his father. He didn't even have his bodyguards with him when he went to Yankee games. They trailed him to and from the Stadium, but stayed with the car. This was father-son time: a fatal mistake.

The Yankees were looking good, and Louie was enjoying himself, so much so that he never notice the two redheads that sat behind him. He was on the third base side, mid-level, where the overhang made the boisterous cheers and sonorous boos bounce all around.

The two redheads cheered when the crowd cheered, booed when the crowd booed, all as if they were in Rome. They blended in and stood out at the same time, just as they wanted to. They were patient and yet on edge. They were waiting for one thing...

The wave.

The wave was a crowd favorite. In every stadium, at every type of a sporting event, someone would set off the wave. The concept was simple: one section would start it by standing up, throwing up their hands and then sitting down. Isolated, it had no effect, but if everyone in the stadium did it—one right after another—the visual effect truly looked like a human wave. It was fun, it was a huge crowd pleaser, and it was also the perfect moment for a murder.

Right before the 5th inning, it happened. It started in the right field bleachers.

"Look, Daddy, the wave is coming!" Louie's son exclaimed, excitedly.

"Yeah, that's a pretty big wave," Louie chuckled.

"Can we do it, Daddy, please?" the boy pleaded.

"You sure you can swim?" Louie teased.

The people rose and sat in a unison that looked choreographed and not the spontaneous creation that it was. As it made its way around the first base line, Louie felt a tap on his shoulder. He turned to see who it was and looked into the pretty smile of one of the redheads.

"Remember me?" she asked.

"Nah," Louie replied coldly. He hated to be interrupted during his father-son outing.

He turned back around, but something in the back of his mind made him remember her eyes, the clear blueness of them, the shimmer—but most of all, he remembered the coldness. He had seen it before; it only took him a second to remember.

"Here we go, Dad!" his son gleefully announced, as the wave engulfed them.

Louie saw his son's mouth move, but he was oblivious to the words. The sound of cheers all around overwhelmed his senses. The people in front of them and behind them stood up, so he was alone deep in the pocket of the wave. As he turned his head back to look at the girl with the cold blue eyes, he felt a sharp, searing sensation run across his throat, starting at his jugular vein and ending across his Adam's apple. It stung, but it didn't burn, and his mind told him what had just happened.

His throat had been cut from ear to ear.

The weapon Alicia had used was a surgeon's scalpel, an instrument designed to save lives, yet just as effective in taking one. Louie began to gurgle on his blood, as he leaned back in the seat, grasping at his throat. The agony he felt was nothing compared to the agony he would've felt had he seen what was happening to his son. At the same time that Alicia was slicing Louie's throat, Amanda was doing the same thing to his son.

Just as he stood up, throwing his little arms in the air, Amanda grabbed him by the forehead and plunged the scalpel expertly into his neck and slit his entire throat in one smooth motion; then she forced his dying body into a slump in his seat. His neck was so small that, had she cut further, she would've decapitated him. Blood sprayed like summer rain onto the man in front of him, but he was having too much fun to notice.

It happened so fast, that by the time the wave had moved onto its completion, the two redheads were making their way up two separate aisles. When they merged with the crowd, they had discarded their wigs and were simple dyed brunettes. People would later tell the police conflicting stories. One story said a redhead that went left; others said a brunette that went right. Still, others said the brunette went left and the redhead went right.

The murder scandalized the City. It was clear that it was a mob hit, but what was unusual was that a child was murdered as well. Everyone knew that La Cosa Nostra didn't involve wives and kids.

But Joey was sending a message and declaring war on the old ways. If you don't recognize me, I don't recognize your rules, and without rules, only the best man would win. He was determined to prove that he was the best man.

The very best there was.

Several days later, Joey jumped out of a cab in front of the Trump Hotel and handed the cabby a $50 bill.

"Keep the change," he told him.

He adjusted the cuffs on his double-breasted silk pinstriped Brioni suit. His hair looked like he had just stepped out of the stylist's chair and a diamond pinkie ring winked whenever it was given time to reflect. His swagger turned heads as he headed inside the hotel.

He had come to see Enrico, who had just arrived from Miami with the latest shipment of X-pills. The drug was beginning to really catch on at the clubs and college campuses, up and down the East Coast. Joey's team was making money hand over fist. Everybody was playing their part, but it was Enrico who had really come though like a champ.

He had the smuggling game down to a science. Instead of using the New York airports, he used Miami International. He told Joey he had a mole in baggage, customs, and maintenance. He knew his trade well, and that impressed Joey. His relationship with the New Yorker was no longer standoffish, but still had an air of tension that Joey felt was time to clear up. Always one to push the button, Joey had come to shove it, open fistedly over the cliff.

Enrico was staying on the 21st floor. When Joey got off the elevator, he almost bumped into a sexy little Asian getting in the elevator.

"Excuse me," he smiled.

"Anytime," she replied, flirtatiously.

They exchanged looks—more like licks—then passed on, each to their respective destinations. Joey arrived at the door and knocked. Several seconds later, Enrico answered it.

"Joey, good to see you! Come on in," Enrico greeted, shaking his hand.

Joey stepped inside, looking around the luxurious suite.

"Living in the slums, I forgot how the other half lives," Joey quipped.

Enrico chuckled.

"What are you drinking?" Enrico asked, standing at the bar.

"Anything but vodka," Joey replied, unbuttoning his suit jacket then sitting down on the couch and crossing his legs, right over left in languid gangster style. "Fuckin' Zev."

"Yeah, I know what you mean. I just dropped off the shipment," Enrico chuckled.

"Everything good?" Joey asked, knowing that everything

was good already, but wanting to see how Enrico rated the situation.

"Good? I'm the best," Enrico shot back, cockily.

Joey held up his glass, as if to toast his arrogance. "I love a guy with confidence," he remarked, then drank.

Enrico sat on the arm of the love seat, eyes intent on Joey. "I heard that the Yankee thing with the kid got the cops riled up," he said.

Joey shrugged. "It's their job to bust balls; keeps you on your toes."

"Yeah, but hits don't usually involve kids. Whoever did it must've been...pissed," Enrico surmised then sipped his drink.

Joey nodded with a slight smirk that seemed to say, "I'll indulge you." He sat his glass down on the end table, turning his attention back to Enrico.

"What is it that you're trying to say, Enrico?" Joey questioned, his tone with an ever so subtle hint of warning.

Unflapped, Enrico simply shrugged and replied, "Just making observations."

Joey nodded and echoed, "Observations...okay."

He stood up and grabbed his drink.

"Come on, I wanna show you something," Joey announced, heading across the room to the balcony. He opened the sliding doors, stepped out then looked back to see Enrico still perched on the arm of the chair. "Whaddya doin'? I said I wanna show you something."

"Out there?" Enrico asked, in a deadpan tone.

"It'll only take a second, I promise. Besides, it's a beautiful night." Joey smiled, but his eyes conveyed something else.

Enrico felt like he knew Joey's game, so he was compelled to play along. He downed his drink and got up, stopping at the bar to fix another. He then joined Joey on the balcony.

"Welcome to New York," Joey declared, as he threw up his arms playfully. "Welcome to my City. Now look," he said, throwing his arms around Enrico's shoulder and taking a sip of his drink. He pointed at the skyline with the index finger of his drink hand. "I wanna make an observation about New York. This place...it stinks. The only thing that keeps it from being Calcutta is that it's godless. But it's beautiful at night. Look at her. The stars twinkle like fairy dust, and somewhere some sucker believes in it, you know? But that's only because you can't see the dirt at night, the grime...the rot, eh? It's like the thing, I forgot the word, but the night. New York wears it like it's a word."

"Façade," Enrico suggested.

Joey pointed at him. "That's a good one. I like that. Façade. Wasn't the word I was lookin' for, but it fits well enough. So I take it that you get what I'm saying," Joey questioned, as he took his arm from around Enrico and looked at him.

Enrico returned his level gaze.

"Loud and clear."

Joey sipped his drink and watched Enrico for a moment.

"You know, Enrico, I like you. You're a smart guy and you're good at what you do. We may've gotten off to a rocky start, but I guess we had to feel each other out, kinda sorta, ya think?"

"I agree," Enrico nodded.

"And me and you...I can see us doing some big things. Sky's the limit. But to do that, you know what we need, you know what's missin'?" Joey asked rhetorically.

Enrico, self-assured that he knew where Joey was going, played his role and said, "What?"

"Trust," Joey stated simply, adding "in our line of business, you've got to have two things: respect from your enemies and trust from your friends. So I ask you for your trust."

"You've never given me a reason not to trust you, Joey."

Joey smiled with genuine warmth. "That's good to know. And I hope that continues to hold, because I'm gonna ask you to take off your clothes."

The statement took a blink to settle in Enrico's mind, and when it did, it threw him because he wasn't expecting it.

"What?" he asked, confusedly.

"Your clothes, Enrico. Take 'em off." Joey repeated, any trace of a smile now gone.

"What the hell are—" he started to say, and then it hit him. "You think I'm wearing a wire?"

Joey made a conciliatory gesture with his hands. "Please... Enrico, this isn't about you, remember? I'm asking you to trust *me*."

Enrico saw the psychological ploy Joey was using, but it was one for which he had no defense. By wording it—not as a question of Enrico's trustworthiness, but of his own—Joey had painted him in a corner, the only way out being compliance.

"This is fuckin' crazy! I'm not taking off my clothes! I'm not wearing a wire! I'm not a cop!" Enrico protested.

"I'm not wearing one either. You want me to take mine off too?" Joey chuckled. "Come on, Enrico. Trust me."

Enrico eyed Joey hard. He knew this was a test he had to pass. He knew that if he did, the sky was truly the limit. But if he didn't...it didn't bear thinking about.

"This is crazy," he mumbled as he began to unbutton his shirt.

Joey leaned back casually against the railing, crossing his feet at the ankles and watching him strip.

Once his shirt was unbuttoned, it revealed the gun in his waistband. He sat it on a small table just inside the door. He took off his shirt, revealing a toned yet muscular physique. He stepped out of his gator sandals then dropped his pants, revealing his powder blue Calvin Klein briefs.

"See? No fuckin' wires," Enrico hissed indignantly.

Joey approached him and peered around him to make sure nothing was attached to his back. Satisfied, he said, "Okay," and then did something Enrico didn't expect...

Joey grabbed him by the back of the neck, pulled into him and kissed Enrico, forcing his tongue into his shocked mouth.

Enrico snatched away instantly.

"What the *fuck* are you doing?" he barked, full of bass.

"Makin' an observation," Joey replied, without a hint of humor, and then reached for Enrico again.

Enrico knocked his hand away and simultaneously threw an overhand right hook at Joey, but it was off balance. Joey easily ducked it and shot a short jab to Enrico's kidney that stung a grunt from his lips. Enrico buckled and stumbled, trying to spin and square off with Joey, but that was made more difficult because he had his pants around his ankles—a fact that Joey had anticipated.

"Like I said, my City," Joey huffed. "Now let me show it to you."

Joey landed a barrage of punches, all body blows, all taking their toll as he pushed Enrico up against the balcony and shoved his head back until he was bent over backwards, looking at New York from twenty-one stories up, upside down. The sight made him dizzy, but also made him fight harder because he felt his life was on the line.

Enrico brought his leg up fast, to try to knee Joey in the nuts, but Joey twisted his body, and blocked the attempt with his own knee. He gave Enrico two powerful blows to the solar plexus that knocked the wind from his body and the fight from his spirit. Enrico slumped against the railing, gasping against Joey's chest.

"This dance ain't over," Joey chuckled in his ear.

He bent Enrico over the balcony rail and ripped his briefs down around his thighs. When Enrico felt that, his whole frame of mind changed.

Rape.

The word leapt into his mind and fired up every survival neuron in his brain. He tried to get a footing, but Joey had him bent over the railing so precariously that it was Joey's weight that kept him anchored to the spot. Nevertheless, he struggled, kicked and cursed, "I'm going to kill you! You fucking cunt!"

Joey delivered several more merciless kidney shots that made Enrico feel like he might piss fire from the burning pain. But just when he thought the pain couldn't get worse, he felt an explosion of intense torture as Joey forced himself deep inside his virgin asshole.

"Arrrgghh!" Enrico bellowed and his scream seemed to blanket New York, but it was swallowed by the angry car horns, traffic, and banter of the New York City streets.

"I'm going to..." was all Enrico could get out, because he felt like he was being split into from the back. The pain was seemingly unbearable. Every man has a threshold, and Enrico wished he could reach his so he could simply pass out. However, just when he couldn't take the fresh hurt any longer and he welcomed mindless bliss, he got a glimpse of something beyond pain. It was as undeniable as it was inexplicable, therefore inescapable. It was so overwhelming that it seemed to overshadow the pain, and the pain turned to hatred; hatred of Joey for knowing it was there.

Joey exploded inside him, filling him with his hot load then emotionlessly let his limp body fall to the ground. Joey pulled his pants up and went back inside the suite. He walked over to the bar and poured himself two fingers of cognac. After several moments, he felt Enrico standing behind him. He turned around and found Enrico with his gun aimed at him. The look on Enrico's face was one of pure disgust; on Joey's was one of cold amusement.

Joey sipped his drink, and raised a questioning eyebrow. "So you gonna kill me now, Enrico?"

The gun trembled in Enrico's hand, not from fear but from rage. The hatred Joey had released in him burned in his veins until it tasted like bile in his mouth. Every fiber in his being wanted to pull the trigger, but every fiber in his being prevented him from doing it.

One look into his eyes and Joey knew it.

"You gonna shoot...shoot," Joey taunted, knowing he wouldn't. He couldn't.

"You dirty son of a bitch," Enrico hissed then gripped the gun with both hands as if to steady it or to stop himself from shooting.

Joey laughed at his impotence. He sat his drink down and stepped closer. Even though Enrico was the one holding the gun, when Joey stepped toward him, he stepped back.

"Why did you even bother to fight? You think I didn't know? You think I couldn't see? Of course you did, and you knew this day was comin.'" Joey downed his drink in once swift gulp, then added, "You can thank me later."

"You...you...you won't get away with this," Enrico vowed. "You ever come near me again, I'll kill you," Enrico stammered.

Joey laughed.

"Well kid, that horse has already left the barn, but don't worry... This'll be our little secret."

Joey put down his glass, then turned and walked out the door.

PRESENT DAY JULY 1997

"Y ou're set to go on trial for your *life*. The government says they have an airtight case, and that several of the most notorious people in organized crime have agreed to testify against you. Aren't you just a little worried?"

Joey gave Diane Reynolds, the host of *Night Talk* his most charming smile and with a light chuckle answered, "Diane, when the truth is on your side, whom should you fear? What the government wants to present to the American people is a gangster movie, starring me as the bad guy. But I'm not the bad guy, Diane. I'm a simple Brooklyn boy who made good. I think the American people will see that. I trust them, and I think they trust me."

Joey winked at the camera, knowing that several million people—including members of the potential jury pool—would be tuned in, hanging on his every word. His plan was to try the case in the court of public opinion, because he knew if he won there, the trial was over before it even got started.

"But, Mr. Diamanti..."

"Joey," he corrected her.

"Joey...the government has charged you with some pretty

heinous things. On top of drug smuggling and money laundering, they also have accused you of several murders, including the 1990 slaying of six-year-old, little Andrew Bonanno and—"

"Excuse me, Diane, I'm sorry, but I really have to stop you right there," Joey objected, leaning forward toward the camera, a solemn look on his face. "To be accused of being a gangster or a drug dealer is one thing, but to be accused of actually taking the life of an innocent child..." he shook his head after letting his voice trail off then concluded, "No Diane, I would never do anything like that, I wouldn't even know where to begin to have anything to do with such a heinous crime. I think it truly shows the government's desperation in even charging me."

Joey pinched the bridge of his nose and shook his head, playing to the camera like the pro he was.

"I don't mean to upset you, Mr. Dia—I mean—Joey, I'm sure this is tough, but..."

"I mean, where do you draw the line, you know? I just think it's disgusting," he remarked, frowning as if the word tasted like it sounded.

"But it's not just that, is it, Joey? The government has even implicated you in an attempted murder much closer to home. So I have to ask, did you put a hit on your own father?"

MAY 1990

"Joey?"

"Yeah?"

"You remember that thing with Peter Amuso?"

"Of course. How could I forget?"

"He just met with a man in Queens, at a diner called Andy's."

"Thanks, and Zev..."

"Yes?"

"I owe you one."

PRESENT DAY, AUGUST 1997

"Listen ... I know Joey Diamanti had Louie Bananas and his kid killed!" Joe Provenzano stated adamantly from the witness stand, slapping the wooden rail with his palm.

"Objection, Your Honor! Speculation!" Rollins interjected, rising halfway out of his seat.

"Overruled. Please continue, Mr. Provenzano," the Judge Bartholomew answered.

Joe Pro nodded.

"See," he began, looking at the jury, "there's things you just *know*, you know what I mean? It's a gut instinct. Now I've been a gangster all my life. I'm now 55, so if I know anything, it's La Cosa Nostra: *this thing of ours*. We're men of honor, men of respect, and no true Mafioso would *ever* kill a kid! But Joey, he ain't a man of respect; he's an animal. I curse the day we inducted him into this thing of ours!" Joe Pro remarked with disgust, eyeballing Joey hard.

Joey simply smiled and gave a little nod.

"Mr. Provenzano, if you would, please tell the court why you feel the way you do," the Prosecutor led him.

"Yeah, I was getting to that. You see, Joey wanted to send a message. One that would not be misunderstood. He wanted us to know he didn't respect the old ways, the tradition. He knew by including the kid in the hit, the police would put pressure on us, which would mean we couldn't move on him right away. It was cowardly, smart...but cowardly."

"So he hid behind the boy's vicious murder, knowing in the environs of heightened police scrutiny, none of the crime families wanted to get involved—thereby isolating the Gambino family to act alone," the Prosecutor interpreted.

"Exactly," Joe Pro nodded.

"And is that what happened?"

"Well, yes and no," Joe Pro continued. "Joey killed a Made Man, but at the time he wasn't one. So even though the Gambino regime already had the green light, he basically became the Diamanti regime's responsibility to get involved out of respect," he explained.

"And did they?" the Prosecutor asked like he already knew the answer, and just wanted the jury to hear it.

"They would've, except Joey did the unthinkable."

"Which was?"

"He put a hit on his own old man!"

MAY 1990

"We're gonna do what?" Te Amo exclaimed, her mouth making a surprised 'O'.

She and Joey were lying in bed, naked and sweaty. She was basking in the afterglow, resting her head on his chest, until he said to her: "I think it's time we hit my old man."

She looked at his face to make sure he wasn't joking.

He wasn't.

"Your own father, Joey?" she questioned.

He shrugged, but wouldn't meet her gaze. "Ask him, *his own son*?"

"So this is what it's about? The hit on you?"

He turned his head and looked squarely at her. "Fuckin' right! That's what it's about. You throw me to the wolves, I eat those wolves, but I still ain't full. He's got it coming."

Te Amo ran her hand through her hair and sighed.

"Even I know killing a Boss changes the whole game. It'll unite the families against you."

Joey smirked as if he knew something that she didn't, or at least something he didn't know she knew. "Yeah, it may...but I doubt it. Reason being, a lotta people wouldn't mind whackin' the Don, but nobody's got the heart. So here I go! I get the job done, and I make my father's enemies my friends," he surmised expertly.

"But what if you fail? Suppose his enemies aren't as powerful as his friends?" she countered, knowing joey was not for turning however much she tried to reason him out of it.

He ran his hand, slowly up and down her back. "Then go back to Miami. Remember me on my birthday, name your first kid after me," he quipped.

"You know I would never do that."

"What? Remember me or name the kid?"

"Leave you," she replied, looking him dead in the eyes.

He smiled, pulled her to him and kissed her gently then remarked.

"Loyalty should taste this sweet. Don't worry, though. We won't fail. It's succeeding that's the problem," he said.

Te Amo nodded.

"So, what's the plan?"

Joey didn't answer for a moment, as he mentally rolled the tape of his father's routines.

"Every Sunday, he goes to Mass. Vincenzo is a good Catholic," he quipped sarcastically. "My mama used to go with him until she got sick. So she stopped. It's the perfect place."

"In a church, Joey?"

He flashed a toothy grin then asked, "What better place to die?"

Te Amo laughed.

"I guess you got a point."

"This Sunday. There's no need to wait. We'll take the girls through a dry run, but I want you to get Enrico up here. He's a face no one's seen, so we'll use him as the driver. We can't get the Russians involved. It's gotta be all us," he explained.

"I'll get him here tomorrow," she assured him.

He nodded.

"Okay. Good deal. But don't tell him why. No need to let the cat outta the bag before we skin 'em."

Te Amo gazed into his eyes, her head at a curious angle. Her expression was half-admiration, half-apprehension.

"Joey Diamonds...What will you do next?"

"Naw, the question ain't 'what will I do?' it's what *won't* I do?" he responded, his smile melting into a sneer of menace.

In the wee hours of that Sunday morning, Joey gathered his team in the living room. Enrico had just arrived, reluctantly, from Miami. He only came because it was Te Amo who called. Since the rape, he had been dealing directly with Zev, avoiding Joey like the plague. But now that he was in the same room as Joey, he found his eyes kept falling on him. It was like the wound you keep touching, even though you know it is painful.

No one knew what the plan was, but only Enrico objected vehemently when Joey concluded the explanation with, "Before he goes to church, we hit him."

"What?" Enrico barked. "Are you nuts? I'm not killing anybody!"

"You're right; you're driving."

"I'm not having anything to do with this," Enrico stated firmly, meeting Joey's gaze. Although it wasn't as firm as it once was.

"Look, Enrico...I know this is out of the blue, but somethin' this big, you keep under wraps 'cause sometimes words grow wings, you follow? Now this way, there's no chance of a leak."

"Count me out," Enrico replied.

Te Amo stood up slowly and approached Enrico.

"That's not possible. We're a team, so we move as one. Never forget, you work for the Reyes family, and *this* is Reyes business," she explained calmly, but with unmistakable authority.

"Does your mother know about this?" Enrico challenged.

Te Amo smiled, but her eyes didn't when she said in Spanish, and close to his ear: "I am my mother's daughter; you want to see?"

She stepped back and looked him in the eye. Enrico realized that her statement was one of sheer bravado. It was an ultimatum. He knew that if he refused, he wouldn't walk out alive.

"Enrico," Joey said, "I know you're not a killer," he remarked and the look in his eyes told him all he needed to know. Joey wasn't taunting him; he was simply stating a fact. "All we need you to do is drive. We'll handle the rest."

Enrico eyed Joey coldly, but when he didn't answer, Joey took his silence as approval, so he turned back to the rest of the crew.

"Pop never takes a lot of bodyguards anymore, especially to church. So it'll only be him and Uncle Vito. This'll be quick and simple, nothing fancy. Bianca, you'll be in a stolen car behind our van. Maria, you'll be in another one out front. You run interference. Anybody wanna play here, just scare 'em; if it's the police, obstruct 'em. We'll pull up, bang bang and we're gone. Five blocks away, Marilyn you'll be waitin' with another stolen car. We burn the van, and it's done. Any questions?"

He looked around. Everyone nodded to themselves, yet remained silent.

Joey then pulled out one of the sawn-off double barrel shotguns and handed it to Te Amo. Then he picked up the other one.

"And this...is what I'm using. I say 'I' because this is personal. I shoot my father; Te Amo, you hit Uncle Vito. Don't take chances; aim for the chest."

She nodded, looking at the weapon in her hands.

"Lupara," she said, referring to the Sicilian name for the gun.

Joey glanced at her, mildly surprised that she knew the correct name.

"The other Dons will know what it means."

"Which is?" Amanda asked.

"Call it, a backhanded Sicilian compliment, eh? Ask me later, I'll explain it better. So...everybody clear?"

They all nodded.

"Let's make it happen."

As they filed out the door, Joey walked beside Enrico and smoothly whispered, "Now that you already know you can trust me, after this I'll know I can trust you." He stepped away without waiting for a reply.

Enrico's first reaction was disgust, but as the words sunk in, he understood them perfectly...

...and he hated himself for it.

———

"Any word?" Vincenzo asked Vito, as they drove to church that Sunday morning.

"Not a thing," said Vito. "The kid's laying pretty low."

Vincenzo nodded, glancing out of the window.

"Then he knows."

"Yeah, well he gotta have figured it, you know? I mean, Bananas was a Made guy," Vito responded.

"Please don't remind me," Vincenzo spat back. "He was a junk pusher, and the penalty for that is that you're done. No questions asked," he vented, adding, "But all the families, the regimes with 'no' on their lips, but 'yes' in their palms...*this* is the result."

"You think maybe—" Vito began, but Vincenzo knew what he would say.

"No," he cut him off, with a sigh of resignation, "No. We

cannot interfere. Joey has violated our honor, and for that he must pay."

———————

Joey rode in the back of the van, with his ski mask resting on top of his head and caressing the Lupara, deep in thought. Te Amo, sitting across from him, watched him. She could only imagine his state of mind.

"Hey," she called to him, giving him a firm but supportive look. "You okay?"

"Yeah," he replied.

Enrico glanced at them through the rearview mirror.

"Te Amo," she said softly to Joey.

He smiled.

"I know your name," he cracked.

"I wasn't saying my name," she told him, looking him in the eyes.

He returned her gaze and replied, "I know."

———————

"You think I made a mistake?" Vincenzo asked Vito.

Vito glanced over at him, and knew by the look on his face exactly what he was talking about.

He shrugged.

"You know, Boss, every man has to decide what his own mistakes are. If this life was good enough for you, then why not give it to your kid? If we were doctors or something, we'd send our kids to medical school, right? So, what's the difference? Otherwise we'd be sayin' this life is no good, right?" Vito surmised.

Vincenzo nodded, taking in the wisdom of a friend.

"Just be glad you had all daughters," Vincenzo remarked, and the two old friends shared a laugh.

Joey could see the church ahead as they approached. Everything was in place. Everything was going according to plan. He held the Lupara in his gloved hands and looked at Te Amo.

"Here we go," he said, pulling the ski mask over his face.

Vito pulled into the church parking lot and began to look for a parking space.

"Make sure you get one up front. Okay? My knee's been acting up lately," Vincenzo remarked.

"No problem, Boss."

Neither of them paid any attention to the beige van idling beside the rear entrance of the church. Nor did they pay attention as it began to inch forward as they parked at the end of the front row, the passenger door exposed.

Vito got out first and walked around to open the passenger side door for Vincenzo. He took a cursory look around, but it was more out of habit than vigilance, because he failed to pick up the slow roll of the van, not even twenty-five feet away. But as Vincenzo got out, the presence of the van could not be ignored.

Enrico briefly accelerated the last ten feet as Joey slid open the van's side door. Vito spun around, just as Enrico stopped right in front of the two men.

Vincenzo looked into the cutout holes of the ski mask and knew instantly that he was looking into the eyes of his son. There was no surprise, no fear, not even anger. Vincenzo's look was one of contented resignation.

Joey knew his father knew, but he didn't hesitate. He met his father's look of resignation with one of determination. He leveled the Lupara and pulled the trigger. The first blast hit Vincenzo high in the chest, throwing him off his feet. The second hit him center mass, crumbling him against the vehicle door. Then he fell, facedown on the pavement.

Te Amo's shot hit Vito in the stomach and chest, pushing him back against the car, as he slumped to the ground.

"Go!" Joey barked at Enrico.

Enrico skidded off.

Mission complete.

"Breaking news: Godfather of the Diamanti crime family, Vincenzo Diamanti, was shot this morning."

"Details are sketchy, but sources close to the investigation are saying Vincenzo Diamanti is dead."

"...is alive in critical condition."

"It is unclear as to his status."

"It is believed to be in retaliation for the Bonanno hit, which left the reputed mobster and his son dead."

It didn't take long for the word to get out, and once it did, it was all that New York was talking about.

The hospital that they took Vincenzo and Vito to was flooded with reporters and cameras, almost before they themselves got there. Frankie Shots brought along twenty guys just to secure the floor where they were being treated, away from reporters and cameras. But the one face he didn't expect to see was Joey's. Joey, Enrico, Te Amo, and Maria got off the elevator and began walking toward Frankie. Several of Frankie's men closed ranks around him and repositioned themselves until they had Joey and his entourage surrounded.

Joey took a casual glance over both shoulders then looked at Frankie Shots.

"Call off your dogs. I'm just here to see my father," Joey said.

"You got a lot of nerve comin' down here, Joey," Frankie remarked, closing the distance between them.

Joey did the same until they were almost nose-to-nose.

"I don't know what you're talkin' about..."

"Oh, you know exactly what I'm talkin' about."

"Like I said, I'm here to see my pops."

"Too bad. No visitors," Frankie seethed.

"So if you'll excuse me, I'm goin' in now," Joey informed him, disregarding his words as if he hadn't even heard them.

But as he tried to walk back, Frankie put his hand on Joey's forearm.

"Maybe you didn't hear me..."

"No, maybe you didn't hear *me*," Joey spat back, "but I'm goin' to see my father, Frankie. If you wanna stop me, we can settle it right here, right now. When the smoke clears, whoever's left standin' wins."

The tension spread across the hallway, radiating from the two of them, until every eye was on them. Frankie's guys slowly reached for their weapons, just as Joey's crew did the same. It was beginning to look like a Mexican standoff with Joey and Frankie locked in an eye-to-eye boxing match. But Frankie blinked.

He gave Joey a smile that was more like a sneer then said, "Okay, tough guy. I *can* still call you that, right?" Frankie quipped. Joey knew exactly what he was trying to say, but he didn't bite. "Be my guest. But one day soon, I'll take you up on that 'settle it' offer. How's that?"

"I can't wait," Joey retorted then walked away, leaving Frankie's gaze to burn a hole in his back.

He walked toward the door at the end of the hall. He

stopped before he went in, took a deep breath, knocked softly then entered.

"Joseph," was the first word he heard, from a voice whose sound could still soothe his soul.

It was his mother.

As soon as he entered the room, she crossed the room from her husband's bedside to her son's arms and embraced him. Even though she was a full foot shorter than Joey, it still felt like he was hugging her knees like when he was little and it felt good...almost too good, and his guilt made him pull back.

"You went away. How come I don't see you anymore?" she asked him, with tears for her husband in her eyes, but a smile for her son on her face. "I miss you."

"I missed you too, Ma. Things..." His voice trailed off, because he couldn't find the words to even describe the situation.

She nodded and squeezed his hand, then took a deep breath.

"Look at what they've done to your father," she whispered, holding back the tears, but not the anguish.

The words cut through Joey like a knife, because he was the "they" of which she spoke. Therefore his guilt was her anguish, and it was killing him inside. He looked at his father in the hospital bed and tears welled up in his eyes.

"I'm...I'm sorry, Pop."

His mother hugged him. "No Joey, this is not your fault. If you had been there, I know you would've done all you could to stop it, but then...I dread to even think about what could've happened to you," she sobbed.

"No, Mama, you don't understand," Joey replied, head bowed.

"These animals...in a church?" She questioned, crossing herself then sent up a quick prayer in Sicilian.

"Don't pray for me, Mama," Joey mumbled.

"Only God can save us from the Devil, Joseph."

"That's just it, Mama," Joey stammered, looking at his mother, his cheeks streaked with tears. "I am the Devil because...I shot Pop."

By the time Joey rendezvoused with his crew, he had his game face back. There was no trace of the remorse he felt in the presence of his parents. They were waiting for him just across the New Jersey border on the other end of the George Washington Bridge, at an open-faced motel that has seen better days.

When he walked in, all conversation ceased and everybody turned to him, the collective question in their eyes.

Stone-faced, he answered it:

"He's gonna make it," he announced in a tone laced with trepidation.

Te Amo was the first to speak.

"So what does that mean?" she asked.

"It means trouble, so we gonna have to get out of town for a while. Regroup," he explained.

"So what...go back to Miami?" Te Amo suggested.

"Naw," Joey shook his head. "If they find out you were involved, your mother's already gonna have questions to answer. We go to Miami, they'll see it as being under her protection."

"But...does he think you're involved?"

"I'm here, ain't I? If he did, that wouldn't be so," he lied. "But chances are that he will, eventually. We wanna be regrouped, if and when he does."

He looked around the room. Every soul present was a cold-blooded killer, yet they all knew what they had unleashed upon themselves, so Joey could sense the apprehension.

"Look, this is a setback, no doubt about it. But it ain't the end of the world. Trust me, I still got a couple of aces up my sleeve," he cracked, then gave them a reassuring smile.

"So where are we going?" Enrico questioned.

Joey turned to him and answered, "L.A. It's an open city. Nobody controls the rackets there. We'll see it comin' a mile away."

Bianca chuckled.

"What's the punchline?" Joey asked her.

"Nothing. It's just that I'm from L.A., born and raised there, and my whole family is Blood. L.A. may be open for you spaghetti heads, but we run it!"

Her joke broke the tension and made everyone laugh, gaining a second wind, especially for Joey. He knew having a gang like the Bloods with you was like an army. He grinned and replied, "Cali is looking even better already."

PRESENT DAY, AUGUST 1997

He blew into the courtroom like a breeze, with a powerful whoosh, but as light as a feather. He knew the importance of a good entrance, and in his mind this was a courtroom drama that he had come to be choreographed to perfection. Several actors in attendance exchanged waves and air kisses as he walked up the aisle and headed straight to the witness stand. Joey watched him impassively, following his movements with his eyes. His hand propped up under his chin. He struck a strong contrast to the somberness of the courtroom with his streak of platinum blond hair worn asymmetrically and partially covering one eye. His face as youthful as a 12-year-old boy; yet he was 45. He was enviably thin and his colorful yet tasteful combination of pastels made his presence feel like a smile. The bailiff brought over the Bible, and he was sworn in.

"I do," he replied with an impish grin, then took his seat on the stand. The Prosecutor stood, approached the stand, and said, "Please state your name for the record."

The blond leaned into the microphone, tapped it lightly to make sure it was on, and replied, "Martin Latrell. But my friends call me Marty."

"And Mr. Latrell, what is your occupation?"

"I'm a movie producer; a very successful movie producer, if I may add," Marty arrogantly declared, sweeping his bangs out of his face and trying unsuccessfully to hook them behind his ear.

"And in your profession, have you ever had any reason to know Joseph Diamanti?"

"My God, yes," Marty quipped, hand to his chest, mimicking a clutching of pearls. "It was horrible; that man's a monster."

"And do you see him here today?"

"He's sitting right over there in the dark Brioni. Look at him! So beautiful! What a waste. I could've made him a star," Marty remarked wishfully. A few people, including some jurors stifled giggles. The Prosecutor cleared his throat.

"Yes, well be that as it may, what were the results of your interactions, Mr. Latrell?"

"Therapy. Lots of therapy," Marty replied, and this time people couldn't stifle their snickers, even though Marty said it with a straight face. "My therapist suggested that I write a book. I'm still considering it." More snickers.

Joey could see the testimony wasn't going as the Prosecutor might have planned. Joey figured he wanted to get a homosexual on the stand as a prosecution witness so he didn't come off as being prejudicial toward homosexuals through his prosecution of Joey. But no gay guy in his circle was going to take the stand against him except for Marty. But Marty was a little too over-the-top, and choreographed to perfection. He reeked of bullshit. Joey smiled smugly at the Prosecutor and the Prosecutor averted his eyes.

"My round, I think," thought Joey.

"Mr. Latrell, could you relay to us how your acquaintance-ship with Mr. Diamanti affected your business?" the Prosecutor asked.

"He tried to take over my production company with his strong-arm tactics. I woke up every morning expecting to find a horse head in my bed," Marty huffed.

More snickers.

"He was really lookin' for another part of the horse," Joey joked, whispering in Rollins's ear.

"So you feel that you were in danger all the time?" the Prosecutor probed.

"Incessantly. It's like in the movies, when you know something is going to happen, but you just don't know when. I *make* movies; I don't want to *live* in them," Marty affirmed.

"And how specifically did he create this constant fear in your life?"

"He extorted several million dollars from me and tried to take over my company," Marty replied.

"And had you refused?" the Prosecutor pressed.

"He said he'd kill me, and I believed him."

The Prosecutor showed several exhibits to the jury, including a picture of Marty with a bruised face, taken by the police after he filed charges for assault.

Content that he had made his point, the Prosecutor sat down and Rollins approached the witness stand.

"Mr. Latrell, you said that your friends call you Marty. Can I call you Marty?" Rollins smirked.

"No," Marty snapped with an attitude.

Rollins turned to the jury, chuckled and said, "Hostile witness," then turned back to Marty.

"Then, Mr. Latrell, let me ask you about any other dealings you had with my client, Joseph Diamanti."

"Totally irrelevant," Marty sniffed.

"On the contrary, Mr. Latrell. I think it is very relevant that when you first met my client, you tried to seduce him," Rollins remarked.

"Seduce him?" Marty echoed indignantly. "*He* seduced *me*! I was the victim!"

"Just like you were the victim in the assault you alleged to the LAPD."

"*Exactly.*"

"An assault you presented to the jury out of context, as if it were in fact my client."

"It *was* your client!"

"But that isn't what you told the LAPD is it, Mr. Latrell?"

Marty rolled his eyes, but didn't respond.

"That was a question, Mr. Latrell."

"No," Marty mumbled.

"Excuse me?"

"No," Marty blazed, stabbing Rollins with the daggers in his eyes.

"You told them it was just a lovers' spat, but you wouldn't tell them who this mystery lover was, did you, Mr. Latrell? You did not tell them that the mystery lover was in fact my client, Mr. Diamanti," Rollins accused.

"At the time, Joey hadn't come out, so he said he would kill me."

"But yet you continued the relationship until Mr. Diamanti broke off the relationship, is that not correct?"

"So?" Marty spat, crossing his arms defensively.

"And how did you feel about Mr. Diamanti when he dropped you?" Rollins questioned, purposely trying to provoke Marty.

Marty looked across the room, directly at Joey.

"I felt he was heartless and cruel, and I hope they throw away the key!"

"Just for being heartless and cruel?"

"Isn't that enough?"

Rollins looked at the jury to gauge their reaction to the last response then said, "No more questions, Your Honor."

Rollins wasn't even back to his seat before the Prosecutor sprung to his feet. His gamble had backfired. He knew about the fact that Joey and Marty had a relationship, but Marty had assured him that he harbored no ill will and just wanted to do the right thing. But Rollins had expertly pulled Marty's heart-strings and made him play a tune that sounded like one of a jealous ex-lover.

"Permission to re-direct, Your Honor."

"Granted."

He quickly approached Marty. Marty's look said he knew he had fucked up, but the Prosecutor disregarded it.

"Despite how you may've felt about Mr. Diamanti person-ally, did that in any way cause you to misstate the facts of the case as you know them to be?"

"Absolutely not," Marty said confidently. "When I said he was heartless and cruel, I meant as a human being, not just to me. Joey Diamanti is a coldblooded murderer, and when he came to L.A., he turned the city crimson with the bloodbath he unleashed!"

JUNE 1990

The Jungle. South Central. Blood control.

The apartment building at the end of the dead-end street is made like a small fortress: one-way in and one-way out. The apartments are built in a square around a common courtyard. One breezeway leads from the street to the inner sanctum of the courtyard. Once inside, anything can happen.

This is where Bianca was born and raised, and where she took Joey to meet her cousin Bone, a true OG in the Jungle. They pulled up in a brand new black Jaguar that Joey bought as soon as he hit L.A. He brought Te Amo and Enrico along for the trip.

"Listen," Bianca warned before they got out of the car. "My family's crazy. They don't play no games. But if they wit' you, nothin' in L.A. can touch you."

"Sounds like my kind of people," Joey replied.

When they got out, all eyes were on them: stone-faced, and it seemed like everybody had on something red, even the old folks. Seeing unfamiliar White faces in the hood usually either means one of two things: police or dope fiends. They didn't like either, so slowly the soldiers took position until someone said, "I know that ain't Bianca!"

"Who you think it is, Blood? What's up!" she rang out, stepping out onto the street.

The stone faces cracked into smiles and laughter, as several people—males and females—hugged her and exchanged the Blood handshake.

"Girl, I ain't seen you since forever! Where you been?" one girl in a red bandana asked.

"Everywhere," Bianca chuckled.

Many more greeted her before she was able to ask, "Where Bone?"

"In the spot! You already know."

"Come on, it's time to meet Bone."

She led them through the breezeway, only to emerge into another celebration.

"Yo Bianca, what up?"

"We up, fool!" she hollered back, making elaborate hand gestures.

Everywhere Joey looked, he saw young Black men and women in a world of their own, brandishing weapons even some armies didn't have, brazenly as if they were legal.

Bianca led them to one of the apartments and knocked. Several seconds later, the door was answered by a beast of a man, bare-chested except for the maze of tattoos that covered his smooth brown skin.

"Baby Girl!" He growled, scooping Bianca off her feet.

He looked like a professional bodybuilder, the size of Schwarzenegger, but it was all courtesy of prison weights.

"Animal, put me the fuck down!" she giggled.

"Girl, where the fuck you been?" he laughed, happy to see his big sister.

"I'm about to be on your ass if you don't put me down," she demanded, but still laughing.

He obliged her.

"When did you get home?" she asked.

"Like four months ago."

"I hope you plannin' on stayin' out."

"Like they say, plans are made to be broken," he replied, cracking a sinister grin. He looked at Te Amo and licked his lips. "Damn, sis, who is this?"

"None of ya B.I. Where Bone at?" she answered.

"Inside," he replied, eyeing Te Amo, who smiled and winked. He then looked at Joey and Enrico and scowled.

"Who the fuck is y'all, the goddamn police?"

Joey smirked and started to reply, but Bianca barked, "They wit' me, nigga!"

They all stepped into the apartment. The L.A. heat died at the door, as the AC on full blast gave them welcomed relief. Showing on the TV was a bootleg copy of Spike Lee's *School Daze*. The apartment was cluttered, but extravagantly furnished. In the middle of the room, in a straight back chair sat Bone. He was getting his hair braided by a slim, light skinned chick. Bone was light skinned as well, and his bare chest was covered with tattoos. He was nowhere as big as Animal, which is how he got his name: Bone. He was tall, lanky, and bone skinny, but he was as deadly as a cobra and could strike just as quickly. Despite his laidback style, when he saw Bianca, his face broke out in a big ass smile.

"What up, Baby Buzzin," he greeted, substituting "buzzin" for the word "cousin" because he avoided words beginning with a "C."

He got up and embraced her warmly. Joey could tell from the tightness of the embrace, and the closeness that this wasn't friendship or anything else. This was *family*.

"Goddamn, you disappeared. How long has it been?" Bone asked, stepping back to look at her.

"Too long," she smiled.

"Fo sho," Bone agreed, then his eyes fell on the rest of her group. "And who's this you got in my spot?"

"These my people, Bone. My girl, Te Amo, that's Enrico, and this is my man, Joey."

Bone took Te Amo's hand, kissed it then said in Spanish, "It's my pleasure to meet you."

"Likewise," she returned.

Bone looked Enrico up and down, but didn't extend his hand. When he looked at Joey, he didn't look him up and down, but he didn't extend his hand either.

"Yeah, but ah, names don't tell me nothin'," Bone remarked.

"That depends on what you're namin'," Joey shot back smoothly.

"Which is?"

"Money. That's the name of the game, right?"

Bone smirked.

"Ay yo, Tonya, raise up; we'll finish later."

Without asking any questions, the girl who was braiding his hair stood up and walked out the door.

Bone turned, walked over to the lazy boy in the corner, reclined and said, "I'm all ears."

"I come from New York," Joey began, "and if we were in New York, I'd be sitting in that chair. No disrespect, but just so you know."

"None taken," Bone nodded.

"Thank you. So I say that to say, if I say it, I got the weight to make it happen. Now, Bianca tells me that you're a good man to know in L.A. if I'm planning to do something big. Which I am. But to pull it off, I'll need an army. That's what I'm comin' to you for," Joey explained.

Bone let a few moments pass, as he sat smiling at Joey.

"An army, huh? An army of killers? You need soldiers, that's what you askin' for?" Bone asked.

"That's the only thing standing between us and a lot of money," Joey assured him.

Bone nodded.

"*Big* money. You need soldiers...a whole team of soldiers. You need butlers too? Waiters? Mo' tea, suh?" Bone chuckled.

"Man, who the fuck is this White boy?" Bone remarked dismissively, looking at Bianca then Animal.

"Hey Bone, I meant no disrespect," Joey assured him, maintaining an unruffled composure.

"Naw, I know what you meant. See, this ain't New York. Out here, *we* the mob," Bone boasted cockily, surmising Joey's identity by force of his swagger. "What you wanted was a bunch of hired guns, but see, that ain't how it works. Animal, what you think?"

Animal looked Joey up and down, then grabbed his crotch.

"I think I'm sweet on his pretty ass. I wish we woulda met in San Quentin, I woulda had a gun for him alright," Animal laughed menacingly, then blew Joey a kiss.

A slight smirk stayed on Joey's face, but he flexed his jaw muscles, a subtle sign that he was getting heated, and Te Amo caught it. But out of respect for Bianca, they came unarmed.

Bianca saw things turning ugly and began regretting the whole trip. There was no question that she would ride for her family if anything went down, but she didn't think Joey deserved such blatant disrespect. She turned to Bone and remarked, "Bone!"

"Bianca!" he barked right back, and the boom in his voice silenced her instantly. After grilling her a few extra moments, he turned back to Joey. "I'm sure the White boy can speak for himself. Ain't that right, White boy? You got a problem with what my homey just said?"

"Actually, I do," Joey retorted, without hesitation.

"So what you wanna do about it?" Bone probed.

"Kick his ass," Joey replied intently, all the Brooklyn in his accent in full display.

Bone and Animal laughed.

"Nothin' between y'all but air and opportunity," Bone remarked.

"Come on outside, White boy. Come kick my ass," Animal growled, shoving the door open and stepping out.

Joey went out behind him, followed closely by Te Amo, Enrico, and Bianca. Bone brought up the rear. Joey definitely hadn't come to fight, dressed as he was in casual slacks, a silk shirt, and ostrich loafers. He took off his silk shirt as a crowd began to gather.

"Animal 'bout to kill this White boy!" some dude exclaimed.

"Two to one, it's gonna be two hits: Animal hittin' him and him hittin' the fuckin' ground," another laughed.

Joey looked at Animal and sized him up. He looked like a brick wall. Animal leered at him, then got in his stance and headed straight for Joey. Joey got on the defense. Since Animal was so big, Joey expected him to throw big haymakers, so he caught Joey off balance when he snapped a quick right jab. Joey managed to roll with it at the last second. It still staggered him and made Joey realize that, had it made full contact, he'd be unconscious.

Joey moved around Animal counterclockwise then clockwise before delivering a strong overhand right that landed on Animal's jaw, but barely turned his head.

Animal sneered.

"You hit like a bitch," he spat.

But Joey had anticipated that reaction. He had deliberately pulled his punch, wanting the big man to feel overconfident, which he did. Animal moved in to mix it up with him. He landed a flurry of punches that Joey bobbed and weaved to avoid and diminish their impact. Then he hit Animal with a kidney shot that made the big man grunt and grimace.

"Bitches should be so lucky," Joey spat back.

Angry, Animal lunged at him. Joey hit him hard on the chin, but Animal scooped him up and slammed him hard on his back, damn near knocking all the wind out of Joey. Animal sat up on Joey and landed two solid blows before Bone snatched him off Joey. "Naw, homey, shoot from the shoulder; you know the drill," Bone ordered.

Joey struggled to his feet, spat out a glob of blood then remarked, "Hey Animal, you hit like that; they should call you Muffin, you big fuck."

The crowd couldn't help but laugh, which angered Animal. He rushed Joey and threw a wild hook that Joey ducked then shot a 6-inch uppercut that staggered the big man. Joey then followed with a hook of his own that connected so solidly that the crowd let out a collective "ooh!"

Animal shook it off then delivered a two-piece of his own, one to Joey's midsection and the other to his jaw. Joey landed a jab before backing away, knowing he couldn't go toe-to-toe with the big man.

"Naw, fuck that; come on back!" Animal dared.

"The White boy still standin'!" Joey cracked, playing to the crowd, and it worked. They started laughing.

Animal moved again, but Bone stepped between them.

"That's it," he declared, because he had seen all that he needed to.

He stepped up to a winded Joey and smiled.

"I like you, homey. You got heart. I knew that if Bianca brought you, you had to be a stand-up guy. But I like to know the heart of the men I do business with," Bone explained then extended his hand. Joey chuckled and shook it.

"Fair enough," he replied. Then he looked at Animal, "Hey Animal."

Animal looked at him.

"Fuck Rocky, I'm the Italian Stallion!"

Animal smirked then laughed and shook Joey's hand.

––––––––––

The Pulse was the hottest club in L.A. A favorite haunt of A-list movie stars and entertainment moguls, it was a super-exclusive spot with lines around the corner, just the place for Joey to make his L.A. debut. He definitely set out to make an unforgettable first impression. His entourage pulled up in two white, super-stretch limousines, directly in front of the club. The drivers got out and opened the doors. Out of the first limo stepped Enrico, Bone, and Animal, all dressed to impress. But Joey took the cake. He stepped out in regal finery, giving L.A. a taste of the star he was destined to become.

"Who is that?" one member of the paparazzi said to another.

"I don't know, but he's too beautiful not to be somebody," the other replied. Then they both began snapping pictures.

Out of the other limo stepped a bevy of gorgeous women that Joey brought along simply as eye candy. Heads swirled and whispers were loud enough to become comments as Joey and his entourage made their way to the big, muscle-bound guard in the tight black t-shirt that read: Security.

"Name," the guard asked, unimpressed by the electricity that Joey's presence sent through the crowd.

"Joey Diamonds, and they're all with me," he replied, gesturing to his entourage.

"Yeah, well you're not on the list," the guard informed him, unfazed. Joey held out a small wad of money consisting of ten $100 bills and replied, "I know, but by the time I will be, I'll run this town and I'll never forget the guy who gave me my first break in L.A., huh?"

The guard heard lines like that before, but looking at Joey's diamond smile and gangster swagger—not to mention the thousand dollars he was offering—made him take the money, slip it into his pocket and say, "Enjoy your evening, Mister...?"

"Diamonds. Joey Diamonds," Joey replied with a wink, then led his crew inside.

Once inside, he scattered the eye candy in four directions, donating them to the decorum of the club while the four of them made their way to a dark booth in the back, Joey's favorite booth in any club. As they walked, he noticed Te Amo and his team of female killers mingling and working the room, just like he instructed them to do.

He and Bone slid into the booth, with Enrico and Animal on the wings, as Technotronic's "Pump Up the Jam" filled the air.

"So this is the place to be in L.A., huh?" Joey remarked, glancing around, unimpressed.

"Not for my pedigree, homey," Bone responded, equally unimpressed. "Who run this scene?" Joey asked.

"Here in Hollywood, it's either the Armenians or the Mob. As for the drugs, it's the Chechnyans."

"What the fuck's a Chechnyan?" Joey questioned.

Bone shrugged and replied, "An ugly Russian. I don't know. They all Eastern Europeans."

Joey nodded, taking it in. He knew the Mob that Bone referred to was the Piazza family, a weak regime operated at the behest of five families back East, but didn't even have a seat on the Commission. As long as they didn't get in the way, he didn't anticipate a problem with them.

"You see the dude up there in V.I.P.?" Bone said, calling Joey's attention with a nod of his head.

Joey casually glanced up and saw him. He couldn't really see his features, but he was surrounded by bodyguards and broads; two of which were Maria and Marilyn.

"Yeah. What about him?"

One of the Chechnyan bosses. It's like three of 'em in L.A. that carry all the weight, but on the street, he's the top dog."

"What's his name?"

"I don't know, but I do know they ain't no joke. So if they the target, it won't be easy." Bone predicted.

Joey looked at him with a curious smirk.

"What are you sayin' man? You can't handle 'em?"

Bone lit his cigarette.

"Lucky for both of us, we never had to find out."

"Until now," Joey added.

"Depends on what's in it for us."

Joey waved his arm around the immediate vicinity.

"The drug scene in Hollywood'll be ours. Exclusive. The only stipulation is that all the X comes from my people and through my people."

Bone eyed him.

"That's it?"

"That's it. Coke, weed, whatever. It's totally your call. Personally, I wouldn't touch it. X'll make you rich, and right now, it ain't on the radar. By the time it is, you can cash in, a millionaire." Joey explained, remembering Seth's assessment of the situation.

Bone contemplated his words as he smoked his cigarette. He flicked his ashes into the tray.

"What are you askin' of us?"

"Certified killers. No lightweights, no questions asked. They work for me, but they answer to you. So any discrepancies, I hold you accountable," he told Bone, looking directly in his eyes.

Bone shrugged.

"Fair enough. So when do we get started?"

Joey sat back, glanced up at V.I.P. again. His eyes and Maria's met. She gave a wink. He smiled.

"We already have."

Joey let Bone and Animal take the main limo, because they picked up a bevy of chicks, while he and Enrico took the other limo.

"So, whaddya think?" Joey asked, slouched and wide-legged in the back of the limo.

Enrico sat diagonally across from him.

"I think they're a fucking youth gang that can't be trusted," Enrico answered.

"I don't have to trust 'em, just control 'em."

"How?"

"What else? Money. With the money they'll be makin', I'll keep 'em too busy to fuck up. And if they do, I'll handle it," Joey assured him.

Enrico nodded.

"As for you, can you work your magic at LAX?" Joey asked.

Enrico cracked a cocky grin.

"I haven't seen an airport where I couldn't."

"Good, because we're expanding: Chicago, San Fran, Texas and every college town in between. Before we finish, every college kid in America will know what X is," Joey predicted.

"Not a problem," Enrico replied, glancing at his watch. "Listen, drop me at the hotel. My flight to Miami leaves at eight."

"Not yet. We're supposed to meet with the girls and compare notes. Half an hour, tops," Joey told him.

Something in Joey's tone made Enrico look at him, and for the first time during the ride, realize that he was alone with Joey. It was the first time since the rape that they had been alone, and Enrico wondered to himself why he wasn't feeling more anxiety than he was. There was no question that he feared Joey, but his greed and ambition kept him in his orbit.

Not to mention a few other things...

Joey read his mind through his expression.

"Does being alone with me make you uncomfortable, Enrico?" Joey questioned, but his tone told Enrico he was toying with him.

"What kind of game are you playing, Joey?" Enrico retorted.

Joey just watched him for a moment then asked, "You ever think about that night?"

Enrico didn't answer, but his glare did.

"And what's the first thing that comes to your mind? Revenge?"

"Believe me, Joey, every dog will have his day."

"That doesn't answer the question."

Several moments later, they arrived at Joey's condo in Hollywood Hills. Enrico looked at the darkened facade. No lights were on. He looked at Joey.

"I guess they ain't here yet," Joey answered before Enrico asked.

"Then drop me off at my hotel," Enrico responded, eyeing Joey directly.

The driver opened Joey's door.

"You're here now, right? Might as well wait," Joey answered nonchalantly as he left the car.

In that moment, after Enrico paused and climbed out of the car, they both knew...

"Will that be all, Mr. Diamanti?" the driver inquired.

"Yeah, Bill. Thanks, we're good."

The driver got in and drove away, as Joey and Enrico climbed the stairs and went inside.

As soon as they entered, Joey reached to turn the lights on, but Enrico stopped him with a trembling hand.

"No...leave them off," he whispered, inwardly cursing himself for the remark. He wasn't ready for the light.

Even in the dark, he could feel Joey's smile.

"What you do in the dark..." he remarked, letting his voice

trail off as he reached for Enrico, embracing him around the waist and pulling him close to his body.

"The truth is, you never stopped thinking about that night," Joey surmised, whispering in Enrico's ear.

"And I hated every thought," Enrico gritted, hating to admit it but feeling a burden being lifted at the same time.

When Joey bent him over the couch and slid his rock-hard dick inside him, the pain almost made Enrico's knees buckle. But once he got past the pain, he knew things would never be the same.

"So what do you think?" Joey asked Te Amo as she drove.

They were driving along Wilshire Boulevard in a brand new, black convertible Porsche 964 Turbo.

She shrugged.

"It's okay."

"Okay?" he echoed with an incredulous chuckle. "I paid $70k for this thing! I give it to you, and all you can say is, *okay*?"

"I said 'thank you' didn't I?" she retorted, adding with arrogance. "Besides, I already have one of these."

"Yeah, but not in L.A." he shot back.

She cracked half of a smirk, but her attitude stayed firmly in place.

Joey knew she wanted him to ask, but instead just toyed with her emotional game.

"I tell you what: we take it back and you can get whatever you want. How's that?"

Unable to contain it any longer, she turned to him at the light and said, "You bit him, didn't you?"

The way she framed the question and the wording she chose made Joey laugh out loud. His laughter irked her even more.

"You're a fuckin' asshole," she spat.

"Whaddya mean, did I bite him? Am I a fuckin' vampire over here?"

"You know what the hell I mean, Joey."

"Of course I know. I'm just sayin'..." he shook his head. "It's no big deal, okay? He wanted to be bit."

She shook her head as she pulled away from the light, shifting gears with aggression. She couldn't put her finger on why the thought of Enrico being with Joey bothered her. But when she went to Joey's apartment and found Enrico there, she just...knew. Was it the look Enrico gave her? A look that revealed much as he groveled in the guilt he felt? Or was it that she sensed that this was more than a game to Joey? She didn't know. But one thing she did know was that she didn't wear jealousy well.

"The other night...was that the first time?"

"What difference does it make?"

"Because I don't think it's a good idea," she replied.

"Why not?" Joey pressed.

"It's...It's bad for business," she answered, saying the first thing that came to mind, so she wouldn't have to say the real reason.

Joey chuckled. "Now I see where you get your green eyes from."

"Fuck you," she seethed, close to eruption.

"I thought that's what we were talking about?" he remarked, loving the game but realizing it was time to throttle back. He changed the subject. "Speaking of business, run the situation down to me again. I want to wrap my head around an angle."

Te Amo looked at him, knowing what he was doing, but she let it go for the time being.

"Bone basically had it right. The Chechnyans control the drug scene in the L.A. club circuit. Not so much the coke—because the Nicaraguans have that—but the designer shit, definitely. There are three main Bosses: Sergei, Yuri, and Vladimir. Vladimir is the biggest of the three."

"So we kill the heads," he surmised, nodding to himself.

"But it won't be that simple. All three keep a team of body-guards, so getting close is out, unless of course you're a woman," she suggested.

"And we've got plenty of those."

"Exactly," Te Amo agreed then glanced at him.

"So you gonna get your hands dirty?"

"I've got Sergei eating out of my hand already. Of course, that might mean I go a little further than usual, but at least he'll go out with a bang, huh?" she giggled.

Joey frowned up.

"Whoa. Whoa. Whaddya mean 'with a bang'? You gotta buff the guy to kill 'em?"

The tables had turned, and Te Amo jumped on it instantly.

"What does it matter? As long as we get the mark, right?"

"We'll get 'em, just not like that," he replied, poker-faced.

She suppressed a smile.

"How, Joey?"

"Send another broad on the team."

"He likes *me*."

Joey glared at her.

"Don't play with me, okay? The cock sucker's a nobody," Joey growled. "If we have to, we'll wait until he goes into the club and burn it to the fuckin' ground."

Te Amo laughed.

"Really, Joey? Kill everybody, just to get one guy?"

Joey shrugged.

"What can I say? They shoulda been in church," he said, and even though he smirked, he was dead serious.

Te Amo laughed harder.

"I love you too, Papi. Now who's jealous?"

He waved her off, dismissively.

"Fuck outta here; I'm just sayin'...I don't want nobody touchin' you," he admitted.

"How do you think I feel?" she quickly retorted.

"Yeah, well some things I can do, and you can't."

"Fuck you! Same rules."

They argued all the way to Roscoe's Chicken and Waffles, but by the time they got their order and sat down, they were laughing again. Neither could explain the chemistry between them. It was crazy, so it made them crazy.

Toward the end of their meal, they heard a girlish voice call out, "Joey?"

They both looked up and saw the redhead from the New Year's Eve party approaching with a buxom brunette behind her. When Joey recognized who it was, he smiled politely and rose from his seat to hug her.

"Hey, how you doin'?" he greeted, unsure of the girl's name.

Reading his tone, she smiled knowingly and said, "Leslie. Leslie Emerson, from New York. Remember?"

"Right! I'm not too good with names. Your face? Well, that I could never forget," he charmed with an impish grin.

Both girls giggled.

"Thank you," Leslie remarked side glancing at Te Amo, more so to size her up. But then she recognized the face and got wide eyed. "Te Amo! Oh my God, it's a small world! Joey, I didn't know you knew Te Amo!"

"Yeah, small world," Joey remarked, while Leslie bent over and gave the still-seated Te Amo a hug.

"Oh my God," she gushed, straightening up. "Imagine the odds! How long have you two been out here? Have you been out partying? Te Amo, it's nothing like you're used to, right?" Leslie rapidly spat, her demeanor clearly juiced up on coke.

Joey stole a glance at Te Amo; she gave him a sarcastic response on the sly.

"Where are you guys, anyway? We *have* to get together. So

much is happening for me, Joey, and I have you to thank! Remember that commercial you helped me get?"

"Yeah."

"Liar," she giggled. "Anyway, *the* Marty Latrell saw me in it, and he loved me! Now, I'm in his new movie!" she exclaimed then hugged Joey again.

"Hey, textbook Hollywood story, huh? That's beautiful," Joey remarked.

Leslie gasped and got wide eyed then said, "I just had a great idea! Marty's showing the movie he just finished on Friday. Why don't you two come with me? It would be great, and Marty would love you, Joey! Who knows? Maybe there's a Hollywood story waiting for you!"

"I'm camera shy, but who knows? Might be fun. I'll be there," Joey agreed, his agile mind seizing on an angle he just recognized. Leslie wrote down her number and gave it to him then kissed him on the cheek.

"Call me for sure!"

"But of course," Joey replied, as the two females walked away. He looked at Te Amo. "That's your brain on drugs."

"Where do you know her from?" Joey casually questioned as they walked to the car.

"Miami. Club-hopping," she lied.

Joey let it go without comment.

Marty lived in a breathtaking marvel of modernity. His mansion hugged the precipice on which it was built, over-looking the Pacific Ocean. The waves licked and crashed along the base of a cliff 50 feet below—hard enough to send the ocean spray spritzing across your face in Marty's backyard where he set up a tent, almost revival-like to showcase his latest release. He was fresh off a blockbuster, so many of Hollywood's

A-list royalty, actors, and directors were there to play to his ego. White-jacketed waiters weaved around air kissers and whispered daggers, as the narcissistic collective nursed their self-esteem.

Joey and Leslie arrived just before the showing began. More eyes were on Joey than on the screen. Even amongst the A-listed, his natural confidence brought out their insecurities—especially among the guys—though not exclusively. The women would swoon in his presence, while he sat back and enjoyed the attention.

After the showing, several actresses couldn't wait to approach...

"Leslie, where have you been hiding this one?"

"You have to introduce me to your friend."

One middle-aged producer—who clearly resembled Bette Midler—bluntly asked, "How much do you charge?" She assumed he was an escort.

Joey chuckled and replied, "For a lady as lovely as you, no charge." Then he kissed her hand.

He said it to be charming; she took it as an offer. She handed him her card.

"Whatever day that's good for you," she added, then walked away.

Joey pocketed the card and said, "I think I'm gonna love Hollywood."

Leslie giggled.

"I think that Hollywood already loves you," she added, before taking his hand and saying, "Come on, let's find Marty."

After mingling and moving through the spacious backyard, she finally caught up with Marty in his cathedral-ceilinged living room. He was talking to two Japanese businessmen.

"Marty," she sang. "There you are."

She led Joey through the crowd and Marty turned to her with an exasperated look on his face.

"My dear...what is your name again?" he asked impatiently, as he returned her hug and air kiss.

"Leslie."

"Yeah right, Leslie. I'm terribly busy." He started to turn away, until he looked up and saw Joey. The rest of his sentiment was swallowed as he gasped, "Oh my God, you are beautiful!"

Leslie beamed.

"Marty, meet my friend Joey. Joey, this is my producer, Marty Latrell."

"Please say you are the angel of death and you have come to take me away," Marty flirted viciously, not knowing or caring how Joey would take it.

Joey chuckled at the irony, because Marty didn't know how right he was.

"Not yet," Joey winked.

"Then whatever it is, the answer is *yes!*"

Joey and Leslie laughed.

"Who's your agent?"

"Nobody."

"Have you ever been in front of a camera?"

"Never even caught on tape," Joey cracked.

"Joey's not an actor, Marty."

"But he must be," Marty replied, looking at her like the God had spoken. "Or else that would be like Picasso never painting, or...or Bach never composing. His beauty can't go to waste! I would *love* to *have* you," Marty remarked, curling the 'L' in love with his tongue and pausing provocatively mid-sentence, before adding, "in my movie."

Joey gave him a subtle look, but chuckled and replied, "I already have a day job."

"Quit," Marty shot back. "I'll make you a star."

"Sounds tempting," Joey charmed.

"Then let me tell you more," Marty offered. He turned to

Leslie. "You don't mind if I steal him, do you?" Then, without waiting for a reply, he and Joey walked off.

Marty introduced Joey to some of the movers and shakers in Hollywood, with comments like "Meet my next star."

"This is the guy that'll make people say, 'Who is that dreamboat?'"

After the who's who tour, Marty remarked only half-jokingly, "Say the word and we'll take my plane, wreck it, and get stranded on a deserted island."

"The end?" Joey quipped.

"No. Happily ever after," Marty countered, and they both laughed. Once the laughter subsided, Marty added, "But really, Joey I could give you a real future in this town."

"I bet you say that to all the girls, but let's do this. I'ma give you a coupla days to have your people look me up. Then we'll talk again, okay?" Joey proposed.

Marty's eyes got bigger, and he covered his mouth with his hand. "Oh my God. I hope I haven't offended you."

Joey shrugged good-naturedly, even though he had had enough of being paraded around like a piece of meat.

"Not at all. I just want you to know that you're dealing with a little more than just the flavor of the month." He winked, adding, "I'll be in touch." Then he walked away.

Joey made his way back over to Leslie as she schmoozed with another up and coming actor.

"We ready?" Joey remarked, cutting in.

"Sure," Leslie replied, after saying her goodbye to the actor. On their way out to his car, Leslie asked, "So what do you think of Marty?"

"I think I'm gonna squeeze that cock sucker until cash shoots out of his ass," Joey responded seriously, although he was smiling when he said it.

Leslie giggled and playfully hit him.

"Oh Joey, you're so bad!"

The valet brought his car and they drove away. As soon as they were in the car, Leslie was all over him.

"I never got a chance to thank you, did I?" she purred seductively, kissing him along the neck.

"No, but I'm sure you will," he smirked.

"Every inch," she whispered, precisely gripping his zipper, tugging at it, and then when it was all the way down, pulling his half erect dick from his pants and bending over as she pushed her hair out of her face.

Feeling her warm, wet mouth on him instantly made his dick rock up, and the greedy way she slurped made it hard to concentrate on the road.

"Let me ask you something?" he grunted, struggling to keep his focus.

More slurps were her response. He knocked on the back of her head like it was a door.

"Hey."

His dick popped out of her mouth.

"Hmmm?"

"Where do you know Te Amo from?"

"New York. Club scene," she answered in broken sentences, anxious to get back to the dick.

"You sure it ain't Miami?"

"New York," she slobbered with a mouthful of dick.

He nodded to himself, then sat back to enjoy the ride.

PRESENT DAY, JULY 1997

"What about the eccentric Hollywood producer, Marty Latrell?"

"What about him, Diane?"

"Why is he set to testify against you? Any idea as to what he might say?" Diane probed.

Joey chuckled.

"Diane, Marty's a helluva guy, and ironically a guy I'd consider a good friend. But..."

"Despite the fact that he's going to be testifying against you?" she asked, incredulously.

"Everything isn't always what it seems, Diane," Joey replied enigmatically, adding, "I mean, maybe he just has a lot to get off his chest."

"Sour grapes?"

Joey gave a hedging shake of the head.

"Who knows? You know, I mean we don't always see eye to eye. Besides, the government, they're the real gangsters because they make offers no one can refuse. So maybe it's more of a... personal decision," Joey suggested.

"Are you implying that he's testifying because the government has something on *him*?"

"*I* didn't say that; *you* did, Diane," Joey chuckled, "but everybody knows that Hollywood's a world of its own, so somebody's gotta know where the bodies are buried, huh? Look Diane, I'm not concerned with what Marty might say, because he can't say anything incriminating against me."

"Well, recently in an interview, Mr. Latrell said, and I quote, 'I was absolutely terrified of Joey Diamonds, but I loved every minute of it!'"

Joey laughed.

"Yeah, that sounds just like Marty. I mean, what can you say to a statement like that? Bottom line, Marty's a good friend in a bad position. Despite our differences and what the government wants to believe about me, I'm one of the nicest guys you'll ever wanna meet," Joey said, cracking the smile he knew would make half of America's heart skip a collective beat.

JUNE 1990

It didn't take Marty twenty-four hours to find out all he needed to know about Joey. He called Joey on the car phone as Joey drove along.

"Yeah," Joey answered.

"I suppose apologies are in order. I mean, there I was treating you like a piece of meat, when you could snap your fingers and have me hung up *with* the meat," Marty joked.

Joey grinned. He knew when his ego was being stroked.

"No need for apologies...or theatrics either," he retorted nonchalantly.

"No, really. I must apologize. How can I make it up to you?"

"By makin' it up to me."

"I'm all ears."

"Fuel up that plane of yours. We're going to Vegas."

"Sounds delish. How does Friday sound?"

"How's now sound?" Joey shot back, playfully but firmly.

There was a pause that Joey knew was Marty wondering how much of the tempo he would let Joey control, as a man used to being in charge.

"Only if I get to blow on your dice," Marty cooed with a hint of growl.

Joey laughed at his feeble attempt, and replied, "Fuel up the fuckin' plane," then hung up.

Several hours later, they landed in Vegas. Marty had a car waiting that took them directly to the MGM Grand Hotel on the Strip. Once there, they headed straight for the suite awaiting them. As soon as they stepped inside Marty said, "Everything's already handled. My guy's got the pencil," referring to the power to make everything complementary just by signing for it—a power usually reserved for casino owners.

"No need for that, because we're not leaving the room," Joey told him as he loosened his tie.

Marty liked the sound of that, but he still asked, "Then why come all the way to Vegas? I've got a nice little hideaway in Palm Springs."

"Because what happens in Vegas stays in Vegas, right?" Joey answered.

Marty's mischievous grin said *message received*.

Joey sat down on the stylish leather couch, crossed his legs, right over left and remarked, "Now, how 'bout a drink?"

Marty allowed Joey to set the tone up until that point, but he decided it was time to assert his control, because he was used to having it.

"Joey," Marty smiled, yet his eyes didn't. "I like for a man to take charge but not take over."

Joey's smile said *message received*.

"Then hey, let me get *you* a drink."

They both laughed and Joey crossed the room to the bar.

"What's your poison?"

"Gin neat."

"Gin neat," Joey echoed, then poured them both the same drink. He handed Marty a glass.

"I see you like it neat," Marty commented.

"Naw, I just wanted to see how you taste," Joey winked, then looked out at the patio. "Vegas kinda looks naked in the sunlight, without all the lights, huh?"

"And illusions," Marty added with a smirk.

"Yeah, true; no illusions. But the view is still breathtaking," Joey said as he stepped out onto the patio. Marty followed him out there, just like he knew he would.

Joey took a deep breath.

"I love the desert air, don't you?"

"As long as I don't have to smell it," Marty retorted with disdain and a wrinkled nose. Then he sipped his drink.

"Well, I think that's pretty much the idea Marty, but hey," Joey commented, downing his drink and sitting the glass down. "Tell me somethin', Marty: would you like to gamble with me?"

"I thought we weren't leaving the room."

"We're not; we can gamble right here," Joey smiled. It wouldn't be until much later that Marty would remember it as sinister.

"Sure, why not? What shall we play? Strip poker?" Marty quipped, wiggling his eyebrows.

"In due time. I was thinkin' more like roulette."

"We don't have a wheel," Marty replied.

"Sure we do, Marty," Joey replied then rolled out a .38 revolver from the small of his back.

Marty was startled when Joey pulled out the gun.

"What're you going to do with that?"

"Play roulette," Joey answered, like it was obvious. He opened the cylinder and dumped the bullets in his palm, then held up one between his forefinger and thumb for Marty to see as he put it in the chamber. With an elaborate slap, the cylinder closed. He cocked the hammer.

"Count me out," Marty said, reaching for the patio door.

Joey took his arm—and with a look of cold amusement that sent a chill down Marty's spine—said, "Marty...that wasn't a suggestion." He then half shoved him back against the railing. Marty looked down from the dizzying height. Trapped between an abyss and a gun, he looked at Joey with pleading eyes.

"Please tell me you're not serious."

"Relax, Marty, it's your lucky day. Five-to-one odds. Vegas should be so lucky. Well, since I'm holding the gun, you go first," Joey told him. Without hesitation, he put the gun to Marty's head and pulled the trigger.

Click!

The metallic click made Marty whole body tremble with terror and relief at the same time as he cried, "Oh, God!" and ducked at the same time.

"No fair, Marty, you ducked. This time, don't move."

Marty crouched, almost in an upright fetal position, holding on to the railing.

"No. No, please don't do this," he begged.

Click! Click! Joey squeezed the trigger twice in rapid succession, sending spasms through Marty's body that found release in a spurt of urine that wet his trousers.

"Oh, my God. Oh, my God. Oh, my God!" Marty, a confessed atheist, recited like a mantra of hyperventilation.

Joey squatted down next to him.

"Marty, I gotta say, you've been kissed by fate. You oughta go downstairs and try your hand, huh? Joey cracked. "Do we need to keep playing?"

Marty shook his head frantically.

"No! Please, no!"

"Because we can."

"No! Please, no!" Marty begged.

Joey watched him for a moment then chuckled and said, "Marty...Ay Marty. Marty, look at me," then turned his face gently to look at him. "I was just pulling your leg; I palmed the bullet."

Joey opened his palm and held up the gleaming bullet.

"See?"

Marty looked at the bullet then at Joey's smile then back at the bullet. Slowly, his breathing stabilized and he laughed with Joey.

"The gun was empty!" Joey roared. To further prove his point, he opened the cylinder. As he tilted the gun, a single bullet hit the carpeted patio with a thud that brought instant silence.

"Oops," Joey remarked, without even a hint of a smile.

Marty turned a sickly shade of purple.

"Now, get up. Go inside."

Marty scrambled to his feet and staggered inside.

"Joey, why are you doing this to me?" Marty squealed.

Joey ignored him, took off his suit jacket then said, "Now, take off your clothes."

Without hesitation, Marty complied. He stood naked and vulnerable under Joey's steely gaze.

"Now, bend over the couch," Joey ordered.

Marty did as he was told.

Joey unbuckled his belt.

"We need to get somethin' straight right now, just so we understand each other," Joey began, sliding off his belt and wrapping it around his hand, the buckle exposed. "You may be a big fish in a big pond, but you're swimming with sharks now. Ya got me?"

"Y-yesss-s," Marty stammered.

Joey brought the belt across his ass like a whip.

"Do you?" Joey barked, hitting him two more times.

"Yes!"

"Are we on the same page?" Joey hissed, punctuating the question with another lash.

"Please," Marty begged.

"Please, what?"

"Pl-please...please fuck me," Marty stammered, so filled with lustful anguish, he felt like his whole body would explode.

Joey smiled. He stepped closer. He laid the cold leather of his belt on Marty's ass. Marty flinched.

"Please...Joey...fuck...me," Marty trembled.

Joey tossed the belt to the side and grabbed Marty's ass, making Marty bite down on his bottom lip.

"Yeah," Joey growled as he dropped his pants and aimed his rod straight for Marty's ass. "We understand one another."

Then he plunged in, with the full length of his dick, making Marty howl like a Banshee and beg for more.

Two hours later, with Marty sore but satisfied, the two of them lay in the bed, Marty's head on Joey's stomach while he traced Joey's belly button.

"Now I know why your eyes are so blue...and cold," Marty commented.

"And why is that?"

"Your soul is empty. You made a deal with the Devil," Marty cracked, only half-jokingly.

Joey smirked.

"Actually, he made a deal with me. I let him operate as long as I get a cut of every soul."

They both laughed.

"And I've been thinking about your little offer."

"Of?"

"To be in your movie. Who knows? Maybe I'll be the next De Niro. Besides, it'll be good business...partner."

"Partner?" Marty echoed, lifting his head from Joey's stomach.

"Nothing major. I just wanna wet my beak, so to speak, eh? I promise it'll be good for both of us."

"But my investors," Marty protested. "I have—"

Joey smoothly cut him off.

"Hey, where's your manners?"

"Huh?"

"Didn't your mother tell you never to talk with your mouth full?" Joey quipped then turned Marty's face to his crotch and filled his mouth full of dick.

Four nights later, Joey met with Bone in a deserted school parking lot in South Central. They parked facing different directions, Joey in his Jag and Bone in his cherry-red drop top '64 Impala.

"Everything's a go on my end," Bone assured him.

Joey nodded.

"That's good to hear, because when we pull this off, we takin' our show on the road. You got the muscle and I'll make sure you get the product, and together we'll be paid...in full," Joey predicted.

"Sounds good to me," Bone smiled. "But listen, we gotta be on point. These fuckin' Chechnyans are like killer bees. We gotta kill 'em *before* they get out of their hives."

"Between you and my girls, that's a done deal."

Bone nodded, then extended his hand. Joey shook it.

"Then we all good, homey. I'm on it."

Both of them drove off in opposite directions. As Joey drove, he went over his plan. Taking over the ecstasy trade in L.A. and beyond was only the tip of the iceberg. His real plan—the plan he hadn't told anyone—was to totally eliminate the Piazza family and start his own family in L.A. The Piazzas were outliers: West Coast puppets for East Coast strings. He would cut the strings and use that leverage to muscle his way into the Commission. He was determined to be a Made Man and to earn the respect of the five families.

Respect.

That was the recognition he craved. No matter who he was or what he was in their eyes, they would respect him, kill him, or die, but he refused to be an outcast. His thoughts turned to his father and the last time he saw him, lying up in the hospital. The look on his face when he told him he had been the one to hit him. The memory made him squeeze his eyes shut. It cut deeply, yet he knew it had to be done. It was imperative that he moved first. Now, all he had to do was wait...

When he arrived at the apartment, Te Amo greeted him with a kiss and a drink.

"Everybody's in place," she informed him with a triumphant grin.

He sipped his drink.

"Okay."

"And Enrico is here."

Entering the living room, he saw Enrico sitting on the couch. When he saw Joey, he smiled, no longer making an attempt to mask his attraction.

"Hello, Joey."

"How's New York?"

"Perfect. Zev sends his best, and in two days LAX will be a go," Enrico explained proudly, knowing Joey would be pleased with him.

His plan was beginning to look flawless.

"If I woulda known it was this easy, I woulda took over the world a long time ago," Joey quipped arrogantly. They all laughed.

Joey raised his glass. Enrico stood up to join the toast, the three of them in a semicircle.

"To plans coming together," Joey triumphantly sang.

They toasted and drank. When they finished, he kissed both Te Amo and Enrico.

Sergei was a fat, greasy pig. Everything was about more for him. He was short, wide, and obnoxious. He feared no one, which meant he took few precautions. Besides his two bodyguards, he was a virtual open target.

He pulled up to his favorite Italian restaurant. They gave the keys to a young, Black valet. Had they looked closer, they would have seen that he didn't quite fit the décor or the ambiance. But again, he feared no one. Inside, they ate, drank, and were merry—unaware of what awaited them.

When they returned to the car, the valet brought the armor-plated Mercedes around. They got in and pulled off. The valet watched, marveling at how easy it had been. He looked around and began to walk away, quickly pulling a black box out of his pocket. The way the Benz was plated, their weapons couldn't have touched Sergei. But if the weapon were already inside...

The valet pressed the button without even bothering to look around. He didn't have to. He heard it as the C-4 he had planted under the seat went off, enclosing the three men in a secure bomb zone that would leave nothing to identify them besides a mixture of metal, blood, and guts.

Enrico and Te Amo caressed and kissed each inch of Joey's body as they slowly undressed him together. Enrico kissed all over his chest while Te Amo sucked from his ear lobe to his bottom lip and headed south, following the path that Enrico laid. As they both covered him with kisses, he thought of Seth's words, the words he used when he turned him out.

"That's the power only gods have, Joey," Seth once said.

As he looked down at Te Amo and Enrico simultaneously

sucking his dick, kissing over the head of his dick in unisexual bliss, he knew then that indeed he was a god.

Yuri and his five bodyguards entered the strip club like they owned it. Yuri was the youngest Boss, but like a young viper full of venom, he was extremely dangerous. Slim and wiry, he walked on the balls of his feet and seemed to have energy to spare. More cautious than Sergei, his only weakness was the strip club, this strip club in particular.

When he went inside, his bodyguards blocked off an area and only left dancers near Yuri. The dancers were enough, especially the blond with the perky tits named Amanda. She danced over, wearing nothing but a G-string and go-go boots with *fuck me* heels. Yuri loved blonds.

She seductively straddled him, lifting one leg high so he could see the juicy pussy lips peeking out of her G-string.

"How much for you to go with me?" Yuri asked as she gave him a lap dance.

Amanda shook her hair out of her face and licked her lips then leaned into his ear and said, "I'm sorry baby, but I'd rather not go where you're going!"

"Huh?" he questioned, not sure if he had heard her correctly over the music.

He would never know because, while she was whispering in his ear, she was also reaching in her boot. She pulled out the razor-sharp surgeon's scalpel, then quickly cut his throat so deeply that had she encircled his neck, she would have beheaded him.

Blood pulsed everywhere. One of the bodyguards noticed, but it was too late. He barked something in Chechnyan while he pulled out his gun. The other bodyguard followed suit.

Amanda wrapped her legs around Yuri's waist, rolled and

pulled his dead weight on top of her to shield her from the bullets. At the same time, she snatched the pistol that Yuri carried in the small of his back and opened fire. She killed one of the bodyguards, but she was the least of their worries. With their backs turned, they never saw the three Bloods stand up and open fire with fully automatic Uzis. The crowd broke out in frenzy, but within seconds it was over. Amanda and the Bloods made their getaway, leaving nothing but six dead Chechnyans and a story to tell.

Te Amo rode him slowly, savoring every inch of his dick while Enrico covered his body with kisses until he reached the spot where Joey and Te Amo met. He began to lick them from her clit to the base of his dick, causing Te Amo to totally lose it and ride him with wild abandon.

"Fuck, Joey," she groaned, biting down on her bottom lip. "It's...so...good...I...can't...hold...it," she squealed as she creamed his dick.

She laid her head on his chest, but Joey pulled her up, urging her body forward until she climbed his face and sat on his tongue. Enrico ran his tongue around the head of Joey's dick, tasting Te Amo's juices. Then he sat on Joey's dick, reverse cowgirl style and began to meet Joey's every thrust with a hungry grind.

Was it possible for one man to bring so much pain and pleasure at the same time? Because while he was giving Te Amo and Enrico mind-blowing pleasure, he was bringing death and destruction to the streets of L.A.

Vladimir's mansion was a virtual fortress. It sat overlooking

L.A. in the Hollywood Hills section. Motion detectors ran along the base of an eight-foot tall privacy fence. Surveillance cameras surrounded the compound, as his bodyguards patrolled the grounds with automatic weapons and guard dogs. Vladimir was by far the most cautious, but he was also the most dangerous.

The limo arrived at his gate and, after careful scrutiny, was let inside. It drove up and then around the circular driveway. It stopped in front of the main entrance and two scantily dressed females got out. Both wore boots up to their knees, short skirts that revealed to the world that they were panty-less as they strutted up the three-step entrance. They were dressed like twins, and their exotic Indian features almost made them identical as well.

Two bodyguards escorted them upstairs to a large bedroom with an even larger bed. It had to be the size of two king-sized beds put together. The whole room was done in red and black, as if they had come to visit Dracula, if one believes in such things. Vladimir liked to model himself after Vlad the Impaler.

When the two girls entered, the bodyguards closed the door behind them. Several seconds later, Vladimir emerged wearing a red robe and carrying a drink.

"It's good to see you both again. Welcome to my home," Vladimir welcomed them with a slight bow.

"Oh Vlad," the shorter one gushed. "I love this bed," she added, crawling up on it and hiking up her skirt.

The other followed her lead, but instead of getting up in the bed, she leaned behind the other and slid her tongue into her pussy, causing her to let out a passionate gasp.

"I'm glad to see you don't waste time," he said, setting his drink down and approaching the bed.

He positioned himself behind the taller one. She tooted her ass up, ready to be entered. However, instead of grabbing her ass, he grabbed her by the chin and back of her head and snapped her neck like a toothpick. Her dead body hit the floor with a thud.

"Neither do I!" he hissed as he grabbed the other one by the hair. But by time he had a firm grip, she had reached into her boot and came out with an ice pick.

She stabbed him in the shoulder, but he backhanded her so hard that she almost lost consciousness and dropped the weapon. He dragged her by the hair to the foot of the bed, wrapped her arms around the post and pulled a pair of hand-cuffs out of his robe pocket. Once she was cuffed, he examined the wound on his shoulder through the rip in the robe. It was bleeding profusely, but there was little pain to a rock like Vladimir.

"Not bad, but you aim too high," he chuckled. "A professional would've known to come under hand; you would've had a better chance of hitting my heart," he schooled her.

He lifted her head with his hand. She spat in his face. He backhanded blood from her mouth and nose, tasted her spit then wiped the rest away.

"So, we know you are no professional. Who are you, then? Who sent you? If you tell me, I just kill you. You don't then you will wish you were dead. Talk."

With her hair in her face and blood dripping from her mouth, she looked like a wild savage, glaring at him.

"You will talk," he assured her.

Vladimir picked up the ice pick and then stood over her. He held her left hand at the wrist, looked her in the eye, and asked calmly, "Who sent you?"

"Your dead madre, puto," she spat.

Vladimir stabbed her in the hands three times in quick succession.

She howled in pain.

"Shhh," he taunted her, caressing her face. "That was nothing if you don't tell me who sent you."

"Tu madre," was all she got out before he plunged the ice pick into her wrist, and then began to wrench it back and forth. She almost passed out.

Vladimir got up close to her and repeated, "*Who* sent you?"

"Go to hell," she seethed.

"Very well," Vladimir remarked then walked around behind her and pulled up her skirt. He looked at her pretty ass and perfectly shaven pussy.

"Tsk, tsk, what a waste," he mused, contemplating raping her. He then took the ice pick and stabbed her in the pussy.

She let out a loud warble that told him she was reaching her threshold for pain.

"Almost, yes? You tell me now, yes?"

But she kept silent.

He stabbed her again, but this time he pushed the ice pick deeper, plunging into her insides, up to his knuckles. She used all her energy left, reared back causing the ice pick to lodge deeper then brought her weight down on it, causing the tip to protrude outward from her stomach. She then collapsed, blood oozing from her mouth.

"Impressive," he remarked, as he removed his hand and the ice pick, both covered with blood. "Inexperienced, but impressive."

She had managed to impale herself without giving Joey up.

"Whoever sent you will soon learn," Vladimir spat.

He had been onto the girls from day one, but he wanted to find out who sent them. Unable to find out through surveillance, he attempted to find out through torture. Now that he had been outwitted, there was nothing left but to send a message.

He called for his bodyguards. Moments later, two entered. They didn't even blink at the sight of the two dead women.

"Bring me my tools," he instructed.

Enrico and Te Amo slept with their heads on either side of Joey's chest, with his arms wrapped around both of them. They looked like a trinity of fallen angels, sleeping peacefully, but their sleep was interrupted by a ringing phone. They all awoke in quick succession. Te Amo reached over and grabbed the receiver, passing it to Joey without speaking, then reclined back into the bed.

"Yeah...yeah. Okay," he said, then hung up. "Fuck!"

The bass in Joey's voice jolted the sleep out of Te Amo.

"What's wrong?"

"Mianna and Anita never checked in," Joey answered grimly.

"What do you think that means?" Enrico questioned.

Joey looked at him like it was a stupid question.

"It means they're dead and Vladimir got away," Joey answered, getting up and pacing the floor butt-naked.

"What about the other two?" Te Amo wanted to know.

"Taken care of. Vladimir's the only one still breathing."

The three of them contemplated the implications of what it all meant, but they didn't have to wait long to find out what happened to the girls. The TV in the bedroom was turned on with the volume down low. A news flash came on and caught Enrico's eye.

"Look, Joey."

Joey turned around, recognized The Pulse Nightclub blocked off with police tape, and grabbed the remote to turn the volume up.

"L.A. woke up to a gruesome morning, Phil. I'm in front of The Pulse Nightclub where the headless bodies of two women were found. Their heads weren't. A man jogging saw them and promptly called the LAPD."

Joey heard enough. He cut the TV off and threw the remote against the wall.

"Son of a bitch! Fuckin' cock sucker!" he ranted.

It was the first loss he had taken, and it made him feel personally responsible for the two slain women. After all, they were doing his bidding.

He paced the floor furiously, thirsty for revenge. All caution was thrown to the wind. He was willing to do whatever it took. Then he stopped pacing and smiled because he had locked in on a solution.

Te Amo met his smile with her own.

"So, what are we gonna do?"

"Vladimir wants to send messages. I'm just gonna let him know I got it. Personally." Joey leered.

Vladimir raced along the Boulevard in his armored 600 Benz. Two bodyguards sat up front and one sat on his left. The sun peeked brightly through the smog, as he contemplated his next move. At first, he thought the girls had been sent by Yuri and Sergei, but once he found out they were dead, he was focused on uncovering his hidden enemy.

"I don't care what you must do or how much you must pay! Find out!" Vladimir barked into his car phone, then slammed it down. In his mind, it was either the Armenians or the Russians.

Several seconds later, he heard the sound of police sirens. He glanced around and saw the police cruiser with lights flashing behind them.

Whop! Whop!

"I told you no speeding, Lechma," Vladimir gruffed.

"I was not speeding, Vladimir," Lechma protested.

Vladimir quickly weighed his options then said, "Pull over."

Lechma pulled over.

The cruiser stopped behind them. People up and down the street were looking to see what was happening. Two policemen got out—one White, one Black—wearing mirror sunglasses and absolutely no smiles. The White one positioned himself by the backdoor, hand resting casually on his holster. The Black one approached the driver.

"License and registration," the Black officer ordered.

"Is there a problem, Officer?" Lechma asked, trying to keep the contempt he had for Black people out of his voice.

"I'm asking the questions, you just answer 'em," he spat.

Lechma gritted his teeth, but he complied.

The Black officer took one look at the license and remarked, "What is this, a joke? This license is not valid! It's a forgery."

"Forgery?" Lechma echoed. "Bullshit."

"You trying to play with my intelligence? I know fake when I see fake. I'm going to have to ask you to step out of the car. All of you! Now!"

The White officer maintained his position by the backdoor and spoke into the walkie-talkie on his shoulder.

"This is Car 59 requesting backup. Possible UUMV."

When Vladimir heard that, he told everyone in Chechnyan to get out. He didn't want a whole bunch of police showing up.

The four of them got out.

"All of you! Hands on the trunk. Assume the position!" the White officer ordered them.

They all complied.

The street was lined with people. It was broad daylight. The cop had called for backup. All of these factors had lulled Vladimir into a sense of security; a lull he would never recover from.

Both the White and Black officer pulled their guns simultaneously. The Black officer shot the driver and the bodyguard from the back seat, point blank in the back of the head in quick succession. The White officer shot the remaining guard then trained his gun on a stunned Vladimir, as a van skidded up and the door slid open. It all happened in seconds. Vladimir never had a chance to react.

"Ay, Vladimir," the White officer growled. "I got your message." Then he unloaded three shots into the back of Vladimir's head. People were running, screaming and ducking as the officers jumped into the van and make their getaway.

Joey straightened his peaked cap, and walked back to the cop car.

With the death of the Chechneyans, Joey and his crew took over the designer drug scene in L.A. The Bloods handled it while Joey kept them supplied and the girls played the face of the organization. Joey Diamonds' name began to buzz, not only in the streets, but in the industry. Marty cast him in a small role in his latest production—the one Joey was also taking a piece of under the table.

The part was for a gangster. That wasn't a coincidence; it was deliberate. Joey told Marty, "I'll only play gangsters."

"Why would you limit yourself like that? You could easily work your way up to romantic leads," Marty stressed.

But Joey just shrugged and replied, "I like being the bad guy." But it was deeper than that. There was always a method to Joey's madness.

"Hey...Next time, you won't be so lucky."

That was Joey's only line, but Marty said that it brought a chill to his spine.

Joey was a natural and, more importantly, the camera loved him. He hung around Marty, learning the ropes day and night. He let his face be seen around L.A. He wanted everybody to know that Joey Diamonds was in charge.

One month after the Vladimir shooting, Joey was on the set

with Marty. Two wrinkled suit-wearing, middle-aged White men made their way across the set and approached Joey.

"Excuse me, could we have a word with you?"

Looking at them—everything about their demeanor screamed *cops*. But Joey played stupid.

"You just had nine," Joey retorted.

They flashed their badges.

"This'll only take a second, Mr. Diamanti," one assured him.

"If you insist."

"We do."

"Then I guess I have no choice, huh?"

Joey led them to one of the trailers, and they went inside. Joey took one of the makeup chairs while the two detectives stood.

"I'm Detective O'Ryan and this is Detective Schmidt," the shorter, pug-nosed detective introduced.

"And what can I do for you, gentlemen?"

"For starters, apologize."

"Okay, I'm sorry. I didn't know she was your wife," Joey cracked.

O'Ryan snorted a chuckle.

"Now, if that was the case, you'd be asking *me* for the apology. No, I was thinking more of two officers you left bound and gagged in South Central, while you used their Cruiser and uniforms to whack Vladimir Kaslov."

"Okay...I'm still waiting for the punch line," Joey remarked.

"There is none, but there is a bottom line."

"And you're taking the scenic route to get to it?"

O'Ryan gave him a leer of a smile.

"Mr. Diamanti, or should I say *Joey Diamonds*, you're making quite an impression out here on the Coast. Now that you removed the Chechnyans, who's next? The Armenians? The Piazza family? Inquiring minds would like to know, Joey."

"Detective O'Ryan, is it? I don't know what you've heard, but I'm just a struggling actor, trying to make a career outta two bit parts. I'll probably end up in porn," Joey replied.

O'Ryan laughed; Schmidt only smiled briefly.

"I like you, Joey, so I'm not gonna bust your balls. *This* time. But I will paint you a picture: Word is, you've got quite an alliance. The Reyes Family out of Miami, the Russians in New York, and now the Bloods. If I didn't know any better, I'd think you were planning a coup d'etat."

"You're right, you don't know any better."

"Maybe, but what I *do* know is if me and my partner here don't see any of the action and I mean soon, then you *will* end up in porn. The receiving end, your end up...in San Quentin. Is that picture clear enough for you, Joey," O'Ryan threatened.

"Listen, Detective. I have no idea what you're talkin' about. If I was half the guy you say I am, maybe I could get laid in this fuckin' town. But I tell you what I'm gonna do: I've always been an avid supporter of the local police back home, so why not here, too? So let's call this...a donation because sometimes I get parking tickets. I speed occasionally, jaywalk; a real pain in the ass, you know?" Joey offered, handing them a wad of bills.

"Jaywalk, huh?" O'Ryan chuckled. "Yeah, Joey, I never thought much for WOPs. They're dumb, greasy. But you, you might just grow on me."

"Yeah, like a cancer," Joey spat with a smile, but wanting to spit in his face.

O'Ryan read his expression and retorted, "I hope not, huh? Because, if I get cancer, so will you." O'Ryan winked. "We'll be in touch."

"I'll bet you will."

"You can bet your pretty ass on it," O'Ryan retorted as the two detectives exited the trailer.

"We love you, Joey."

"I wanna fuck you, Joey."

"Joey Diamonds."

Joey arrived in L.A. in more ways than one. He and his entourage pulled up in front of The Pulse in a stretch limo. He got out with Te Amo on one arm and Marty on the other, the rest of the girls bringing up the rear. As he approached the front of the line, he stopped in front of the guard.

"Remember me?" Joey smirked.

"How can I forget?"

"Me neither. I told you I never forget the guy who gave me my first break," Joey reminded him.

The guard smiled, happy to be remembered.

"Just doin' my job."

"Not anymore, 'cause you work for me. No more peanuts; we pay in bananas and they come in big bunches, eh?" Joey laughed then playfully slapped the guard on the cheek.

The guard laughed.

"Thanks, Mr. Diamanti. I'm Mike."

"Call me Diamonds, call me Joey; just make sure you call me in the morning, okay?" Joey instructed him, gave him a card, shook his hand, then went inside.

Inside, Joey watched the team control the crowd, as he sat back in the V.I.P. like a king overlooking his kingdom. While he, Te Amo, and Marilyn were nursing drinks and he was smoking a cigar, the waitress brought over a bottle of Cristal.

"Where'd it come from?" Joey questioned.

"The group of gentlemen to your left," the waitress gestured with her chin.

Joey didn't even bother to look. He was already aware of the presence. It was the underboss of the Piazza family, Tommy Scarlata. Joey knew the Piazzas would make a move, sooner or later. Now the move was being made, so he made one of his own.

"Send it back," Joey instructed her, flicking his cigar ashes in one of the champagne flutes that came with the bottle.

"As you wish, Mr. Diamanti," the waitress replied, taking the bottle and the flutes away.

Te Amo didn't say anything, but she questioned him with her eyes.

"You'll see in a minute," he replied to her expression.

A few moments later, Tommy and his two bodyguards approached Joey's booth.

"Hey Joey, whatsa matter wit' you, eh? I send you the bubbly—the best in the house—and you send me back your disrespect? What am I missin' here?" Tommy questioned, keeping his tone light with his presence imposing.

Joey wouldn't even grant him the respect of looking at him. In a tone that sounded bored, Joey answered, "Because you and your boss are a couple of pussies that don't even deserve an acknowledgement, let alone respect."

Both bodyguards started to lunge. Te Amo and Marilyn flinched to stand up, but Tommy restrained his bodyguards, and the girls restrained themselves.

"Hey guys, whaddya gonna do, beat up three ladies for mouthin' off?" Tommy chuckled and his bodyguards did too. "That's what happens when you try to be nice to a faggot that uses broads for muscle."

The bodyguards roared with contemptuous laughter. Joey finally looked at Tommy. He always reminded him of Jackie Gleason, but despite what he called him, he knew that Tommy was a seasoned killer.

"Hey Tommy...go fuck your dead mother in the ass," Joey spat, calmly but with pure venom.

This time, his bodyguards lunged, but Te Amo and Marilyn stood simultaneously, with nine millimeters pointed in their faces. They stopped dead in their tracks. Joey puffed his cigar.

"You–you–you cock suckin' son of a bitch!" Tommy stuttered, choked with rage. "I'm gonna kill ya!"

"Make your next move your best move, Tommy. Now get the fuck outta here," Joey hissed in a tone like a rattlesnake.

Tommy eyed him hard.

"You're a dead man, you fuckin' son of a bitch! A dead man!" Tommy vowed, then reluctantly let his bodyguards lead him away.

When they were gone, Te Amo and Marilyn sat down.

"One question," Te Amo asked, "Was that necessary?"

Joey contemplated her question for a moment.

"New York's been too quiet; somebody's pulling the Piazza's strings. I figure we rile 'em up, we'll find out who."

"They're definitely riled up."

"Well, we'll definitely find out who then."

PRESENT DAY, AUGUST 1997

"Now, will you please explain to the court what was going on in New York while Mr. Diamond was causing such an uproar in California?" the Prosecutor asked Joe "Pro" Provenzano.

Joe cleared his throat and replied, "The question with all five families was what to do about Joey. See, the Commission asked—"

"Excuse me, Mr. Provenzano, didn't mean to cut you off but—"

"Then why did you?" Joe Pro said sharply, showing how much he hated to be cut off. A few snickers were scattered around the room.

"Could you explain who and what the Commission is?"

"Why didn't you *say* that? Okay, so the Commission is the central body, the government of the underworld, so to speak. The Boss of each of the five families makes up the main body, and then a few families around the Country, too: like Buffalo, Cleveland, St. Louis, and a coupla other places. They all have a vote on who gets made, and if a Made Man can be whacked. It also governs territory, et cetera, et cetera. Are we clear?"

"Crystal," the Prosecutor replied.

"So yeah, where was I...oh yeah, everybody's like, 'what the hell do we do about the kid?' We go to his father, Vincenzo, but Vincenzo wants to give him a pass. Even though he tried to kill him, it's still his son, so it's understandable. Only, it's outta Vincenzo's hands because Vincenzo is a Boss and the cardinal rule is you can't kill a Boss without the approval of the Commission," Joe Pro explained.

"So you're saying, Mr. Provenzano, that Mr. Diamanti had unilateral power to protect his son, even though he himself was the victim?" the Prosecutor started trying to put it in court jargon.

To which Joe Pro replied, "Uni—wha?"

"Unilateral power to—"

"Look, Mr. Prosecutor, I said what I said, so if you let me say it, you'll understand," Joe Pro retorted.

A smattering of laughter scattered through the courtroom.

"Please proceed, Mr. Provenzano."

"So yeah...you can't kill a Boss. So Vincenzo's hands are tied. But outta nowhere, up steps Salvatore Romano, Boss of the Romano family. He says, maybe Joey didn't do it, but everybody knows he did it! Nobody else would've hit the Don. But the Don won't say either way, and since the Romanos carry just as much weight as the Diamantis, Sal's non-vote becomes a veto. But it puts us all in a pickle, because no one can touch Joey, and he's busy putting the squeeze on the Coast," Joe Pro said, breaking it all down, play-by-play. He stopped to clear his throat then began talking again.

"And it's obvious he's trying to spark a war with the Piazzas because of the disrespectful statement he made about the underboss Tommy's mother. Something had to be done. So it was decided that since Sal wanted to give the kid the benefit of the doubt, he would talk to the kid. Whole time, Vincenzo's gotta be screamin' because he and Sal hate each other's guts. So everybody knows that Sal's got an angle, but no one knew what it was. And that's how Joey became a member of the Romano family," Joe Pro concluded.

But it was much more complicated than that.

AUGUST 1990

Vincenzo sat on the back patio, quietly soaking in the scenery. It was a hot day, but not so much under the awning that extended from the house. His gaze ran along the rise and fall of the landscape, and for a moment he was reminded of his childhood in Castellammare del Golfo, a small village on the west coast of Sicily. At such moments, he often contemplated how his life would have turned out had his father, a respected Don in Sicily, not fallen out of favor with Mussolini and was forced emigrate to the United States.

"Such is life," his thoughts mused, resigning himself to the man he had become: a man he was proud to be, yet he hadn't always been proud.

All thoughts were interrupted when Vito escorted Frankie Shots out to see him.

"Boss, it's Frankie."

Frankie shook his hand, then kissed him on both cheeks, and sat down beside Vincenzo.

"Thank you, Vito, and if you don't mind, have the butler bring out some coffee and some of those cookies Frankie loves," Vincenzo requested.

"Sure Boss, no problem," Vito replied, then disappeared inside.

"Beautiful day isn't it, Don Vincenzo?" Frankie remarked.

Soon, the butler came out with a tray of coffee, cookies, and two cups. He poured them each a cup of coffee then left.

"Do me a favor, Frankie, indulge an old man. Speak to me in Sicilian; I'm feeling homesick," Vincenzo asked.

Frankie knew he had something heavy on his mind, because he only spoke freely in Sicilian.

"Whatever you wish, my Don," Frankie said in Sicilian.

Vincenzo felt more comfortable speaking in his mother tongue.

"Frankie, over the years I've seen a lot. This thing of ours is changing; it's not what it was. I'm not saying it's good or bad; I'm just stating a fact. A man must deal in facts, don't you agree, Paisano?" he said in Sicilian.

"Of course, my Don."

Vincenzo nodded.

"For me, facts are simple. The hard part is facing them as they are and as you wish them to be. I am old, but this is a young man's game. I can no longer keep up with the changes, nor do I want to. As the sun sets for me, I would like for it to be over the hills and plains of Castellammare del Golfo.

Frankie's chest heaved, but he maintained his composure to make sure he was hearing correctly.

"What is it that you ask of me, my Don?"

"My friend, it is you who may ask of me. Yes, you have been like a son to me. I have taken you in, and you have made me nothing but proud. You may be sottocapo, but one day you will be capo de tutti capi, eh? Mark my words, until that day, I ask you to take over the Diamanti family." Vincenzo explained.

Inside, Frankie was charged, but he kept his composure.

"For you, my Don, anything."

Vincenzo smiled at him warmly, then patted his hand.

"I know you won't let me down. Just know, being the Boss is not easy. You must be a fox *and* a lion. But knowing when to be which is the key to success."

"I understand, Don Vincenzo."

Do you? Vincenzo mused to himself, but he kept his own counsel and said, "Now...there are some things that we must discuss."

Frankie stayed silent and attentive, so Vincenzo continued.

"The books are not to be opened at this time, because for now you are only acting Boss. I don't want the other families to feel...put upon."

"I understand," Frankie nodded.

"Also, we have several problems within the family—problems that I want dealt with right away."

When he said "problems," Frankie knew that Vincenzo meant he wanted some people killed.

"I'll handle it," Frankie assured him.

Vincenzo leaned over and whispered nine names in his ear, several of which sent a chill down Frankie's spine.

"Don Vincenzo," Frankie began slowly, looking the Don in the eye, "several of these men are close to my heart, and I fear that if they have fallen out of favor, somehow I have fallen out of favor. And if I have, please tell me how, and I will correct it."

"Frankie," Vincenzo replied, wearing the warm smile of a killer you could call a friend, "I just made you a Boss and you think you earned my displeasure? These men are not your responsibility...but the problem is."

"It will be handled," Frankie reiterated, even though his jubilance was not tempered. To be made a king, but to lose your army leaves you more vulnerable.

"Lastly... I withheld my true intentions from the Commission only because I didn't want them meddling in our family affairs. But I am giving you a free hand to deal with the situation as you wish," Vincenzo explained.

"Then I will hold to outward appearances until the time is right to react," Frankie responded.

Vincenzo playfully slapped Frankie's cheek.

"*That* was the decision of a fox," he remarked, and Frankie took it to be a compliment.

Vincenzo started to get up, so Frankie rose quickly to assist him. Once they were both standing, Vincenzo took Frankie by both shoulders and said, "You've earned this day, Frankie. May you always get what you deserve." Then he kissed him on both cheeks and embraced him.

Joey's operation was expanding across the country. He had already set up distribution in San Francisco and Seattle. Then he moved across the Midwest and Texas. He benefitted from the gang infrastructure, so wherever the Bloods were, he had a ready-made retail operation, and the Russian Jews kept him supplied. His hands never got dirty; he simply made millions connecting supply with demand, taking a hefty cut for the trouble.

He moved into a beautiful place in Beverly Hills that he bought for seven million dollars.

When Te Amo first walked in with him and the realtor, she quipped, "Take out the ceiling, expand the walls, and it just might be big enough to fit my ego."

It stayed unfurnished for weeks. When Enrico returned from expanding the operation into Chicago, he came to see the new place for the first time. When he arrived, he saw Joey's newest toy: a black on black Ferrari Testarossa with the license plate that read *Vapors*. He smirked to himself as he went to the door and found it cracked. He pushed it open and walked inside. His footsteps echoed on the marble floors and bounced off the cathedral ceilings of the atrium. He admired the double set of stairs that hugged both walls and headed up the one to his left. The place was gigantic; so big that it swallowed the sounds that Enrico started to hear as he headed down the hall to the master bedroom. The sounds were muffled, yet unmistakable. In his mind, he stopped and refused to go any further. The guttural moans were that of a man in the throes of passion, not a woman. But he hadn't stopped. He kept going, right up to the door and pushed it open.

Inside, the room was totally bare except for the single mattress in the middle of the floor on which Joey was fucking Marty. He had him on all fours like a dog in heat, pounding away at his ass from the back. Marty's eyes were closed and he was oblivious to the voyeur, but Joey was looking directly at Enrico. His smile told him Joey had meant for him to see this scene. That's why the front door was open. The sparseness of the room and the raw energy of the act made the whole scene dirty, like the room was in an abandoned apartment in a condemned tenement in the Bronx and not a multi-million dollar mansion.

"Come to Daddy, my little Spanish rose," Joey remarked, taunting him.

"Fuck you," Enrico hissed then stormed out of the room.

He made it halfway up the hallway before he stopped, balled up his fist and turned back. He stopped when he heard Marty exclaim, "Oh my god, Joey! Oh yes!"

The passion in Marty's tone made Enrico sick to his stomach. He felt tormented. Part of him wanted to go back and beat the shit out of both of them, while a part of him wanted to cry. He hated the way that Joey could toy with his every emotion. At the same time, it brought him closer knowing that he was so connected to another human being that they could bring out his deepest and darkest, despite the pain. In that moment, Enrico felt truly alive.

Before he met Joey, he knew he was attracted to men on

some level. It wasn't a conscious admittance, but a subconscious acceptance that he buried and Joey easily found. Now, he realized he was falling in love with a man that would ultimately destroy him. Enrico slid down the wall and sat with his head in his hands. He heard the shower water go on. He heard the muffled voices, the laughter then silence, and the moans began again under the sizzle of the shower. Enrico stared off and zoned out, focusing on a single ray of heat that came through the window and cut across the hall. His trance was only broken by the sound of approaching footsteps. He looked up and saw Marty—fully dressed—coming up the hallway. He refused to make eye contact or to even acknowledge Enrico's presence as he walked by and disappeared down the stairs.

Then Joey stepped out of the bedroom, wearing a white, terry cloth robe and smoking a cigar.

"So, how you like my new place?" Joey asked, openly toying with Enrico's emotions.

"Dígame," Enrico seethed in Spanish.

"Because I'm going to break you," Joey answered, coldly and truthfully.

"Why?"

"Why not?"

The raw bluntness of Joey's statement struck a nerve and Enrico lashed out. He swung at Joey with every ounce of hatred, love, and pain he had been bottling up. Joey weaved, easily avoiding the wild blow then pushed Enrico's face firmly against the wall and pinned him there with his body.

"Still think you can fight it, huh Enrico?" Joey growled lustfully in his ear.

"Get off me," Enrico protested weakly, but he liked the feeling of Joey's body pressed against his, and he was strangely turned on by the thought that Joey had just been inside another man.

"Is that what you really want, Enrico? Huh?" Joey asked, kissing Enrico along his neck.

"What I want is for you to stop playing these games."

"Stop fighting and I will!"

"What's in it for me?"

"Freedom."

Enrico laughed.

"All you want is a slave."

"Joey released Enrico then turned him around to look at him.

"Slavery is freedom," he quipped.

Looking in his eyes, Enrico understood the power of hypnotism, as Joey urged him lower and Enrico bent slowly to his knees.

The seeds of Joey's downfall were appropriately enough being planted where it all started: in the clubs in New York City, with a young debutante home on summer vacation from Harrogate Ladies' College, an exclusive boarding school in North Yorkshire, England.

"Pregnant?" her mother echoed, the force of the word sure to send her back into therapy. "By whom?"

"I...I don't know, Mother," the young debutante cried.

She then explained, in graphic detail, how she took "some little pill" and it made her feel really, really good. But made her do really, really bad things with four or five guys—two of whom went to the same country club.

When asked what this little pill was, all she could say was "X."

"X?"

"X", she repeated, and then she showed her mother one, much to her mother's chagrin.

The mother took the pill to the father who, being a very generous donor to the Democratic Party, almost literally dumped the pill on the Mayor's desk and demanded, "The purveyor of this trash must be locked up indefinitely." The mayor couldn't promise indefinite imprisonment, but assured him that the person would definitely be locked up. The police came discreetly to the debutante's home and had her go through some mug shots of some known purveyors.

"That's him," she said, remembering the guy's face because he had been cute. She flirted and ended up giving him a blowjob in exchange for the pill (which, of course, she didn't mention).

The guy's name was Sammy Bilotti, a Gambino wannabe that ran narcotics in and around the clubs in Manhattan for the Gambinos. Two days later, he was picked up and thoroughly interrogated.

"Come on, Sammy, this is bullshit! This is the Mayor's daughter we're talking about," Salley lied.

"I swear to God, I don't know what X is! I never seen it in my life," Sammy equally lied.

"What did you do, Sammy? You wanted to boff her, didn't you Sammy?" Pirelli speculated.

"She's a real looker; I'da boffed her," the first Detective chimed in.

"How about it, Sammy boy. Did you boff her?"

"Hey guys, gimme a break. She gave me a blow job, and I..."

Salley slapped the table. "You dumb Guinea fuck! She's only sixteen!" He lied.

"Huh? No, she was in the fuckin' club!"

"Ever hear of statutory rape, Sammy? You know what niggas do to sweet Guinea rapists on the Island?"

"Niggas with great big schlongs, Sammy," Salley added.

They were talking so fast that Sammy didn't have time to formulate a thought, let alone think.

"Jesus! All this over a little fuckin' pill?" Sammy shook his head.

"I thought you said you never saw it before, Sammy. How'd you know it's little?"

"I'll tell you what ain't little...the schlongs, Sammy. I swear to God they're this fuckin' long," Salley remarked, holding his hands about two feet apart.

"And that's not even counting the head!"

"Okay! Alright! Let's deal! I'll give you some Russians!" Sammy offered.

"Russians?" Pirelli scoffed. "What I look like, Joe McCarthy over there? Give me Gotti. I want you to run this all the way up the flagpole and give me Gotti!"

"I can't give you Gotti! How?"

"Guinea punk rapes Mayor's daughter, marries schlong. Is that the newspaper headline you want lining your cape, you dumb fuck?"

"Okay, okay. Rizzo, I'll give you Rizzo! That's the best I can do, I swear to God!"

The two Detectives finally stopped their rapid-fire verbal assault, and stole a glance at one another. Mike Rizzo was a strong Capo for the Gambino family. He had been promoted when Bonanno had been killed. Rizzo was definitely a strong entry into the Gambino hierarchy.

"You willin' to wear a wire?" Salley inquired, almost openly salivating.

"A wire? Are you fuckin' crazy? If Rizzo thinks I'm recording him... Look, all I do is turn in the money to this guy. That's it."

"So, wear a wire. One time. Get the guy to acknowledge the transaction and it's a done deal. You're back at the club boffing the Mayor's other daughter."

Sammy thought about it, lit a cigarette and replied, "One time, no more. Any more, and I'd rather be fitted for the schlong."

"I'm telling you, Joey, the script is perfect for you!" Marty gushed. "You said you wouldn't play anybody but a gangster. Well, this is about a gangster from Italy that comes to take over the American Mafia, and in the midst, he falls in love with a blind girl who teaches him true love. Perfect!"

Marty, Joey, and Te Amo were having dinner at Spago's in L.A. Joey liked the place so much that he was contemplating becoming part owner. He thought about what Marty said then looked at Te Amo.

"Whaddya think?" he asked her.

"I think you're nuts. A movie, Joey, really? A little too high profile, no?" Te Amo objected.

"Trust me, it's insurance," he replied enigmatically then looked back at Marty. "I'm in. What's the catch?"

Marty sipped his wine then answered, "It's my current production for Stonewall, the investment house in New York that's been bankrolling me, and who my last three films have grossed them over 300 million worldwide. Suddenly, they have cold feet. They say it's too gay, too controversial. I say, controversy sells, not gay controversy. The fuckin' pricks. Anyway, I need them to be persuaded to open the spigot again."

Joey chuckled.

"So you wanna use me as muscle, huh? Multimillion dollar shakedown?"

"For a million dollar kickback, your own production and five percent off my backend, who's shaking who?" Marty quipped.

Joey laughed.

"Touché," he remarked, holding up his glass to Marty, giving him a solitary toast. "Touché, eh? Okay, I'll take care of it."

"Should I kiss your ring, godfather?" Marty joked.

"No, but I got somethin' else for you to kiss, smart guy," Joey snickered.

A few moments later, Enrico approached the table. Te Amo almost didn't recognize him. His eyebrows had been waxed and arched. He had taken his hair out of the ever-present ponytail and was wearing it loose. His style of dress was different and his movement more fluid and graceful. He was, in a word, effeminate.

"Enrico?" Te Amo questioned, incredulously.

"Sorry I'm late; we had a little problem," he explained.

"Where?" Joey wanted to know.

"New York."

Te Amo was still looking at him. "Wow, you look...different."

Enrico looked unsure of himself, until Joey said, "I think you look great," then his face beamed with pride.

"Thank you, Joey."

Te Amo looked on in amusement. Marty looked on with pity in his eyes.

"Well I guess the crux of my problem has been dealt with; I'll let you discuss yours," Marty said as he stood up and looked at Joey, adding, "If you'd be so kind as to see me out."

Joey dabbed his mouth with his napkin and stood up. He and Marty headed for the door. The twins, sitting at a table by the door, caught Joey's eye. He nodded subtly. They rose and went out the door, both carrying purses that packed a lot more than mascara.

In the parking lot, they spread out to flank Joey and keep an eye out.

"Joey, I look at us as friends; something we will be long after we tire of one another's embrace."

"True, so speak freely."

"Thank you. What I just saw...was appalling. Something like that, you could never do to me, because I know who I am.

But that also works to your advantage because you at least know who you're dealing with," Marty explained as they approached his Spyder Convertible. "But Joey, if you continue to make people who you want them to be, when the time comes, will you know who they are?" Marty jeweled Joey.

Joey chuckled and nodded.

"I got you."

"No, you don't. You're young, and power intoxicates. Just remember what I said, okay?" Marty told him, kissed him on the cheek and got in the car.

Just as he was pulling off, Bianca pulled up. Joey bent down in the window and gave her a kiss.

"What's up, beautiful?"

"The Piazzas."

"What about 'em," Joey scowled.

"Nothin' crazy. They say New York wants to have a sit down."

"Where and when?"

"They said that's up to you," she replied.

He thought about it for a minute, then a smile spread across his face.

"Tell them...we'll meet in the Jungle."

"How'd I know you would say that?"

He leaned in, kissed her, and playfully bit her lip.

"Don't start nothin' you can't finish," she remarked, with a wink.

"Since when do you know me to do that?" Joey quipped, as he walked back inside.

———

Two days later, the Italians arrived in the Jungle—three carloads deep—full of soldiers along with the Underboss of the Piazza family and the representative of the Commission. When they got there, Animal and several other Bloods blocked their entrance.

"All y'all ain't comin' in here," Animal informed them with a menacing look. The Italians, far from intimidated, didn't push the issue.

"No offense, but we didn't know what to expect," Tommy Scarlata remarked. "How's about somebody get Joey for me?"

Animal got on the walkie-talkie. A few minutes later, Joey walked out. He looked at all of the soldiers standing around the cars.

"You sure you guys just came for a sit down?" Joey quipped with a smile.

"Just...coverin' all bases, Joey. You're kinda unpredictable," Tommy commented, holding his tongue.

Joey chuckled.

"I understand, Tommy, and it's no problem with me. You coulda brought an army, I'm only a guest over here, same as you. So I tell you what: you can bring a soldier apiece, how's that?"

"No. No soldiers, Joey. Can you guarantee our safety?" the representative asked, looking Joey in the eyes.

"You have my word, Mr. Massino," Joey replied, solemnly.

Joey knew exactly who the massive fat man was: Peter Massino, or better known as Peter the Pope. He was the Consigliore of the Romano family. He was a legend and helped Salvatore Romano take over what was the Colombo family. Joey knew that if they sent the Pope as the rep, the Commission was taking him very seriously.

"That's good enough for me," Massino replied, as he turned and whispered in his bodyguard's ear.

The bodyguard nodded, made a gesture to the other soldiers and they all got back into the cars.

Joey, Tommy, and Massino walked under the breezeway and entered the Jungle. As they walked, Joey put his hand on

Tommy's shoulder and said, "Mr. Scarlata, I want to apologize about the other night. I was totally out of line. I understand if you don't accept it, but I offer it with all my honor."

Tommy looked at Joey. He knew what Joey was doing; Joey wanted to set the tone to show Massino he wasn't a hard man to talk to. Still, looking in his eyes, it was hard for Tommy not to at least want to believe him.

"Forget about it, kid; I already did," Tommy replied.

The two men shook hands. Joey led them to Bone's apartment. They entered and sat down around the kitchen table.

"What can I get you guys to drink?" Joey offered.

"Some coffee," Massino replied.

"Make that two," Tommy added, following Massino's lead.

Joey sat three cups on the table then filled them up. Once done, he put the coffee pot in the middle of the table and sat down.

"First off, allow me to say...Don Massino, it is an honor and a privilege to sit at the same table as you, as well as you, Don Scarlata. I am young, eh? Full of piss and venom, but one thing I'm not is insensitive. So please, take my words in that vein," Joey said showing that he could be just as respectful as disrespectful.

Massino sipped his coffee, looking at Joey the whole time. He had the kind of gaze that lesser men called chilling. He put his cup down and said, "The ruthless are never insincere. They mean everything they do. So tell me: what is it you're doing, Joey?"

Joey shrugged.

"Just trying to wet my beak."

Massino snorted. "Is that what you call it? Seems to me that you're pushing for a war out here, huh? It's not enough that you bury the Chechnyans, but now you're pushin' into territory clearly belonging to the Piazza regime? So Tommy sends you a gift: a peaceful prelude to a sit down and you tell 'em to fuck his mother. Tommy, no offense."

"None taken."

"Is that what you call wettin' your beak?"

"Don Massino, I saw an opportunity, and I took it. I mean after all, I'm an outlaw, right? Why do you expect me to play by the rules?" Joey shot back.

Massino pointed a fat, savage-like finger at Joey.

"We didn't make you an outlaw. That's between you and Don Diamanti. The Commission has yet to vote on your status. Until then, I've been sent to make you an offer."

"I'm listening..."

"Your aggression ends *today*. You will respect the Piazza regime's interests and relinquish any and all operations that impede on such interests, without their consent. The drugs you can keep, but you'll kick back thirty percent to the Commission and ten to the Piazza regime. In return, the Commission will recognize you as under the protection of the Piazza regime as long as you're in California, until we rule on your status," Massino proposed.

Joey sipped on his coffee. What Massino proposed was really no offer at all. And on top of that, they wanted nearly half of his California money in return. But he understood the ways of the elders. They wanted to see if he was willing to submit to an order from the Commission, to see if he would agree to such humiliating terms as penance for past sins. The two older men watched him, impassively but closely. Joey sat his cup down.

"Don Scarlata...Don Massino, I accept whatever conditions the Commission imposes. I will comply totally. I ask only one thing in return."

"Which is?" Massino inquired.

"That the two of you both accept my sincerest apologies that this meeting even had to take place."

Massino smiled.

"Apology accepted."

Joey turned to Tommy.

"As for you, Don Scarlata," he said—getting up and grabbing a briefcase that he had by the refrigerator. He sat it on the table, popped the clasps, and opened it. It was filled with money. "This is from me to you. It might not be a bottle of champagne, but I hope it conveys the message of my friendship."

Tommy's greedy eyes scanned the money. His estimate was that it was at least $100k. He was right. He got up, shook Joey's hand, embraced him and kissed him on both cheeks.

"You've got class, kid. Keep that up and you'll go a long way." Tommy advised him. Massino got Joey's message. It told him that he had anticipated such a situation and was ready to put the cherry on top. Massino nodded approvingly.

"Tommy, do me a favor. You can go. Let me speak to Joey alone," Massino requested.

Tommy shook Massino's hand, then Joey's, grabbed the briefcase, and left.

Massino pulled out his cigar. Joey pulled out his lighter and lit it for him. Massino puffed until it was lit then sat back and said, "I liked how you handled that, Joey. Tommy's right. You've got class."

"Comin' from you, Don Massino, that's a real compliment," Joey answered. He could tell that Massino caught the subtle dig at Tommy.

Massino puffed and smiled.

"You're a lot like your old man. Brutally honest, without having to be brutal, you get me?"

Joey nodded.

"Do you know why I was sent out here as representative?"

"No."

He paused.

"Because you've been vouched for by Big Sal," Massino informed him proudly.

Salvatore Romano, his father's archenemy. The picture was becoming clearer, but still not yet in focus.

"My thanks to the Don, but I'm confused."

"Don't be. What's between your father and Sal doesn't have to be between you and Sal...or does it?" Massino quipped.

Without hesitation, Joey answered, "No, not at all."

"That's good, because he wants you to come back with me and meet with him personally. Will you do that?"

"I'd be honored. All I ask—"

"He guarantees your safety," Massino interjected. "As a matter of fact, it's been his vote that kept the hit off your head."

Interesting, Joey thought.

"Then I guess my only question is: when do we leave?"

Massino and Joey flew into JFK the next day. They were taken via a black Lincoln directly to a diner in Queens. It was called Andy's.

Now, Joey understood.

He got out of the car and Massino was driven away in the Lincoln. A Romano foot soldier stayed with Joey.

"Let's get a cup of coffee," the soldier suggested.

They went inside, ordered two cups of coffee. By the time they took one sip, the soldier looked outside.

"Our ride's here."

They left without paying.

The two of them got into a dark blue Buick and were whisked away. They shot through Queens—running red lights at the last minute and making a series of right turns, until they were back where they started. They took the Expressway into Manhattan and switched cars in Chinatown. Joey got into a silver Mercedes-Benz, driven by a small, quiet man that reminded him of Joe Pesci. Two hours later, they ended up at the same diner, only this time they entered through the back door, through the kitchen and into a small office.

Sitting behind the desk was Salvatore Romano. He had been there the whole time.

He sat, smoking a cigar, hands folded over a protruding gut while he watched the Yankee game on a small black and white TV sitting on the desk.

"Have a seat, Joey. I'll be with you in a minute," Sal told him, cigar clenched between his teeth.

Joey sat.

Mattingly struck out. Sal tuned off the TV, stood and rounded the desk. Joey stood.

"Joey Diamanti," Sal intoned, looking him over, sizing him up. "It's good to finally meet you."

"It's an honor to meet you, Don Romano," Joey replied politely.

Sal waved him off.

"By the time we're done, you'll be calling me Uncle Sally, eh?" he chuckled, then shook Joey's hand, embraced him and kissed both cheeks.

"Have a seat," Sal offered.

Joey sat down in the same seat but Sal took the other seat next to Joey and pulled himself closer.

"So, how's L.A., Joey?" Sal inquired, making small talk.

"The broads'll do but there's no place like New York," Joey responded.

"Yeah, I feel the same way. I never go any further than Vegas if I can help it, you know?"

The two men regarded one another with smiles on their faces, but their eyes were poker players.

"I guess you're wonderin' why you're here," Sal began.

"I already know."

"Then why are you here?"

"Because you asked me to come," Joey quipped with a smirk.

Sal chuckled.

"I like wise guys, Joey. A man oughta be able to enjoy a good laugh, ya think?"

"I agree," Joey affirmed.

"It relieves tension, you know? Because in this business, there's a lot of tension, a lot of bad blood. Like between your father and I. Your father's a helluva guy, but he could never enjoy a good laugh. He took himself too seriously, and a lot of things that could've been avoided weren't. Am I makin' sense over here?" Sal probed.

"I follow you perfectly."

"Then I want you to look me in the eyes and tell me you're your own man and not just your father's son," Sal challenged.

Joey looked him in the eyes and replied, "I am my own man and not my father's son."

Sal didn't miss the fact that Joey left the word 'just' out, nor did Joey want him to. Sal nodded.

"I heard a lot about you, Joey. I hear you're a stand-up guy—that you don't take no shit from nobody, but you're a reasonable guy."

"I try to be, Mr. Romano."

"And I hear...you're, uh...left-handed," Sal remarked, using the limp-wrist gesture as a euphemism for Joey's sexual orientation.

Joey smiled.

"More like...ambidextrous."

Sal chuckled.

"Then you must have one helluva curve."

Both men laughed.

"Listen, I have no problem with what a man does behind closed doors. This is America, for Christ's sake. Even in Sicily, I knew a guy that fucked sheep. Forget about it, whaddya gonna do, eh?" Sal remarked. "What's important to me is loyalty... honor...and respect. You got that, you get no argument from me."

"Is that what you're asking of me?" Joey inquired, looking Sal in the eyes.

Sal returned his gaze and replied, "Well, first and foremost I'm asking you for your friendship. Let everything else stem from that. I think you and I, we can do some big things together, Joey...big things, starting out there on the Coast."

"I thought I was to be under the Piazza protection?" Joey smirked.

Sal sat down in the chair and waved him off.

"The Piazzas couldn't protect their own ass with both hands. Fuck the Piazzas. You're a smart guy, Joey. I'm sure you already knew that you'd be under my protection, but the Piazza's responsibility."

Joey nodded. "Once I saw Don Massino, I figured as much."

"Then you understand protocol. The only reason the whole fuckin' Commission ain't gunnin' for you is because I went to bat for ya 'cause I don't believe you'd kill your own old man, and I believe you deserve our respect despite being...ambidextrous," Sal explained.

"Then I'm forever in your debt," Joey remarked.

Sal accepted his spoken homage.

"Besides...between you and me, your father's been...cleanin' house. Jimmy Casso, Lil' Joe Pipes, Benny Bagels... That's just a few of the good souls no longer with us, and if you notice, all these guys were kinda partial to Frankie Shots. So what does that say to you?" Sal quizzed.

"All I need to know," Joey answered.

"Yeah, but he also made 'em actin' Boss, so I figure, you promote a guy into a position of *power*, but you take away his *strength,* that's like the guys are made king but you cut off their johnsons before they were allowed near the broads."

"Eunuchs," Joey corrected Sal.

"Yeah, eunuchs; Frankie Shots is a fuckin' eunuch."

They both laughed.

"But never mind that. You're my guy on the Coast, so bring me my money personally, got me?"

"Sure, Boss," Joey smirked.

Sal smiled and pointed at Joey.

"Hey...I'm not your Boss yet. But keep your nose clean and I will be, eh?"

Sherman Brothers was one of the main investment banks on Wall Street that were investing in movies. They even had a Hollywood Division, and Andrew Wynn was the President of the Division. He was young, brash, and full of himself. He had decided not to give Marty the rest of the money for his Stonewall production, and liked to let it be known that he had such unilateral power.

"Hey, fuck Marty Latrell. I own that cock sucking weasel," he bragged into the speakerphone as he swiveled in his leather chair and looked out on the sunset from an office that rivaled Gordon Gekko in the movie *Wall Street.* In fact, everything about Andrew reminded people of Gekko, down to the suspenders and slicked-back hair, because Andrew tried to pattern himself after the character's swagger.

"But Marty's made you guys a lot of money," the voice on the other end reminded him.

"Are you kiddin'? *I* made Marty! Without Sherman Brothers, he'd be a fuckin' pariah. Sometimes you just gotta remind a guy who's boss," Andrew boasted.

"Whatever you say. Hey, there's this new club that every-body's talking about..."

"Can't. Got a date with the twin blonds."

The line got quiet.

"Bob, you still there?"

"I hate you, Andy," the voice said, playfully. "I can't even ask if she has a sister, because you're fucking her too! You're my hero."

Andrew laughed. "Gotta go. Life awaits," he replied, then broke the connection.

Andrew grabbed his jacket and headed out the door for the elevator. By the time he reached street level, an all-white limo was awaiting him. A sexy Latina driver got out to open the door.

"Good evening, Mr. Wynn."

He looked her up and down, tasting her with his eyes.

"I hope you'll be a part of it," he leered.

She opened the door. The twin blonds said, "Hi Andrew!" simultaneously, then giggled like vixens.

"Looks like you already got your hands full," the driver quipped.

"Always room for one more," he winked.

"I'll keep that in mind," she winked back.

He got in. They peeled off. One twin pulled out the cocaine.

"Alright! Let the good times roll!" he yelled, taking the rolled up hundred dollar bill from the other twin and scarfing several lines of coke. He loved the way cocaine made him feel. Invincible. All-powerful. They called the titans of Wall Street "masters of the universe." Cocaine made him really feel like one. Mix that with cognac, plus the jiggle of bare breasts and girlish giggles, and he didn't even notice that he was in a garage in the Bronx...

Until it was too late.

"Hey, where—"

Click-clack! Click-clack! was all he heard. It was the sounds of the twins—Amanda and Alicia—cocking their twin .45's that they were holding. They were just as pretty, but in a lethal kind of way.

"What the hell is going on? Do you fucking cunts know who I am?" he bassed, the cocaine fueling his narcissism.

"Do you know who I am?" came the reply, but it was a male's voice. He looked up and saw Joey looking down on him from outside the car.

"I—I don't understand."

"Get out the fuckin' car."

Amanda grabbed him by the collar and guided him out of the car. When he got out, Maria the driver had a gun on him as did Amanda. Alicia took out two pairs of handcuffs and cuffed him to a metal pole on the wall.

Joey put his hands in his pockets and looked at Andrew.

"Now...I asked you a question. I said, 'Do you know who I am?'"

"Yes," Andrew said, while nodding nervously. He recognized Joey Diamonds instantly.

"Do you know what I do?"

"Yes."

"Do you know what I can do to you?"

"Please don't."

"I'll take that as a *yes*. So we don't have to play any games, and we can get straight to the point. You owe Marty; Marty owes me. But I can't get paid unless you pay. You see our problem here, Andy?" Joe quizzed him.

"Yes, I – I – I do. I had no idea, Mr. Diamonds, that you were involved."

"So, now that you know, whaddya gonna do?"

"Marty will get the rest of his money, you have my word."

Joey playfully teased Andrew.

"I can see how you got so rich, Andy; you're quick. You like to get to the point, which saves a lot of time and keeps me from playin' hardball. Besides...you don't want the pictures to get out."

"Pictures?" Andrew echoed, confusedly.

Joey smiled and nodded over Andrew's shoulder. He looked and saw Alicia strapping on a black, 12-inch dildo while Maria took the lens cap off a camera.

Joey walked up to Alicia, looked at the dildo then said, "Hmmm, interesting choice of color," then he ran one finger along the dildo. "Wow...no Vaseline. I'll see ya, Andy."

Joey walked away as Amanda snatched Andrew's pants off.

"No – no – no – please – no," Andrew begged.

As Joey left, all he could hear were Andrew's glass-shattering screams and the incessant click of the camera in action.

JULY 1997

"But my question, Joey, is: are you a gangster?" Diane smiled, yet her gaze was intense.

Joey threw his head back and laughed.

"Diane, come on. Gimme a break, huh? I'm an actor, I'm an entrepreneur, a self-made man, but a gangster?" He shook his head. "But I get it, you know, because we've been doing this since the beginning. Adam blamed Eve, God blamed the Devil, and Americans blame gangsters: outlaws, the bad guys. Somebody so you can also say, "Hey at least I'm not *that*." But at the same time, we still admire the bad guy. So it's a love-hate relationship. We need to feel good about our own BS," Joey surmised.

"So you're simply society's scapegoat?"

"The modern-day version of the horned one himself."

"Well, aren't you capitalizing by putting out a movie called *The Purple Don* during your trial?" Diane probed.

"That was totally the decision of the studio," Joey replied, but leaving out the fact that he was part owner of the studio.

"Tell me, Joey, if you weren't an actor, what would Joey Diamanti be? *Who* would Joey Diamanti be?"

Joey shrugged nonchalantly and replied, "A plumber."
"A plumber? Why a plumber?"
He smiled, devilishly and answered, "I like to lay the pipe."

PRESENT DAY, AUGUST 1997

"Please state your name for the record."

"James O'Ryan."

"And, Mr. O'Ryan what do you do for a living?"

"Well, for the last eight years, up to about six months ago, I was a Detective with the LAPD."

"And what happened to change that?"

"I was arrested for possession of cocaine and ecstasy," O'Ryan admitted.

"I see," the Prosecutor mused, as he paced in front of the witness stand. "And at any given time during your eight years as Detective, did you know the defendant, Joseph Diamanti?"

"I did."

"In what capacity?"

"I worked for him," O'Ryan answered.

Rollins stood up.

"Objection, Your Honor."

"Overruled."

"When you say you worked for him, could you be more specific?" the Prosecutor probed.

"Yeah. I was a dirty cop, and I was on Diamanti's payroll. It's not a fact that I'm proud of, but it's a fact."

"And how long did this arrangement go on?"

"Between a year and a half to two years," O'Ryan estimated.

"What were some of your duties for Mr. Diamanti?"

"I would tell him if any of his illegal interests were under investigation, or if any of his people were working with the police. I also helped Mr. Diamanti plan and carry out the murder of Dominick Piazza and Tommy Scarlata, Boss and Underboss of the Piazza crime family in L.A.," O'Ryan explained.

Rollins jumped to his feet.

"Objection, Your Honor! My client is not charged with the murders Mr. O'Ryan refers to."

"But he is charged with drug dealing and racketeering. I simply want to establish a pattern of conduct," the Prosecutor rebutted.

"Tread lightly, Counselor," the Judge Bartholomew warned the Prosecutor, and then he turned to Rollins and said, "Overruled."

The Prosecutor walked back over to the witness stand.

"And for what reason were these two men murdered?" the Prosecutor questioned.

"Because Joey's—I mean Mr. Diamanti's Boss—Salvatore Romano wanted them dead. Romano is the Boss of one of the biggest crime families in New York. He's been wanting to control the action out of L.A. for a long time, but L.A. is what you call an open city.

"Meaning?"

"Meaning, any family can set up operations out there, as long as no toes get stepped on. The Piazza family was the only family in L.A., but they had no power in New York. Romano wanted to get them a vote on the Commission, and then have the Bosses whacked so he could move his people to control the vote. It's all a whole bunch of greaseball stuff. Anyway, once Romano finagled this, he had Mr. Diamanti whack the Bosses," O'Ryan told a spellbound jury.

"What role did you play?"

"I was to claim that Tommy Scarlata was my informant, so Romano could justify killing a Made Man to the Commission. Now if the Boss' crime family, the Piazzas, knew their Underboss was a rat...that makes them a rat by default. If the Boss was too blind to spot the rat, that makes him too dumb to be the Boss. Either way, they had to go," O'Ryan concluded.

"And how did Mr. Diamanti benefit?" the Prosecutor asked.

"The double murder is how he got his button."

"His button?"

"How Joey Diamonds became an official Made Man in the Mafia."

MARCH 1991

E nrico stood nude in front of the full-length mirror. He didn't know if he liked what he saw because he didn't know *who* he saw. Was this the new him, the him he'd always been or was it the him Joey had created? He didn't recognize his own mannerisms, his own style. His walk felt artificial and uncomfortable; even his thoughts felt as much as implants as the implants he was contemplating to fill out his hips.

Enrico had begun to take hormone supplements, estrogen, and he could see his breasts starting to come in. He anticipated them like a girl on the verge of puberty, combined with a cancer watching the burgeoning of a growth. He was torn emotionally. But one thing he was sure of was his love for Joey. All of this was for Joey. It was what Joey wanted, or rather what Enrico discerned that Joey wanted. Joey only smiled encouragingly or remained impassive, which Enrico read as disapproval.

They would lie in bed and Joey would tweak his nipple and remark, "If you had a little more to grab, eh, I'd have the best of both worlds." A few days later, Enrico told him, "I'm going to start taking estrogen." Joey would smile and kiss him passionately.

So gradually, Enrico came to the idea to announce to Joey, "I'm going to have a sex change operation."

"Are you sure?"

Enrico searched Joey's eyes to find his own sense of certainty. When he thought he had found it, he answered, "Absolutely."

Joey took him to bed and fucked him royally.

So as he stood in front of the hospital mirror, about to undergo surgery, he didn't know what was looking back at him, but he knew whoever he was, he wanted to be loved.

"Mr. Valdez," the nurse began as she entered. After seeing that he was naked, she turned her head, adding, "I'm sorry. I didn't know you were..."

"It's okay," Enrico replied in an apologetic tone, as he slipped back on his hospital robe. "I was just...saying goodbye, I guess."

She gave him a matronly look.

"It's a big step."

"I know."

They exchanged an awkward glance.

"The doctor will be in momentarily."

"Thank you, nurse."

"You're very welcome," she smiled warmly then walked out and closed the door behind her.

As they whizzed him into O.R., Enrico wished Joey was there to hold his hand. But Joey was becoming a big star. His bit role in Marty's movie had gotten the town, as Hollywood insiders called it, *buzzing*. So Joey was off negotiating another film.

"Count back from ten," the doctor told him.

"When I wake up, I'll be who he wants me to be," his heart told him, but his head was saying something different.

"10, 9, 8, 7..."

Meanwhile, Joey was in New York, doing what he did best: living the Diamond life. His role in the movie may have been small, but since he was already larger than life, the perception was only magnified. Everybody wanted to take a picture with him, be seen with him, and party with him. But everywhere he went, he kept Te Amo with him.

"You're going to be ripped to pieces," Te Amo said while smiling for the paparazzi, posing with Joey.

"Whaddya mean?"

"Look at all those women that want to be in my shoes," she remarked.

Joey looked around and had to admit that the plastic expression on many a female's face looked more like pageant-style clenched teeth and not genuine smiles. So Joey turned to Te Amo and scooped her off her feet, making her giggle uncontrollably.

"So, give 'em to them," he suggested, and she did, kicking her shoes off and launching them into the crowd like a bouquet at the end of a wedding. The NY Post headline would read the next day:

Who's That Girl?

He carried her into the club and sat her on his lap. As the night wore on, many came by the table to pay homage; gangsters and civilians like. The civilians came just to be seen, but the gangsters came because Joey had begun to share his ill-gotten gains with each of the five families, even the Diamantis. He was making so much money off the ecstasy distribution network that he could afford to be generous, and that generosity he used like political leverage in Congress. He was not only a ruthless adversary; he was a valued ally. He was Machiavellian in all his dealings.

"Joey, there's a guy here that wants to see you," his body-guard Mike whispered in his ear.

"Yeah, who?"

"Anthony Braza. Says he's Gambino."

"Never heard of him," Joey sniffed.

"He says you'll remember him once you see him."

Mike pointed and Joey followed his finger. When Joey saw him, he immediately recognized him from the New Year's Eve party of 1989: the guy he beat up.

"Oh yeah, the guy I knocked on his ass," Joey chuckled. "Sure, I'll humor 'em. Send 'em over."

Mike went over and came back with the guy. He approached with his hand extended. Joey reached out and shook it.

"How you doin'? Sit down. I would offer you a drink, but you and alcohol don't get along so good," Joey quipped, good-naturedly.

"Mr. Diamanti, my name's Anthony Braza. I'm a friend of the Gambinos. And I just wanted to apologize for that night. I never got a chance to, and it's been kind of killin' me ever since. So when I saw you over here..."

Joey held up his hand.

"Hey Anthony, forget about it, eh? I'm not the type to hold grudges."

Anthony breathed easily, and it looked as if he had finally taken a breath after a year.

"Thank you, Mr. Diamanti."

"Call me Joey."

"Thank you, Joey."

"Okay, Anthony. Is there anything else?" Joey asked, already bored with humoring a nobody.

"Actually...there is," Anthony replied, carefully.

"Then let's hear it."

Anthony looked at Te Amo on Joey's lap, then at Joey.

"No offense, Mr. Diamanti. I mean…"

Joey studied Anthony's expression for a moment, then turned to Te Amo. "Slide over for a minute."

When she did, Anthony got closer to Joey and whispered in his ear, "I thought you outta know that I got this cop, you know what I mean? He can tell me what color underwear the Mayor's wearing, you get me? Beautiful fuckin' arrangement. Anyway, he tells me that he knows a few things about the hit on you."

Joey looked at Anthony intently.

"Anthony, you're talkin' about a very sensitive subject with me."

"I can only imagine, but I'm tellin' you…Joey this guy, he don't miss."

"So why'd he tell you?"

"Cause he's in my pocket and don't know how to get in touch with youse."

Joey pinned his eyes with a gaze so direct that Anthony squirmed under it.

"Honest to God, Joey, I wouldn't bullshit about somethin' like this."

"You better not…Listen, you give Mike your number. Set up a meeting with this cop and I want *you* there, capeesh, Paisano?"

"Sure thing, Joey. No problem."

"Okay…and if this thing's legit, you got a friend for life," Joey promised.

Two days later, Mike drove Joey to a section of Hoboken, NJ near the docks and warehouses. He pulled up behind another car and parked. Joey got out, and then got in the back seat of the other car. Waiting inside was Anthony Braza and a middle-aged man with a potbelly and graying temples.

"How you doin', Joey? This is Detective Clooney," he introduced.

Clooney turned and extended his hand over the seat.

"How are you, Joey? I've heard a lot about you," Clooney said.

"Yeah, apparently more than most. Tell me what you know," Joey replied, cutting straight to the chase.

Clooney looked at Anthony.

"Ay, Joey, no disrespect, but Clooney here usually sells this type of information," Anthony told Joey.

"Yeah, I'm sure he does, and I'm sure it's all very lucrative, but what I'm askin' for is an introductory offer, a sample of the goods. You prove to me what you have is that good, and I'll make you both very rich men," Joey counter offered.

Clooney looked through the rearview into Joey's cold blue eyes. Even in the dark, Clooney could see the determination and confidence. He knew Joey was a rising star, one he wanted to hitch his wagon to.

"Okay," Clooney relented, "but next time—"

"Next time I'll pay you triple, and then I put you on the payroll."

That was all Clooney needed to hear. He handed Joey a bulky manila folder. Joey took it and slid out the contents. There were mug shots, surveillance photos, several typed pages, and even a cassette tape. Joey glanced at a couple of the photos, but in the dark, he couldn't see much.

"Okay, so walk me through this," he told Clooney.

"The four mug shots are the shooters that tried to take off the piece of work on you. They were brought in from Cleveland."

"Cleveland?" Joey repeated in an impressed tone. "They're a regular Murder, Inc. They grow killers like weeds. Who brung 'em in?"

"That I don't know, but I can paint you a picture. It'll be up to you to connect the dots."

"I'm listening."

"I'm assigned to the New York State Organized Crime Task Force, a pie job if there's ever been one because nobody really gives a fuck; it's all political, you follow me? It's a tap dance for the Feds. Anyway...the way it works is there's supposed to be a unit assigned to monitor each of the five families."

"Who are you assigned to?"

"The Diamantis," Clooney smiled and looked at Joey in the rearview.

"The Big Dog! Congratulations," Joey quipped.

"I said *supposed*. Actually our budget is non-existent, so I basically cover them *all*. But after they tried to clip you, I start getting mixed signals from my Diamanti surveillance."

"Mixed signals?"

"Yeah, like every other family figured it was your old man 'cause you were..."

"I know what I am. G'head."

Clooney cleared his throat.

"Yeah so, that was the consensus, only I hear Benny Bagels on the phone sayin' that your old man was pissed and he wants Frankie to find out who tried to clip you," Clooney explained.

Joey couldn't believe his ears. His old man *hadn't* tried to kill him! It felt like a two-ton rock had just been lifted off his heart.

"Okay," Joey said, barely audibly.

"But Benny says, the guy doesn't give a fuck; the guy says to make it look good. I don't know who the guy is. Listen to the tape; it's all there," Clooney explained.

"Go on," Joey replied. He knew exactly who the guy was.

"Then a few days later, Benny Bagels keeps sayin' that he can't get Vinnie Boom Boom on the phone because he wants to make sure his ass in covered in Cleveland. So I think...Cleveland? Somebody else was talking about Cleveland and Vinnie Boom Boom."

"Who?"

"Peter Amuso."

Joey's ears perked up, because now he could see it all.

"But this was a week before the hit. So I trace back and I monitor all flights to and from Cleveland outta LaGuardia, JFK, and Newark."

"Smart guy."

"Thanks, I try. The night of the hit, I got four guys leaving from Newark. But I don't know I've got a jackpot until I cross check, and the same four guys came into JFK three days *before* the hit. I run the names, all aliases but one: a James Weston. He has a charge on his alias, so I get a mug shot. I call in a favor in Cleveland and boom, it's Jimmy Callahan, an Irish killer who runs a crew that'll make the Westies look like fuckin' pansies.

Joey sat back, trying to digest the intricacies of the plot. It was complex, but oh so simple, and it had been in his face the whole time.

Joey ran his hand through his hair.

"Who else have you told about this?"

"Nobody," Clooney replied.

"Don't fuckin' shit me, Clooney! Who knows?" Joey barked.

The sudden change in tone caught Clooney off guard.

"Nobody, Joey, I swear to God."

Joey felt like he was telling the truth, because he didn't know what Joey knew. He didn't know what filled in the blanks that made it all make sense. One thing was for sure: Clooney thought the Gambinos were involved. That's why he had taken the information to Braza. That's what Joey wanted him to keep thinking.

"Okay," Joey finally said, after a prolonged silence. "Okay," he repeated, this time with more finality, as if he had decided on a course of action.

"So whaddya think?" Anthony asked, looking back at Joey with a content smile on his face. He felt he had made a friend for life.

"I think somebody's playing a very dangerous game, and I can't afford to let them find out I know," Joey replied, and with that he lifted his .456 and hit Anthony and Clooney, point blank, two apiece in the heads, drenching the windshield and inside of the front of the car with brains and blood.

Joey sat back in the seat, thinking. Several seconds later, Mike ran up to the car, gun in hand. He snatched Joey's door open.

"Boss, you okay? What happened?" he asked.

Joey looked at Mike.

"I fucked up...I shouldn't have done that. But I had to."

Mike couldn't understand, but he had no time to process it.

"We gotta get outta here!"

"Yeah. Find the shells."

"Huh?"

"We gotta find the fuckin' shells. I hit 'em with an automatic!"

Mike knew that Joey hadn't planned on killing them, because he would've never used an automatic. He wiped the back of the door handle then opened the passenger door so the interior light would come on.

Anthony's bloody body flopped out.

"Fuck!" Mike spat.

With the light on, all somebody had to do was drive by and see it all. They frantically searched the back floor. Seconds seemed like minutes, minutes like hours until they found all four.

"Got 'em. Let's go," Mike exclaimed.

Joey tucked the bulky manila envelope so nothing would fall out. Then they fled, leaving behind the single biggest mistake Joey Diamonds would ever make.

"Chief Sorenson, what was Detective Clooney doing in New Jersey with Anthony Braza, a reputed Gambino mobster?" the reporter questioned.

"That, uh hasn't been fully investigated, but we think Braza was one of the Detective's informants," the Chief responded.

"Chief Sorenson, wouldn't that type of information be well documented?"

"No comment. Listen, we are investigating all possible avenues, but rest assured, we *will* find out what happened. The budget of the Organized Crime Task Force will be substantially increased and will be an effective factor in ridding New York of—"

Joey cut the TV off and sat in the darkness of his own thoughts. He was in the bedroom of his New York City condo in the Trump Towers. He knew killing the cop could be a problem, but letting him live would've been more of a problem. Whoever was behind this couldn't find out he knew, so Joey went with the old adage: the only way two people can keep a secret is if one of them is dead.

His thoughts turned to that guy. He listened to the tape. He heard every word. He knew who Benny Bagels was. What about Frankie Shots?

Frankie had been behind the hit, but his father hadn't. That was both a relief and a problem. Frankie could've never made such a move without a powerful ally, and Joey felt like he knew who it was. But he needed to be sure. Absolutely sure. And then...Te Amo entered.

"Why are you sitting in the dark?" she asked.

"Thinking." He paused.

"Enrico is on the phone," she said then handed him the cordless.

He took it. She looked at him. He looked drained.

"You sure you're okay?"

"Never better," he replied.

She knew it was a lie, but she let it go and walked out.

"Yeah?"

"Joey?"

"Yeah Enrico, it's me. How you doin'?"

"I'm fine. How are you?"

"Just peachy...Listen, I'm right in the middle of somethin' here, so talk to me."

"Oh, I'm sorry. I could call back," he offered, feeling awkward in the moment.

"Yeah, but you called now. Enrico, please."

"I just wanted to tell you that...I did it."

[Pause]

"Did what?"

"The surgery," Enrico replied, a little impatient because Joey should have known what surgery.

"Yeah, right... Listen, I'll be back on the Coast in a coupla weeks; we'll talk about it then."

"Joey, you haven't heard a word I said."

"Sure I did. You said you're having surgery."

"*Had* Joey, *had*. I had the surgery," Enrico seethed.

"Yeah, *had*. I'll talk to you later."

Joey hung up then went into the living room where Te Amo, Mike, and Maria were. They looked up when he entered.

"Te Amo, get Zev on the phone. Tell him we're gonna need a few guys."

She nodded and took the phone from his extended hand.

"Mike, get us six seats. We're going to Cleveland. Maria, call Amanda. Nobody else needs to know," he announced then walked out. From then on, everybody would be on a need-to-know basis.

Salley and Pirelli, the same Detectives who'd nabbed Sammy had worked Sammy's wiretap into the indictment of Mike Rizzo. They had Mike in the same interrogation that they had Sammy. They played a few tapes for Rizzo, and Rizzo turned green. He knew it was over.

"Yeah, Rizz, we're calling 'em the greatest hits of Mike Rizzo; you like?" Detective Salley taunted.

Rizzo replied, "I want my—"

Pirelli stopped him, saying, "Hol' up. Think about what you're doin'. We've got you on this tape, not only making drug deals, but badmouthin' Gotti. You questioned his right to take over after Big Paul. You even have him responsible for Big Paul's death. Now, if you lawyer up, this tape becomes public knowledge because we'll use it to justify no bail. So, you're fucked either way!"

"Unless," Salley chimed in, "unless we can find a way to...compromise."

"What's John gonna think when he hears this tape, huh? He's not gonna be too pleased."

"I'm not a fuckin' rat," Rizzo protested.

"And you're not a dead man either...yet. Mike, you fucked up—maybe not with us, because maybe you can win the case—but can you win with John? With that temper?"

Rizzo thought about what he said. He knew he had said too much. His mother always said his big mouth would get him in trouble one day, and she was right. But she never said his mouth would get him out of trouble one day, too. But today would be that day, not because he was afraid of doing time; he was afraid of *not* doing time and suffering John Gotti's wrath.

Rizzo sighed hard; it was the sigh of resignation.

"Listen...If I do this, I want witness protection for me and my family."

The Detectives looked at one another, and then back at Rizzo.

"Whatsa matter, Rizzo, you don't trust us?"

"Fuck you. NYPD is a joke. Federal WP or I lawyer up," he replied.

Salley reached out and shook Rizzo's hand.

"We'll make it happen."

The Shamrock Pub was packed to capacity. It was Friday night, and Cleveland's working class Irish were out to drink, fight, throw up, and pass out. A perfect night for a robbery...or what would seem like one. Te Amo, Maria, and Amanda had gone in first and were flirting it up with Jimmy Callahan and his crew: two Irish men, two Italians. All killers. The Shamrock was their watering hole of choice; a fact that Joey found out easily through the Calamini family goons.

Once the girls were in place, the four of Zev's Russian goons with ski masks ran into the club, waving AK-47's, letting off a few short bursts of gunfire, accompanied by shouts of: "Everybody on the ground! This is a stickup!" Those in the room quickly fell flat on their faces.

Jimmy and his crew were slow to get down, but once one of the Russians drove home the point by driving the rifle butt into one of the Italian's noses, they knew it was a serious situation.

"Do you fucking bastards know who the fuck I am?" Jimmy laughed as he got down. "You're gonna be dead, on the front page of the news if you don't shut the fuck up!" Te Amo growled as she cuffed Jimmy behind his back.

"I'm Jimmy Callahan!"

"Good; that means we got the right guy!" she replied.

The Russians grabbed the four-man crew and dragged them out the back to an awaiting van, driven by Mike. They all jumped in and then skidded off.

Once they got to the abandoned warehouse and unloaded

the four-man crew, Joey took Mike aside and said, "Dump this van, torch it, and get back to New York ASAP. Anybody asks, I never left, got me? I never left," Joey carefully instructed.

"I got you, Boss."

"Okay, go."

Mike left. The Russians tied the four men to chairs. One handed Joey a .45. He walked up to the first man who was Italian. He shot him in the kneecap without warning. The man bellowed in pain.

"You guys recognize me, huh? I'm the guy you tried to kill, but you obviously missed as you can see. I wasn't killed. Now... who ordered the hit?"

No one said a word. They all stared ahead, all resigned to die. Joey shot the same guy in the other kneecap. He bellowed like a beached whale, but didn't say a word. Joey put the gun in his mouth and hissed in his face, "You fuckin' piece of shit, who ordered the goddamn hit?"

Joey looked in the guy's eyes and could see absolutely no fear. He slowly extracted the gun from his mouth then blew his brains all over the Italian next to him. Joey stepped back and eyed the three remaining men. His eyes stopped on the other Italian.

"Was that your brother? Because you guys look alike. But I'm sure you don't want to look like him now, do you Guido?" Joey taunted, but despite the man's obvious fear, he kept his mouth closed.

"You had a little accident, huh?" Joey remarked, referring to the urine running down the man's leg, forming a puddle at the bottom of the leg of the chair.

Joey's crew laughed.

"Your brother, now he was a tough son of a bitch," Joey snickered, referring to the dead man. "Even after I blew off both kneecaps, he still kept his mouth shut. What a waste. I would've loved to have him in my crew. Oh well."

Joey stepped closer to the dude.

"Hey, you got brains on your face," Joey remarked, using the dude's shirt to smear it even more, as he put the gun between his eyes.

"What's the matter? You don't look so tough no more. I can imagine what's going through your mind right now. Probably, 'I fucked up' has crossed your mind," Joey chuckled. "Now I'll ask you like I asked your fuckin' brother down there: you cock suckers tried to kill me. I wanna know who ordered the hit?"

"Go fuck yourself," the dude hissed.

Joey laughed.

"You Goombahs outta Cleveland got balls, I'll give you that. So let's see what happens here," Joey said, then pointed the gun at the guy's testicles and blew them off.

The guy bellowed and slumped in the chair. Joey grabbed a handful of his hair then began to savagely pistol whip the man's face. When he finished, the gun and Joey's hand were covered with blood. He wiped it on the guy's shirt.

"Who...ordered...the...fucking...hit?" Joey barked in the guy's face.

The guy just glared at him through the one eye that wasn't swollen shut. "Fuck you."

Joey raised the gun and blew the guys brains out. His lifeless body slumped and twitched in the chair. When Joey pointed the gun on the third man, he wasted no time in blurting out, "Frankie Shots, it was Frankie Shots that gave us the hit!"

Just hearing the name made Joey's blood boil. He had figured as much, but hearing it made it worse.

"Smart guy," Joey remarked, referring to the third guy. In return, he made his death quick by putting two in his head at point blank. The fourth guy, Jimmy Callahan started laughing. Joey aimed his gun at him.

"I never thought I'd see somebody die laughing," Joey cracked, with a straight face.

"You dumb Italian fuck," the man roared with a pronounced Irish accent. "You can't see the forest for the trees! You think that was a hit?" Jimmy guffawed. "You don't know jack!"

"So introduce me," Joey shot back.

Jimmy spat at Joey, the spit landing near his shoes.

"Go fuck your mother!"

"So be it," Joey replied then pumped three slugs into Jimmy's face, the force of which blew him and his chair backwards.

Joey looked at the dead men with disgust. He hadn't broken them, so all he had gotten was revenge.

"Burn it to the ground," Joey growled, heading for the door.

"You look like Te Amo."

Those were the first words Joey spoke when he first laid eyes on Enrico after the operation, but that wasn't what Enrico heard. What he heard was, "You're a fake, you're a fraud, you're *not* Te Amo, nor could you ever be!"

It was said with the intent of ridicule, as if to humiliate and add insult to injury; it was said in front of Te Amo. The irony was that Enrico hadn't wanted to *look* like Te Amo; he simply wanted Joey to *see* him like Te Amo. He had achieved the form without the substance.

The three of them stood in the living room of Joey's West Coast mansion, three points in a strange triangle. Te Amo could see the pain in Enrico's eyes, and her heart wept for Enrico. She knew Joey was being intentionally cruel.

"No. No, not at all, Enrico. I think you look beautiful

Enrico...or should I call you something else?" she ventured timidly.

"Call 'em Two Amo. Get it, Two...Amo?" Joey snickered, adding, "I mean, what is this all about?"

"What do you mean, Joey? We *talked* about this," Enrico replied, fists clenched, as if that would assist him in holding back the tears.

"I'm going to go," Te Amo announced, turning for the door.

Joey protested, "Go for what? What's the problem?"

Te Amo looked at him, shook her head, and walked out.

Joey shrugged, "Suit yourself."

Joey loosened his tie and sat down on the couch.

"Enrico, Enrica, whateva, get me a drink."

Enrico glared at him then fixed him a drink. He came back and handed it to Joey.

"Now...can we talk?" Enrico questioned intently.

Joey looked at him. He had his haircut asymmetrically to highlight his newly acquired femininity. His chest swelled with estrogen and his hips curved with shapeliness. He looked every bit a woman, but he was simply a figment of Joey's imagination.

"Whaddya want me to say?" Joey asked. "Congratulations, you're a broad."

Enrico smirked with an expression behind which he hid to stifle the pain.

"I should've known you would do this. Why do you do it? Why do you play games with people's lives like this?"

"What makes you think it's a game?" Joey shot back.

"Because you don't take anyone seriously enough to acknowledge that they have the right to exist independent of you," Enrico accused.

Joey smiled but his eyes stayed cold.

"Don't ever think you can figure me out, *Enrica*," Joey said, emphasizing the changed ending of the name with a mocking tone. "...because you'll fail."

Joey got up and started to walk away.

"It's not my fault that your father won't accept you for who you are, Joey," Enrico blurted out, no longer able to hold back the tears.

Joey stopped and turned around.

"What'd you say," he hissed in a dangerously calm tone.

"Because he won't accept you for who you are, you want to turn me into someone else so you can reject me too!" he cried.

"Shut your fuckin' mouth!" Joey barked.

"No! I won't! I won't let you make me into you! That's where I draw the line! Haven't I stood by you? I busted my ass to help you build this empire so I've earned my rights, Joey! I've earned them!" Enrico cried.

"Right to what?" Joey growled.

"Your love," he sobbed. "Is that too much to ask? You broke me, Joey. You win. I'm not fighting it anymore, so why are you fighting me?"

Despite his rage, Enrico had found refuge in the only emotion Joey reserved for the broken: pity. So when Joey reached to caress his face, what Enrico took as tenderness was really the condescension emanating from Joey's god-complex. He thought Joey wanted to break him; the truth was much more evil than that.

Enrico kissed the palm of Joey's hand and then his wrist, then he seized his mouth with his own with a passion that had him peeling away Joey's clothes as he fell to his knees to worship at the fleshly temple. Joey watched this tempest, allowing himself to be ravaged. Enrico took Joey's swollen manhood into his mouth and began to feast with tongue and lips with feverish abandonment.

Joey pulled Enrico to his feet, opening his mouth and placing his mouth on his developing breast. Enrico gasped deep in his throat as Joey undressed him then laid his back on the floor. Enrico wrapped his legs around Joey's back, as Joey slid his dick deep inside him and began to stroke him slowly while running his tongue over his nipples.

"Oh my God, Joey, I love you so much...so much," Enrico cried, the long, slow strokes sending vibrations through his whole body.

For the first time, instead of simply fucking him, Joey made love to Enrico. Out of pity, he felt Enrico deserved a little heaven, because he was headed for a whole lot of hell.

PRESENT DAY, AUGUST 1997

The bad blood between the NYPD and the FBI is legendary. When you add the external tension between the New York District Attorney's office and the Justice Department—the layers of bureaucracy, backbiting, and jealousy—it's a wonder how cooperation ever occurs. But to do so, you have to do what Detectives Salley and Pirelli did: you have to cut across enemy lines and go straight to the boss. The head honcho. The U.S. Attorney for the Southern District of New York. Even though there is a Southern District and an Eastern District, the Southern District covers Manhattan. Geographically, it receives the more high-profile cases, ergo the accolades, political appointments, and the all-around spotlight. So, coming to the U.S. Attorney (Southern) made the most sense. Besides, this U.S. Attorney was formerly an Assistant D.A. in Manhattan under Robert Morgenthau, the legendary New York District Attorney for what seemed like a millennium, so they were familiar with him.

His name was Steven Rein, but everyone called him the Prosecutor. He was tough and unbending; some would even say unscrupulous. But he almost always got his man, with a conviction rate nearing 100%. No other name was needed, although his appearance belied his reputation. He was balding and bespectacled. He spoke with a slight lisp. But for any lawyer and/or defendant to underestimate him was a veritable death sentence. Sometimes literally.

The detectives were ushered into the Prosecutor's office. It was an impressive ensemble of mahogany and gilded decor. It reminded them of the New York Public Library. The Prosecutor sat behind a large mahogany desk. The office seemed to swallow him, as the Prosecutor sat somewhere in the back of its throat. But they weren't fooled by appearance; they knew that this was Oz and the Prosecutor was the Wizard.

"Good afternoon, gentlemen. How are you?" the Prosecutor greeted, as he rose and shook their hands.

"Fine, sir, fine. I'm Detective Salley, NYPD," Salley said.

"Detective Pirelli," the other introduced himself.

"Pirelli? You worked the double homicide of those two models in '87, right?" the Prosecutor recalled.

Pirelli smiled, happy to be remembered.

"Right."

"Helluva job," the Prosecutor complimented, as they all sat down. "So, what can I do for you gentlemen?"

"We've got an offer you can't refuse," Pirelli joked, doing a bad Brando impression.

The Prosecutor chuckled politely.

"My favorite kind."

"Ever heard of Mike Rizzo?" Salley asked.

"Not offhand."

"He's a Gambino Capo. We got 'em six ways to Sunday, so we can easily wrap a bow around him and deliver him," Salley offered.

"If?" the Prosecutor quipped.

"*If* he can get witness protection," Salley answered.

"What can he give us? Gotti?"

"We're still working our way up the wiretaps. As of now, he can tie the Gambinos and the Russian Mafia to an ecstasy ring comin' out of Israel. Really big," Salley explained.

The Prosecutor nodded, contemplating. He knew the FBI was working an angle in the ecstasy craze. There were a lot of missing links, so if this Rizzo could plug the holes...

"So, what's the catch?" the Prosecutor probed, knowing the horse trade process like the back of his hand. "Why me? Why didn't you take it to the State Task Force?"

Pirelli shook his head.

"Because they're a bunch of buffoons, the whole operation has been compromised. Besides, you're the best and most of this shit falls under your jurisdiction."

"And?" the Prosecutor smirked.

The two Detectives looked at each other. Salley nodded subtly, a gesture that the Prosecutor didn't miss.

"And...maybe soon, we'll be looking to move up in the world, and we know, a word from you over at Justice wouldn't hurt," Pirelli admitted.

The Prosecutor chuckled.

"A man once said, 'never trust a guy unless he's got a horse in the race.' Listen Detectives, I'd like to talk to Rizzo. If I can pick his brain, if he's the little train that could, then we've got a deal."

The three men stood up and shook hands.

"We can set it up for tomorrow morning," Salley suggested.

"Sounds great," the Prosecutor replied, and just like that began the journey to the biggest showdown of his career.

APRIL 1991

He named her "Giuseppe" after his favorite Italian restaurant in Brooklyn, and whenever he took her out, he had Giuseppe's chef flown out to the Coast to cook his favorite dishes.

The Giuseppe was a 120-foot yacht that cost Joey a mint. It was a major expense, but it was actually Marty who was footing the bill because it was in the name of his production company. Marty had recently been named head of Climactic Pictures, and with his promotion came more power in Hollywood for Joey. It was no secret that Joey was the real power behind the throne.

Joey had taken the Giuseppe out with Marty, Enrico, and Andrew Wynn aboard. Joey helped the Sherman Brothers make a lot of money and therefore helped make Andrew more powerful at the firm. So despite the nature of their initial meeting, the next several had been pleasant enough.

"See, the secret to great spaghetti," Joey began, leaning around the table to fill everyone's glass with red wine, "Is not the sauce... No. It's letting the starch from the pasta enrich the sauce and the sauce soak into the pasta, you see? This is why I love spaghetti with just butter and Parmesan; it's clean, it's honest, eh? Everybody thinks it's the sauce, right? But the sauce is like a beautiful, red dress on a broad. You take it off and whaddya have? Fuckin' clumps and rolls all over the place. You're askin' her, 'how the fuck did you get all that in the dress?' Fuckin' disgusting. I like 'em nude so you know what you're gettin' into."

"I happen to like red dresses," Marty smirked, taking a bite of his linguini in clam sauce, "as long as it matches my heels."

They all laughed.

"And you look good too, huh? Salud!" Joey toasted and drank his wine.

"So Andrew, now that I'm running the show over at Climactic, what can I expect from Sherman Brothers?" Marty probed.

"I don't see why we couldn't finance a full slate," Andrew replied cheerfully, cutting his eye at Enrico, something he had been doing all day.

"I'm going to hold you to this," Marty warned him playfully.

"Hey, you keep churning out those numbers you have had the last few quarters, and a full slate is a worthy investment."

"And speaking of worthy investments," Joey remarked, as the waiter came and cleared away the dishes and as he handed out cigars. Everyone took one except Enrico. "Whatsa matter, you watching your weight or something?" Joey quipped, eyeing Enrico.

"No, I just rather not," Enrico replied.

Joey shrugged.

"Suit yourself. These are 'imported' from Cuba. Illegal in America and they say that crime don't pay," Joey smirked.

They laughed and lit up.

"Smooth...but a slightly peppery something," Marty remarked.

"You gotta get me some of these, Joey," Andrew requested.

"Not a problem, Andy. Remind me."

"I will."

"Hey, Andy."

Andrew looked up.

"You know, I couldn't help but notice that you've been checking out Enrico. I mean it's been happening all night, so I couldn't help but notice."

A lump formed in Andrew's throat.

"Oh, hey Joey, I didn't mean anything by it."

"Of course you did, but it's not a problem; she's fuckin' beautiful," Joey said, looking at Enrico then ran the back of his hand, lovingly over Enrico's cheek.

"No really, Joey I don't...go that way. No offense," Andrew assured him.

"You sure?" Joey smirked. "You coulda fooled me."

"Absolutely."

Marty looked at Joey and saw the glint in his eye. He knew he was about to be devilish.

"You know Andy, I've never been in Missouri, but in many ways, I'm a Missourian," Joey told him.

"I don't understand."

"Show me," Joey retorted, then turned to Enrico and said, "Baby...take off your clothes."

Enrico slowly rose and, without hesitation began to remove his top and khakis.

Marty looked in Enrico's eyes and could see, even though he didn't hesitate in complying with Joey's command, that his eyes were full of trepidation.

"Joey, you don't have to do this," Marty said.

"And you shut your fuckin' mouth," Joey told Marty suavely, but the ice in his tone totally froze any response Marty could have made.

Joey looked at Andy, who seemed to squirm under Joey's direct gaze.

"You say 'absolutely', but if all your spaghetti's been cooked in sauce, then how would you know?"

Andrew cleared his throat. "Joey, this really isn't necessary."

Enrico stood beside Joey's chair, stark naked. His breasts, perky and firm, his hips those of an alabaster Venus in Venice.

"Look at her, Andy...ain't she beautiful? My creation. I'm like Michelangelo, only I used human flesh, huh." Joey chuckled.

Andrew averted his sneer, but his eyes kept returning to Enrico's succulent flesh.

"Enrico," Joey began, "check his spaghetti."

Enrico went around to Andrew and put his hand on his dick. He looked at Joey and nodded his head. Joey chuckled.

"You see, Andy, sometimes we learn things about ourselves that we didn't even know."

"I – I – I, no it's not me. It's the image, the...contrast," Andy stammered, attempting to justify his erection.

Joey held up his hand to silence him.

"Andy, no need to explain. Enrico, teach my friend Andy here what he always wanted to know, but was afraid to ask."

"No!" Andy yelped, trying to bark. "No! I must draw the line. I will not!"

"Interrupt me again," Joey said, elevating his tone only slightly, "Andy, I own you so this is not a request. So, sit back, relax...and don't look a gift horse in the mouth," Joey cracked, putting the cigar in his mouth and clenching it with his teeth.

Andrew knew that Joey was referring to several factors simultaneously in terms of why he owned him. He still had those pictures, which could ruin his career. Plus, the fact that one word from Marty could get him fired and end his career—any word from Marty's mouth was put there by Joey. Lastly because, in their world, Joey had power over life and death. He relented and fell silent.

Enrico looked at Joey, his eyes pleading as he lowered

himself to his knees. The look he received was one that a condemned man feared, but signaled no expectation of reprieve.

Enrico undid Andy's trousers then slid his dick in his mouth and began to deep throat him. Andy squirmed, clenched his fists, his eyes fighting the feeling he so much wanted to enjoy, but didn't want to give into Joey. Joey smirked, watching the internal play out so vividly in the external. When Andy gripped the cigar so tightly that it broke, that act seemed to be symbolic, because at that moment he grabbed the back of Enrico's head, and getting a handful of hair, began fucking his face. Enrico bobbed faster, the slurping sounds filled the room, and when Andrew came, he bucked the table, rattling the glasses and letting out a growl that sounded like a roar.

As soon as Andrew's cum shot into his mouth, Enrico jumped up and ran to the railing, spitting Andrew's cum overboard and throwing up right behind it.

Joey rose slowly and went to the railing. He leaned over slightly, looking into Enrico's sickened face and cracked, "What's the matter? Seasick?"

Then he took Marty by the hand and led him to the master bedroom.

JULY 1997

"You know what I think it is, Diane? Why people hate when I'm around but love to keep me near?" Joey began, rhetorically.

"What's that, Joey?"

"Besides, this gangster they want to make me out to be? It has nothing to do with that. I'm simply the thing they would be, if they only had the cajones to be."

"And what is that?"

He paused for effect.

"Free."

MAY 1991

"Hey Joey, anybody ever tell ya, you're supposed to let the Boss win?" Sal chuckled as he stood holding his cue stick, watching Joey run the balls off the table. Joey, getting ready for the next shot, looked at Sal, hit the cue and scratched —obviously on purpose.

"Oops," Joey cracked.

Sal laughed. Joey rolled him the cue ball. They were in the rec room of Sal's large mansion. Very few people ever came into the house. To most in the Romano family, this was like the holiest of the holies in Solomon's temple. Here is where you spoke to god: Sal. Therefore, it was swept for bugs every six hours. Totally clean, and even then Sal took his own precautions.

Sal placed his stick on the table.

"Hey, forget about it, but if you ever tell anybody, I'll whack youse."

Joey playfully zipped his lips.

They walked over to the bar. Sal played bartender. He took out two glasses and dropped a cube into each one, then poured two fingers of brandy. He slid a glass to Joey.

"Salud!"

"Salud."

They drank.

"You know, Joey, you're doin' a helluva job out there on the Coast," Sal remarked.

They clinked glasses, signaling a toast.

"It's a fuckin' goldmine, Sal. There's so much more I could be doin', only I can't, you know?" Joey signified.

Sal nodded.

"I know what you mean, and that's kinda what I wanted to talk to you about."

"Okay."

Sal leaned on the bar counter close to Joey and lowered his voice.

"Don't quote me on this but...I've been doin' this a long time and my gut, it's rarely let me down. Well, there was the ulcer, but you get my drift."

"Certainly."

"Okay, so again, don't quote me but my gut is tellin' me, I don't know. I think..." he wrote *Tommy* on the bar, the image in the wax just enough for Joey to make out, "...is a rat."

"Yeah?" Joey responded.

"You don't sound surprised," Sal commented.

Joey looked Sal in the eyes.

"Nothing surprises me, Sal."

"That's good...anyway, yeah I think he is."

"So you want me to keep an eye on 'em?" Joey probed, feeling Sal out.

"Naw, naw; it's just my gut, you know? Hey, don't youse got a..." he tapped his chest, right where a badge would be, indicating a cop "...out there on the payroll."

"Yeah, a coupla of 'em," Joey informed him.

"Maybe he could verify what I'm feelin', ya think?" Sal

asked, giving Joey the look Joey understood totally. It was the look that one killer could communicate to another killer.

That's when Joey knew. Sal wanted him to kill Tommy Scarlata, and he would use the cop to go along and say Tommy was an informant. The Commission then wouldn't retaliate against him for killing a Made Man.

"Sure, I can arrange that," Joey replied, using the word *arrange* to let Sal knew he understood.

Sal's smirk conveyed that he did as well.

Sal again poured them both two fingers. Sal took a sip.

"But you know...if so and so's a rat then..." Sal mused then wrote Dominick Piazza on the bar "...he's gotta know, right? Which makes him a rat too in my book."

"I couldn't agree more," Joey seconded. "But what if he don't know?"

"Then he's too stupid to be a Boss!"

They both laughed.

"I mean, gimme a break, eh? Your Sotto Capo is a fuckin' rat, and you don't know? Minchia!" Sal cracked.

"But being stupid's not a crime," Joey reminded.

"I know, which means the cop knows they're both rats. Capeesh, Paisano?"

"Of course. Then what happens?"

"Well, in the absence of leadership, the Commission will take over the family until a new Boss can take over. Of course, until then, we'll need a guy out there to run things for us, somebody that knows the Coast. You know the Coast, Joey."

Joey smirked.

"Like the back of my hand."

"The only thing is, you're not a friend of ours. You got no button," Sal reminded him, then downed his drink, looked Joey in the eyes and said, "So I guess we'll have to do something about that, huh?"

It could not have been plainer. Sal was offering to sponsor

Joey's induction into the Mafia in exchange for the murders of Tommy Scarlata and Dominick Piazza. It would be a deal Joey couldn't refuse, but he was in awe of the intricacy of the whole power structure. He was but a cog.

Te Amo pushed her hair out of her face and sat up, straddling Joey. The room smelled of sex as the rain beat against the windowpanes in sheets. Te Amo studied Joey's face for a moment then asked, "What have you done to Enrico?"

"What has Enrico done to himself?" he shot back.

"You know what I mean, Joey."

Joey shrugged.

"I despise weakness."

"Love's not a weakness."

"That depends."

She cocked her head to the side and traced the contour of his face.

"How can such beauty be so ugly?"

Joey smirked.

"I guess it's really in the eye of the beholder, huh?"

Te Amo shook her head.

"If you destroy him, who will take his place? You need him. He's one of the best," Te Amo reminded him.

"This is true, but don't worry. I know when to say when."

She slid off him, and lay beside him, propping her head up with her hand so she could continue to look him in the eye.

"And what about me? I'm starting to feel...shut out of things."

"Whaddya mean, 'shut out'? You're with me all the time."

"Exactly my point."

"I can't keep you close?"

"That's what you do with enemies."

"You watch too many mob movies."

"You *are* a mob movie."

Joey laughed, but Te Amo wasn't trying to be funny.

"I'm serious, Joey. Everything with you is so calculated, so... scripted. I feel like I'm being written out," Te Amo admitted.

Joey returned the seriousness of her gaze, and replied, "Things are different than they were in the beginning. Stakes are higher. I got a lot more to lose, so I gotta play things closer to the chest."

"Do you trust me?" she asked.

"Baby, sometimes...I don't even trust myself."

With that, he got up and went into the bathroom, shutting the door behind him.

New Orleans. Another successful delivery.

Enrico sat in the hotel bar, nursing a drink. As usual, everything came off without a hitch. Success had become commonplace. There was no longer elation or relief; that had long ago been replaced with anxiety. It was like, the longer the streak of success, the longer a mistake loomed. Enrico was a stickler for details. Everything had to be perfect because Joey would have it no other way, and the thought of letting Joey down made Enrico physically ill. He had to get it right every time, just to prove himself worthy, just to bask in Joey's approval, not wallow in his ridicule. Enrico understood the game Joey was playing, but when you're in love, you mistrust your head and over trust your heart, which tells you, *if only I can do better, be better, then he'll see it and understand.* You keep chasing that carrot, oblivious to the pain of the stick. But slowly, it takes its toll and soon you start to crack, and that's when things fall apart.

"Um...excuse me?"

Enrico heard the voice. He looked up from his thoughts and

into a friendly, smiling face. He was moderately handsome. Average: average brown hair, average brown eyes, and a smattering of freckles, but his smile was warm and inviting, so Enrico couldn't help but return it.

"Yes."

"How are you? I hope I'm not imposing, but I saw you sitting alone and well, I was sitting alone and I was wondering..." he let his voice trail off, hoping that Enrico would fill in the blank.

"I'm not what you think I am," Enrico replied, downing his drink.

The guy continued to smile.

"No, trust me, I know exactly who you are. Can I join you?"

Enrico looked at him, studied him for a moment and answered, "Sure."

He sat and extended his hand. Enrico shook it.

"I'm Paul Simms."

"Celeste Myers," Enrico replied with his alias.

They engaged in the type of small talk that people do when they'd rather be talking about something more in-depth, but must keep up appearances. It's the kind of small talk that lingers on until the liquor gives you the excuse to say what you wanted to say. It's the why you drank the liquor in the first place: to give you the courage to say it.

Talking to Paul was a relief for Enrico. He hadn't talked to anyone in so long. He lived in a world where nobody trusted anyone enough to talk, lest something slips. And on top of that, the one you need to talk to the most is the one you can talk to the least.

Paul may have not been Joey, but he was a welcome relief from the loneliness.

Paul checked his watch.

"Listen, would I be out of line if..."

Enrico cut him off, not so much out of eagerness, but out of not wanting to name the thing, so his mind wouldn't know what to name it and feel guilty about it.

"No...no, you wouldn't."

Their eyes met, gazes full of hunger.

"Are you...staying here?" Paul asked.

Enrico nodded, a sexual lump in his throat.

"Are you?"

"Your place or mine," Paul quipped, being cliché-like on purpose.

"Whichever is closer."

"I'm on the ninth floor."

"Then it's your place."

Paul paid for the drinks, and they headed for his room. Once they got through the door, they were all over one another. It felt so good for Enrico to be ravaged with anticipation; every part. His breasts sucked, his ass crack licked, his asshole sucked and then to be fucked passionately with all the intensity that makes a one-night stand worth doing again.

When he woke up wrapped in Paul's arms, he felt guilty— not for having done it, but for fully intending to do it again.

They exchanged numbers. Paul tongued him down at the door.

"When will I see you again?" Paul questioned intently.

"I travel a lot. I could be anywhere."

"I'll find you."

They kissed again. Enrico left, feeling renewed. He drove to the airport, never knowing that he was being followed...

It was Dominick Piazza's 67th birthday. Every Capo and Made Man of the Piazza family was present, but many from New York who were supposed to come declined at the last minute.

That should have been a sign.

But, as they say: *a just man sleeps soundly*. Dominick was a just man, soundly asleep to the footsteps in the dark. Joey arrived with Detective O'Ryan, but didn't introduce him, and nobody asked for an introduction. It was a gathering of old men, a celebration of the old ways and not all of them pleasant. Joey sat next to Tommy Scarlata, to his left. To Tommy's left at the head of the long, rectangular table sat Don Piazza. As the night wore on and the liquor worked its way into everyone's systems, Joey stood up to toast Piazza. He clinked a fork against his glass to get everyone's attention. Once he had it, he said, "I wanna toast the Don...since coming to the Coast, this man has opened his home to me, his family, his respect to me, and I wanna thank him."

The majority of the men clapped. Joey turned to the Don and continued, "Don Piazza, you are a prince among men. Happy Birthday!"

"Salud!"

Everyone drank up. Then Joey turned to Tommy.

"And this guy? What can I say about this guy? Stand up, will ya Tommy? Let the family see you."

Tommy waved Joey off at first; then as the cheers continued, he relented. He stood next to Joey. Joey put his drink down then put his arm around Tommy.

"Tommy, some things just can't be put into words, you know? So why try? Sometimes you gotta let the moment speak for itself," Joey remarked. Then he pulled Tommy to him and kissed him on the mouth. Hard. There was nothing sexual about it. It was Sicilian tradition: the kiss of death.

Tommy felt it in his bones. He tried to push Joey away, but Joey grabbed him tightly by the collar. While he kissed Tommy, he had reached down and grabbed the steak knife that he had placed in front of himself during dinner and plunged it into Tommy's chest. Tommy grunted and tried to break away, but Joey was relentless. Over and over Joey stabbed Tommy in the neck and chest. With each thrust, Tommy sank lower and lower, until Joey sat him back in his chair and proceeded to stab him six more times. When it was all said and done, Joey had stabbed him over seventy times. Blood was everywhere—all over the tablecloth, all over Joey's tuxedo and sprinkled on Joey's face like freckles.

Winded slightly, Joey sat down and tossed the knife on the table. He smoothed his hair, lest anything was out of place. Then he remarked, "Tommy was a rat...a stinkin', filthy rat. And this...is what happens to rats. Any questions?"

Don Piazza jumped to his feet, livid.

"You fuckin' piece of shit! You disrespect me like this!" Piazza looked around, spit flying from his mouth, "And no one does nothing? Kill this piece of shit!"

No one moved.

Joey wiped his bloody hands on the end of the tablecloth.

"They don't work for you anymore, Dominick. As of now, the Piazza regime is under the control of the Commission until new leadership can be found."

Pizza looked around the room. Many couldn't meet his gaze, and didn't speak up. The coup was complete. Every Capo in the family had signed on so as not to get signed off.

Piazza turned to Joey.

"Can I know for what crime I am going to die for?"

"Come on, Dom, you already know. You're a rat, too," Joey spat. "The Detective here can verify that."

Dominick looked at Joey and then chuckled. He shook his head.

"Well, if that is what our honorable society has come to, then I'd rather die honorably than live amongst such filth," he spat, then spat—literally—on the floor.

His words brought a tinge of guilt to Joey, because he knew Piazza wasn't a rat, but his greed for power was stronger than his respect for honor.

Joey held up his drink, which was sprinkled with blood, inside and out.

"Happy Birthday, Dom; now get him outta here," Joey instructed, then downed the drink. He looked at O'Ryan. "I don't want either body to be found."

Then he got up and walked away.

"Vinnie Boom Boom! How are ya? Well, I can see for myself, huh Vinnie?" Joey quipped as he walked into the motel room in Queens.

Vinnie was handcuffed to the bed, butt-naked. Bianca and Marilyn were sitting on each side of him, fully clothed.

"Ay Joey, what the fuck is this all about?" Vinnie asked, trying to sound calm, but Joey could see the nervousness under the facade.

"Vinnie, word on the street is that you really go for the Black chicks. It took us a minute, but I figured Marilyn and Bianca could track you down, and here you are," Joey remarked as he took Marilyn's spot on the bed.

"Joey, please. What's goin' on? I swear to you, I have no idea," Vinnie vowed.

"Oh, you don't? Good thing you're not a choir boy, Vinnie, 'cause God don't hold our kind accountable for the bullshit," he chuckled. "I'm gonna say one word, and if you don't start talkin' then I'ma start with your left nut," Joey threatened, pulling out a .32 revolver. "Cleveland."

Vinnie's body tensed as if he were about to speak, but Joey put the cold steel to his left nut and Vinnie thought again.

"Whatever you wanna know, Joey."

"The truth. Who brung 'em in?"

Vinnie sighed.

"Frankie, Joey. Frankie Shots."

"He wouldn't have done it without my old man, if some-body else wasn't backin' him. Who was the someone else?" Joey probed, jamming the pistol down into Vinnie's groin and making him see stars.

"I swear, Joey, I don't know. I only dealt with Bagels. Benny Bagels, but he made it clear he had Frankie's nod!"

"What about Peter Amuso? Where does he fit in?"

"Pete set it up in Cleveland. He was freelance! A go-between!" Vinnie answered.

"So this wasn't Gambino? You tellin' me Amuso set me up, but fuckin' Gotti knew nothing?" Joey gruffed.

"I don't know, Joey. I swear to fuckin' god! All I know is Frankie wanted to send a message!"

Joey frowned. "A message?"

Vinnie nodded vigorously.

"It wasn't a hit, Joey; it was a message. Bagels made that clear. He kept tellin' me, make sure I don't hit neither one of 'em, make sure I don't hit neither one of 'em!"

The clarity of the situation smacked Joey in the face.

"Are you sure? He said neither one of 'em!"

"Like a thousand times!"

"How long before the hit did he say this?"

"A week, maybe two. I don't know, Joey. I swear to ya!" Vinnie begged.

Te Amo...

His head was spinning, but he didn't let it show.

"Joey, I woulda never got involved had it been a hit," Vinnie tried to explain.

Joey chuckled and patted Vinnie on the cheek.

"Of course. I mean, after all it was only a message, right?"

"Joey. Never!"

"Hey, lemme give you a message, eh," Joey spat coldly, then gave Bianca a nod.

She spat the razor into her hand, grabbed a fistful of

Vinnie's hair then snatched his head back and slit his throat, ear to ear. His eyes bulged and blood gurgled out. In less than a minute, he was dead.

Make sure you don't hit either one of 'em, he thought, because now it all made sense.

Te Amo.

PRESENT DAY 1997

"So Mr. Provenzano, you said that Mr. Romano's 'angle' opened the doors for Mr. Diamanti to be inducted into the Mafia?" the Prosecutor reiterated.

Joe Pro shrugged. "More or less."

"Could you be more specific about Mr. Romano's angle?"

"Romano wanted to control the West Coast, without 'controlling' it, if you get my drift," Joe Pro explained.

"So, Mr. Diamanti would be the means to that end," the Prosecutor replied.

Joe Pro gave him the pursed lip of an impressed expression.

"You catch on quick, counselor. You must be Sicilian," Joe Pro cracked.

Many in the courtroom chuckled. Even the Prosecutor had to smile.

"So, yeah, the Piazza hit was Joey's ticket, but only after the sit down with Romano and Don Vincenzo, Joey's father. I mediated, and that's how I came to be involved," Joe Pro explained.

"Could you elaborate," the Prosecutor requested.

"You see," Joe Pro began, shifting uncomfortably in his seat, "Romano needed my vote on the Commission to pull this thing off. Besides, I'm the last of the original Bosses, so my say carries a lot of weight. So Sal, he knows I can see what he's doing, so he cuts me in. Let's me wet my beak."

"Pay you off," the Prosecutor interpreted.

"Exactly. So once I'm on board, no one can oppose him, and Joey takes over the Coast in the name of the Commission, but once he's made, he's really an extension of the Romano regime."

"How so?"

"Because, when the books were opened, he got listed as one of Romanos, ya see?" Joe Pro remarked.

"I do."

"Okay...but before the Boss of Bosses died in prison—God rest his soul—he sent for Joey. Now I can't say what happened at the meeting, because I wasn't there, but when Joey came back, he helped the goombahs push me out," Joe Pro spat with disgust and locked gazes with Joey.

"Push you out?"

"Yeah, he backed the friggin' guy Carmine Graziano over me! Sixty years in this business, and I get pushed by young punks! Joey backs the guy, and Sal figures, hey no Joe Pro and I can control the Commish myself. But what he don't know is, Joey's caught on and now the pawn's gonna be king. Sal pushed out his only ally 'cause he thought he had a friend!" Joe Pro laughed, still looking at Joey. "The kid's smart, but I couldn't stand by and do nothin'. So I switched governments, and here I am."

Joey sat and listened to the words because they were directed at him. It was true that he had helped push Joe Pro out, and now he heard why Joe Pro decided to become a cooperating witness.

Sour grapes. Plain and simple. Joey would learn from that mistake in the future.

"Now, Mr. Provenzano, just for the record, you spoke of the

'Boss of Bosses'. Who were you referring to?"

 "The Don of Dons. My Don, Don Tino Gigante."

MAY 1992

It felt good to be back in Miami.

Enrico loved to travel, but Miami would forever be his home. He had just come from Chicago; another successful drop and a weekend with Paul. He had seen him several times over the past few weeks, and on each occasion their time together grew sweeter. Paul's embrace made him crave Joey's cruelty in order to justify the affair. Fueled by his guilt and need for attention, each tryst gave Enrico reason to look forward to the next.

Enrico unlocked the door of his condo. He paused in the darkness. Sniffed. His stomach flipped and the butterflies fluttered, all against his will.

"Hello, Joey," Enrico greeted. He couldn't see him in the dark, but he could smell him. The place smelled like Courvoisier.

Joey clicked on the lamp. He was sitting on the couch, a bottle of Courvoisier in one hand and a .45 in the other.

"I gotta watch you too?" Joey slurred.

"You're drunk," Enrico stated, matter of factly.

"I had to get up the nerve."

"For what?"

"To kill you," Joey replied, holding the gun out, aimed at Enrico.

"You're not going to kill me, Joey," Enrico chuckled.

"Yeah? What makes you so sure?" Joey questioned.

"You would've packed a revolver."

Joey smirked. "Yeah, well maybe I oughta kill you."

"Why?"

Joey struggled to his feet, hit the Courvoisier and approached Enrico. "Because I can't trust none of you," Joey replied. His cold blue eyes cutting through Enrico. "Nobody can be trusted."

"I've never given you a reason to say that about me, Joey," Enrico remarked, because Joey's gaze was beginning to become unnerving.

Joey stopped directly in front of Enrico.

"But you will."

"You act as if you want me to."

Joey caressed Enrico with the fingertips of the hand that held the gun.

"Who is he, eh? Who is he?" Joey questioned, smelling and kissing Enrico's neck, running his tongue from his ear to his throat. "I can smell him all over you."

Enrico closed his eyes and enjoyed the seduction.

"Nobody," he whispered.

"Nobody as in nobody, or nobody as in he doesn't matter?" Joey quipped, kissing Enrico, caressing his tongue with his own.

After the kiss, Enrico groaned, "Both."

Joey dropped the Courvoisier, spilling the remnants on Enrico's plush carpet. He used his free hand to grope Enrico's body lustfully.

"You gonna betray me, too? You gonna betray me like Te Amo?" Joey asked, pulling up Enrico's skirt.

"Never," he gasped. "Never."

"Never say never."

"I love you," Enrico declared, covering Joey's neck and face with kisses and licks.

He fumbled with Joey's jeans, the heat of the moment building, until Joey dropped the gun, lifted Enrico off his feet and impaled him with his hard, pulsating dick, as Enrico wrapped his legs around Joey's waist. Joey spread his cheeks and plowed into him deeper, making Enrico cry out his name, his screams shattering the thin Paul facade over his raw passion for Joey. They spent the night fucking passionately; sleep only coming when it couldn't be denied. In the morning, Enrico asked, "How did she betray you?"

Joey smoothed Enrico's hair.

"Forget about it. I was drunk."

"You never get drunk enough to say what you don't mean," Enrico countered.

"It doesn't matter; it's just the nature of a woman."

Enrico studied Joey's face then asked.

"Do you think I would ever betray you?"

"I don't think about it. Should I?"

"No."

"Then you've answered your own question."

Enrico's guilt made him kiss Joey like he was apologizing. The nature of a woman; that's what he would blame his betrayal on.

They parted in the underground garage. Joey went to New York, while Enrico would stay in Miami, awaiting another shipment. Neither knew that they were under surveillance.

"What do we have here? A secret lover?" one agent quipped as he and another agent watched the monitors in an unmarked van.

"I thought his lover was Paul."

"I guess queers cheat, too."

Laughter.

The agent looked at Joey again.

"Hey Dave, can you get me in closer?"

The camera zoomed in. The agent's eyes got as big as plates.

"Holy shit! Do you know who that guy is?"

"You know him?"

"Who doesn't? I worked O.C. long enough. Hell, half the country knows that face!"

The other agent got amped.

"Looks like this case just took on epic proportions."

"We snag the queer tonight."

"I'll get the S.A.C. on the phone."

That night, Enrico was leaving a phone booth where he had just set up the final points for the incoming flight. All of a sudden, three unmarked Crown Victorias skidded up and surrounded him.

"Out of the car!"

"Now! Now!"

"Move!"

It all happened so fast that Enrico didn't know if he was being arrested or kidnapped. The agents wasted no time cuffing him and shoving him into the back seat of one of the unmarked cars. Then they all drove off. The agent in the passenger side turned halfway around in the seat.

"You've got until we reach the Federal building to either play ball or go away for a very long time."

"I want to talk to my lawyer. I have nothing to say," Enrico shot back calmly.

"Suit yourself, but listen to what we've got and see what you're up against," the agent retorted.

He started flipping through black and white surveillance photos.

"We have a baggage handler in Milwaukee, two plane mechanics in L.A., two warehousemen in New York, and a stewardess. Each one is ready and willing to name you the boss of an international smuggling ring. You want a lawyer? I say you call two, 'cause you're going to need 'em!"

On each picture, Enrico recognized faces. Some were of people while they were talking to Enrico, one of the Feds' favorite psychological ploys. Enrico saw that this wasn't just a bust. He had been the focus of an investigation. The agent saw the look on his face and thought he had one on the hook.

"What if I agree to...cooperate?"

"Then we drop you off and no one knows you got pinched. But from that moment on, you work for us. You *belong* to us. You try and fuck us, we'll fuckin' fry you," the agent threatened.

"Okay," Enrico agreed. He needed to buy some time as well as warn Joey. At that point, he was ready to sacrifice everyone except himself and Joey.

The passenger nodded to the driver. The driver hung a right and they headed for an out-of-the-way motel. Once inside, they took the cuffs off Enrico, sat him at the small table in the room and sat a tape recorder in front of him.

"Now...tell us about Diamanti."

Enrico looked at the little spinning wheel of the recorder, licked his lips and began to talk.

"Why are you having me followed?" Te Amo asked.

They were at the premiere for Marty's newest movie. Te Amo hadn't seen Joey for days. He wouldn't accept her calls, he hadn't been home or anywhere she could reach him. When she spoke to his bodyguard Mike, he was evasive. She couldn't even get a straight answer out of Bianca when she confronted her.

"Bianca, never forget who you work for. You work for *me*, not Joey," Te Amo warned her.

Bianca had simply smiled and walked away.

That's when Te Amo noticed that she was being followed wherever she went. It was obvious. They didn't even try to hide it. She didn't recognize the faces. She figured they were free-lance. Regardless, she didn't like it, and she intended to confront Joey about it. She knew he'd be at the premiere because he was in the movie.

She spotted him in Marty's living room, talking to a female director. By the way the woman reacted to her presence, Te Amo knew that Joey had fucked her. Te Amo cut off all conversation with the bluntness of her statement.

"Why are you having me followed?"

Joey looked at her coldly, as he turned to the director and said, in Italian, "I'll talk to you later."

The woman nodded and stepped off. He turned to Te Amo.

"You speak that way in front of strangers? Maybe instead, I should have you baby sat," he spat, walking off.

Te Amo jumped in behind him.

"Fuck you, Joey! Answer my question."

"I don't know what you're talkin' about."

They went into Marty's study and closed the door, shutting themselves off from the party.

"Joey, you're making it very clear that something's wrong," Te Amo accused. "You don't return my calls, you haven't seen me in weeks, and you put a bunch of fuckin' amateurs on to follow me? For what? What are you trying to tell me, Joey? Here I am! Say it to my face!" Te Amo vented, getting all her stress out in one rant. She was fuming because she felt rejected and didn't understand why.

"You're paranoid, okay? I don't return your calls? You're a big girl; you can figure it out. I'm bored witcha. Whatcha need, a bullhorn? Go home. Maybe I'll write," he replied coldly.

Every word felt like a slap in the face, but Te Amo didn't let it show.

"I'm not one of your flunkies, Joey, or one of your floozies— female or otherwise," she smirked. "Don't forget, I'm a boss too. You think I'm calling you for you? I'm calling because you seem to have forgotten the facts of our agreement."

"You wanna be a boss, be a boss," Joey shrugged. "Matter of fact, why don't you take over the whole operation, Coast to Coast? I'm getting out of the distribution business. So it's yours...Boss."

The two of them eyed each other down, neither being able to say what they truly wanted, because the stakes had gotten too high for emotions.

"You think that's it? You think you can just use me, use my family, and then toss us the crumbs," Te Amo gritted. "You'd better think again."

"Whaddya want from me? I offer you a multimillion-dollar operation and you call it 'crumbs'? I'd offer you my soul, but the devil's got first dibs," he cracked.

"You know what, Joey? You can go to hell," Te Amo retorted, then walked out.

"I'm already in hell," he yelled after her, "and it feels like home, you muthafucka!"

As soon as Enrico walked into the hotel room, he walked straight into Paul's kiss and embrace.

"I came as soon as I could," Paul told him. "Now, talk to me. What's going on?"

"Like I said over the phone. I got busted, but Joey doesn't know."

"That's all you said, though. And truthfully, I'm not sure if I understand."

Enrico sighed.

"I'm sorry. I've been dealing with criminals for so long, I've forgotten how our world must look to honest, law-abiding people."

"You make me sound like Opie," Paul joked, making Enrico smile. For that he was thankful.

"The reason Joey doesn't know I got arrested is because I made a deal on the spot to cooperate."

"Oh, I see."

"What else was I supposed to do? They have me over a barrel and they didn't give me any time to make a decision." Enrico tried to explain, but Paul took him by his arms and looked him in the eyes.

"Hey Celeste, you don't have to justify anything to me. I'm here for you. Just walk me through it so I can understand."

They sat down on the edge of the bed.

"My intention was to just get away with telling them as little as possible and then warning Joey that the operation was blown. But the first thing they asked about was Joey!" Enrico told him.

"Joey? *Your* guy, Joey?" Paul probed, a tinge of jealousy in his tone.

"Paul, I'm sorry."

"No, no. It's okay. Go on."

Enrico took a deep breath, then replied, "I didn't know what to do. I know they got more outta me than I know and now, I'm not sure what to do. I want to tell Joey, but do I tell him they asked about him? But then he'll want to know why I didn't just take the pinch. Then what can I say? He'll know I said something and…I don't know what he'll do."

Paul blew air, audibly.

"Wow. Umm, from what you've told me before, this X is a pretty big thing and this Joey is pretty...demented. I don't know if telling him is a good idea."

"But I've got to do *something*, Paul! I mean, they even want me to wear a wire," Enrico confided.

"A wire? You mean a recording device?"

Enrico nodded.

"What did you tell them?"

"I said I had to think about it. They gave me a few days. I don't know what to do!"

Paul hugged him to his chest.

"Whatever you decide, I'll support you," he vowed.

"Thank you, I needed to hear that," Enrico replied. He kissed Paul, wrapping his arms around his neck and laying him down on the bed.

The final straw came a few days later. Enrico came back to his condo to find Maria and the girls topless and prancing around the pool, along with a few girls Enrico had never seen before. The scene irked him, but what sent him over the edge was walking into his own bedroom and finding Joey in bed with Bianca. She was riding him, reverse cowgirl style, gripping his ankles, facing the door and making fuck faces like a porn star.

"Oh, fuck Daddy, put your thumb in my ass while you beat this pussy," Bianca moaned as she ground her hips into Joey, taking every inch of his big, hard dick.

Enrico was livid as he stood there, frozen. Neither even acknowledged his presence, even though it was obvious they could see him standing there.

"What the hell is going on?" Enrico raged. He felt totally disrespected. Not only was Joey fucking someone else, but in his bed with total disregard for his presence or emotions. He knew right then and there that Joey cared nothing about him.

"Join us," Joey offered, but Enrico knew it was more of a taunt.

Bianca's loud moans and squeals followed him up the hall as he headed back out front, fuming.

Twenty minutes later, Joey came out in his Speedo bathing suit, mingling as if nothing ever happened. Enrico kept imagining that Joey reeked of sex, until all he could smell was the scent of Joey's cum all over everything. He was sick to his stomach.

Joey's mobile phone rang. Enrico was closest, so he answered it.

"Yeah," he said, answering the phone as Joey approached. Then he hung up and told Joey, "It was Sal. He said to tell you, '*congratulations.*'"

Joey smiled and caressed his cheek. "C'mere and say hello to the next Don." Joey pulled Enrico close and kissed him sensually, causing Enrico to tingle all over. He hated that Joey could do that to him so easily.

Joey smiled at him like he could read his mind, and he wore his smile like a taunt. "Everything is going according to plan," Joey winked, then smacked Enrico on the ass and walked away.

Enrico watched him with a hate only love could muster. He had a plan, too—one Joey wasn't planning for—and he contemplated it with a taunting smirk of his own. Enrico picked up the mobile phone and called Paul.

"I'm...I'm going to do it. I'm going to wear the wire."

Joey couldn't remember ever being this nervous. His stomach was doing flips, and he couldn't get there fast enough. He was going to be a Made Man. He dreamt of this day since he was a little kid. Watching the older guys, watching his father and Vito, he idolized their every move. He had played out this day in his mind, over and over. The perhaps greatest thing missing from this fantasy come to life was his father officiating the ceremony. The thought made his heart hurt. But he knew, once he was Made, his father could no longer deny him. He would be a man of respect, worthy of his father's respect.

The trip around Manhattan took two cars and three hours, just to make sure they weren't tailed. An induction ceremony was highly secretive. They ended up at an apartment building in Little Italy. The two men accompanying him escorted Joey upstairs. When he entered the room, there were several guys sitting around the room, including Joe Provenzano and Sal Romano. No one spoke to Joey. Some nodded curtly; others didn't even do that.

Finally, Sal stood up and approached Joey. He looked at him sternly, without a trace of humor.

"Do you know why you are here?" Sal asked.

"No," Joey said, because he knew it was tradition not to know.

"You are going to be a part of this family. Do you have a problem with that?"

"No."

Sal nodded then motioned for Joey's hand. Joey gave him his hand. Sal pricked it with a very sharp dagger. He sprinkled the blood on the card of a Saint, then gave the card to Joey. Joey held it while he lit it then cupped the burning card in his hand.

"Repeat after me: if I should betray my friends," Sal recited.

"If I should betray my friends," Joey echoed.

"I and my soul will burn in hell like the Saint."

"I and my soul will burn in hell like the Saint."

The card stung his hand, but it was worth it. Joey dropped the smoldering ashes, as a wide grin spread across Sal's face.

"Congratulations, kid. Welcome to the family."

"Thanks, Uncle Sally," Joey replied.

The solemnity of the moment over, everyone gathered around Joey, giving him hugs and kisses.

"I knew this day would come," Joe Pro greeted, kissing Joey on both cheeks.

"It's a beautiful day, eh?" Joey announced, smiling proudly.

He had come full circle, from hated homosexual pariah to the newest, celebrated member of one of the oldest traditions in Sicily. Not only was he a Made Man; he was Self-Made Man, and he was proud enough to bask in his own limelight.

PRESENT DAY, AUGUST 1997

The Prosecutor looked hard at Joey.

Joey had a smirk on his face, and was leaned back in his chair next to Rollins like he didn't have a care in the whole damn world. The recess was over, and the Prosecutor was about to wipe that smile off Joey Diamonds' face once and for all.

"Oyez, Oyez!" The bailiff announced, "All rise. The Supreme Court of New York is now in session, the Honorable Judge Hendon Bartholomew presiding."

Everyone in the court rose except Joey. He just slicked back his hair and straightened his tie.

Bartholomew—used to Joey's insolence by now let it pass, showing that he knew rising to the bait would only show that it bothered him. So with a roll of his eyes he sat down and then everyone else sat, except the Prosecutor. "Your Honor, the prosecution would like to call a witness who does not appear on the sheet for today, if it pleases the court."

The judge looked at Rollins. Rollins whispered in Joey's ear, Joey shrugged, and Rollins stood, "No objection here your honor."

The Prosecutor smiled, and "the State calls Ms. Tia Amo Reyes."

Joey sat bolt upright, his face dropping through the floor like a fifty-pound lead weight through plywood. The Prosecutor almost heard the wood splitting.

Te Amo sashayed into the court in a virginal white Versace knee length dress that made her brown skin shine with the inner light of truth. Her eyes were skimming the floor, just ahead of her toes as they clipped to the stand, and the court attendant, holding out the Bible said, "Do you solemnly swear that you will tell the truth, the whole truth, and nothing but the truth, so help you God?"

Te Amo leaned forward, gripping the Bible so tight her knuckles flared, but her voice a near whisper. "I do."

The Prosecutor was going to enjoy this. "Ms. Reyes, can you, for the court, please tell us your relationship to the defendant Mr. Joey Diamanti?"

"We were lovers."

Joey whispered in Rollins ear with some agitation. Rollins nodded and placated Joey with a gesture.

"And, Ms. Reyes, when you say *were lovers*, are we to take from that your relationship ended some time ago?"

"Yes, just before he was arrested. We had a falling out and there has not been a reconciliation. We have not spoken for two years."

The Prosecutor was just warming up now, he walked away from Te Amo, eyeing the gallery, playing to them. When they'd got the notion that he was performing for each and every one of them, he turned back to face the witness stand. "I know Ms. Reyes that you approached the Federal Investigators of your own free will; you weren't part of their investigation I understand."

"That is correct. I had no dealings with Joey's...I mean Mr.

Diamanti's life outside our relationship. He didn't get involved in my business, and I didn't get involved in his."

"I see, it was just a pleasure based relationship?"

"Yes. For the most part. I knew he was bisexual, and that he saw other people, but that didn't concern me."

Joey was bolt upright in his chair, Rollins was putting his hand on his wrist to calm him, turning from the witness's testimony.

"So, I understand however, that you have some evidence that will shed some light on the charges of murder that have been laid against Mr. Diamanti?"

"Oh yes."

Te Amo looked at Joey for the first time, and her eyes were cold. The Prosecutor had to hold his papers in front of his crotch, so the jury couldn't see his hard on.

Joey licked his lips, his fingers drumming on the table in front of him.

"I think my testimony will tell you exactly what kind of man Joey Diamanti is..."

JANUARY 1995

J oey wasted no time in using his Made Man status to whip up a wave of destruction that washed from L.A. to the East Coast, drowning those in its path as it went.

The protection of the Romanos was a gift from the heavens. Not only did it give him a free hand in L.A., as Bone and his crew ran the day to day operations of distributing the X as it came in from Israel, but he had the Piazza soldiers under his command, and was getting a good slice of income from their gambling, girls, and protection scores.

Cleveland was no longer an issue, there was nothing or no one there with the cajones to face up to him, and those that raised their head above the parapet to spit any venom in his direction were removed from the field with extreme prejudice. It felt good to flex his muscles in his new appropriated clothes of underworld respectability.

His father—recovered from the shooting, but now effectively retired—handed over the day-to-day running of the Diamanti family to Frankie Shots, and he was neutered effectively now that Joey was effectively a Romano.

Joey didn't speak to his father, but he no longer felt the need to check with him when he wanted to see or talk to his mother.

Life was good.

Even if Enrico was still a problem, it was one that Joey could deal with when he needed to. The look of jealousy had damped down in his eyes a little, and when he wasn't out of town, he spent all the time he could with Joey. Sitting patiently while Joey conducted business or making himself available for Joey's dick and whatever he wanted to do with it, whenever he wanted to do it.

The only fly in the ointment was Te Amo. Joey was convinced now that she'd known about the hit the whole time. Known when it was coming and that it wouldn't have resulted in any injuries to her or Joey.

The meeting at the funeral had obviously been a set up, and so had the meeting with her mother on the yacht. The Queen of Cocaine had kept her nose out of Joey's business on the West Coast, but perhaps her markets in Miami needed to expand, and what better way to keep a constant flow of information from Joey's activities, than by putting Te Amo into his operation, and have her Blood affiliates do all the legwork?

But Joey couldn't work out why the hit had been set up in the first place. For a lot of the time he considered it had been done by his father, but the revelation that it had been Frankie Shots working on the orders of the Gambino family had come as unwelcome news. But then again, Sal had been his savior. Joey was untouchable now. There could be no further attempted hits on him while he was a Made Man and the Commission had not given their consent.

But this was all material to be dealt with in the future.

Right now, he was in New York, and it amused him to no end to know that he was about to make an offer Joe Pro could not refuse.

The old gangster, his face a mixture of worry and contempt,

sat with his hands on the table. Behind him were two of Cleveland's finest, now in Joey's pocket. Giacomo *The Snake* Sentelli and his cousin Nunzio Basico. Both slightly older than Joey, and who saw where their bread might be buttered in the future. Snake and Zio stood with their palms crossed in front of their suits, heads slightly bowed like Pall Bearers. Joe Pro couldn't have missed the symbolism, especially as they'd brought him to the back room of Joey's club on the Lower East Side, screwed into a coffin that had been slid onto the back of a hearse.

"You cocksucker, Joey."

"It has been known."

"May you burn in eternity," Joe Pro said in Sicilian.

"I hope you enjoyed your ride in the coffin. Gives you something to look forward to in your later years."

"You're not going to kill me, you crazy little faggot."

"That is true."

"Then what's all this for, you dumb fuck? I don't care if you're under the protection of the Romanos, I certainly don't care you're a Diamanti. You have no family because you're a piece of shit, Joey. No one wants you. You're just being used."

"Perhaps. Or maybe I want to get what I want. I don't care, old man. Like you, there is no need for me to care at all. Because one day, you'll be dead. And me? Because I have been charged by the Commission to tell you some facts of life."

The color drained from Joe Pro's face, and his eyes glittered, not with tears but with the dampness of anger and fear.

"What the fuck..."

Joey launched himself to his feet and slapped the old man across the chops.

"Don't speak until you're spoken to!" he screamed, spittle bursting from his mouth and spraying over the old man's cheek as it turned.

"I've killed men for much less," Joe Pro hissed, wiping the back of his hand across his face.

"Just be grateful I'm not killing you."

Joe Pro took a couple of breaths. His hands came back to the table, and he was calm again. Joey was impressed, but he wasn't going to show it.

"That's better. I want to keep this civil if I can."

"So. What's the deal?"

"It's not a deal. It's an instruction."

"Go on."

"Congratulations on your retirement. I'm sorry we don't have a clock for you."

"Retirement?"

"Yes. Go to Florida. Go to Vegas. Go to Timbuktu for all I care, but your time in New York is done."

"On whose authority?"

Joey raised his hand again. Joe Pro didn't flinch.

"Okay okay, it's on your authority. I assume the Commission has nodded this through?"

Joey sat back down. "Of course. You're old, Joe. You're old guard. Things are changing."

"And you're changing them."

"In part, but the millennium is coming, technology is advancing. This thing we do needs men of vision, men not afraid to embrace new alliances, get involved with new product, find new ways to diversify."

"When did you get your MBA?"

Joey smiled. "I just graduated."

Joey reached down under the table, pulled up an attaché case, placed it flat on the table and sprung the locks. It was full of one hundred dollar bills.

"One million..."

"Jeez that's small change. You know how much I'm worth? I don't even know how much I'm worth."

"This morning we took inventory of your account codes, keys to your safes, and the portfolio of legit businesses in your personal collection. I know exactly how much you're worth, Joe Pro, and right now it's one million dollars."

Joe's eyes were wide and filled to the brim with the hottest anger.

"There will be one of these, every six months wherever you decide to settle...away from New York."

"People aren't fired from the Mafia."

"And you're not being fired. Look at it as a chance to spend more time with your money."

"My sons?"

"They have a simple choice: continue running their end of the family, for me and Sal, or they can be retired too. But I hear the benefits aren't as...beneficial. Your final act here in New York will be to tell them of your decision to retire, and that they are to answer to me, until further notice."

"I would rather die."

"And that's why we're keeping you alive."

Sal sucked on a cigar as thick as a baby's thigh, and he sniggered smoke out of his nose. "You took him there in a fucking coffin?"

Joey nodded, his own cigar smoldering between his teeth, "There were flowers too. You sent a wreath. It was very sweet of you."

Sal's mouth exploded a gale of laughter. "I like your style, boy."

"I'm style *and* substance."

"Ain't that the truth?"

Joey took the cigar from his mouth and considered the end like it was a dick he'd just taken from between his lips. Hungry for the taste and the pleasure.

Sal's eyes crumpled a little. However much the boy was

bringing in the cash, he was still not utterly comfortable with Joey's overt expression of his sexuality. Sal was old school, and when Joey made these kinds of gestures, he felt uncomfortable. For a man like Sal, feeling uncomfortable was not a situation he was used to. Joey could see the effect his mouth and cigar were having on the older man.

He knew exactly what he was doing.

"So," Sal coughed, laying down his cigar and getting up from the desk. He went to the window, peering through the blinds over the white expanse of Central Park, frozen in its blanket of fresh snow. "What's next, Joey? You're not the kind of man to rest on his laurels. I know you've got ideas. Let's hear them."

Joey loved the feeling of being drawn further into the Romano circle. Being a Made Man was one thing, but now Sal was looking to him for ideas. It put him into a fine position from which to expand, not only the ambitions of the Romanos but also to advance his own.

"Florida."

Sal turned from the window with a raised eyebrow. "The Trafficantes have Tampa sewn up tighter than a spinster's snatch Joey, and there's balance we don't wanna..."

"Not Tampa, Sal. Miami."

Sal's eyes screwed up like they were caught in a wave of smoke, even though his own cigar was still back on the desk. Joey could see the calculations going on behind Sal's craggy face. Miami was not an area the New York Families had traditionally seen as a place for expansion of business. The Cubans, the Colombians, and the rest of the Hispanic diaspora ran through the city like threads of shit woven into a golden carpet. The X operation Joey had run with Enrico through the Miami airport had been strictly limited, and in the great scheme of things—although profitable in its own way—small potatoes.

To beef up their presence in Miami would not cause ripples, it would generate tsunamis.

Sal raised his hands. "Joey, no. It's not that I don't think you could; it's whether we *should*. You want to start a war? We got things good here in New York and now L.A. The richest time I can remember, and plenty of that is down to you. We don't need the distraction..."

Joey flicked the end of his cigar with his tongue, and Sal looked ever more uncomfortable...but he wasn't going to say anything to the boy.

Joey in turn knew that he wouldn't.

Sal would be happy for Joey to run the operations out West and to contribute to how things were shaping up in New York. In those respects, right now, Joey was irreplaceable. But that might not last forever, so Joey knew he had to press his advantages now while he could. "I'm not going to start a war."

"I don't see how we could move fully into Miami without starting the mother of all conflicts, Joey. Like I said, you have style boy, but you don't want to run before you can walk."

"Sal," said Joey, standing up. "I was born running."

Her skin was golden brown, her body firm and pliable. The white bed sheets were dazzling in Joey's eyes as he pressed down on her shoulder blades and stroked in and out of her warm wetness. The slow rocking of the cabin on the gentle swell of the harbor complimented his rhythm perfectly, making him feel at one with nature in all its glory. He was the swell, he was the shift, and he was the motion.

Her hands reached forward under his weight, grabbing and tugging at the sheets in ecstasy. Joey slid home and held the pressure against her as her body shuddered through the orgasm he'd created. Her head pushed away from the pillow, a throaty purr escaping her lips.

"Joey...I..."

"Shhh," Joey said raking his nails down her spine, causing her back to arc in an ever tauter curve. "Just enjoy it..."

She rolled her head over and around on her neck, as he pressed in harder. The pressure pulsing warmly across his thighs.

Joey cursed inwardly as he felt the moment slipping away from him with a sudden jolt. That unwelcome feeling when the man isn't sure if the erection is sustainable, as if his dick could lose interest and be followed in quick succession by the mind.

A tiny flicker of doubt shivered in his head.

But Joey knew how to deal with this.

He took his left hand from her shoulder blade and pushed the palm gently against the back of her skull, pressing her back down onto the pillow. Muffled sounds of pleasure vibrated against his hand; he hadn't pushed down too viciously, but it had the effect of lifting her desire, and she began grinding her ass back up, rotating her hips.

Joey spat on his fingers and in one practiced movement slid an index finger between his belly and her ass, into the puckered hole above her pussy. She gasped, squirmed a little but accepted the invasion gladly. When Joey shifted, and slid his middle finger in to join the first, there was a small vocalization of surprise, but again she rolled with it. Pushing back, meeting the thrust of his fingers.

When he was in past the second knuckle on both fingers, Joey widened the hole against the resistance of the muscles. Opening her up enough for the next round of their sex.

Joey closed his eyes.

It wasn't the woman on the bed he conjured up in his mind, her legs working wantonly against the mattress, toes curling. It was Enrico.

The attention in his dick came back on point almost immediately as he thought of his erstwhile lover and friend. Enrico was no longer in Joey's orbit.

It was Joey who had pushed him away. Enrico had got crazy and moody over Joey fucking Bianca that day three years ago. Joey was on the verge of becoming Made and Enrico was playing spoiled brat and spurned lover.

Joey kept him around for another few months, but even taking that ass against Enrico's will had lost its allure. Joey didn't need Enrico bitching and carrying on like a jealous teen. So in the end, after the most insane argument as they always were, Joey had told him to get the fuck away from him. He could still work for the family, but he didn't want him in the same bed any more.

Joey knew that in the end he would be cutting off his own nose to spite his face, because Enrico—when he wasn't bitching or whining—was an exceptional lay. But Joey knew he needed to have his focus on consolidating his position. So he had cut Enrico out of his life with extreme prejudice.

He'd not taken any of Enrico's calls, and he'd worked the X end of the business through other parties, who would give Enrico his orders by proxy.

But there were times, like now, as he pushed his dick into the woman's tight ass, when flashes of Enrico would be conjured up from his memory to help with sexual focus. Joey admittedly liked women more in the aesthetic sense, and he could happily fuck them with his head in the right place. But *this* fuck wasn't pleasure. It was business. It wasn't about getting his dick sucked, it was about cementing a deal, and for that Joey needed the image of Enrico.

He needed Enrico front and center in his head.

The woman bucked back, hungrily swallowing Joey's dick to the root. She wanted it hard, and she wanted it fast. In that respect, she was the opposite of Enrico, and so Joey—to replicate what he needed—told her to slow down. "Take it easy baby...I don't want to finish before I have to..."

She groaned and shivered beneath him, but pleasingly did as she was told. Joey made his back strokes long and smooth, as his thrusts built gently.

In Joey's head, Enrico was golden against the same white sheets, sweat pooling in the small of his back, his shoulder muscles bunching, his fingers starred and his ankles bending up to press against Joey's thighs as he always had when they fucked in this way.

Joey could feel the blood rushing hard through his head, his heart was a gunshot, and his loins were full of electricity.

He was nearing the point of no return. On the bed the woman who was Enrico in his head, was orgasming in long, unending shudders of pleasure.

Joey's dick was a piston, the rush building from his nuts to the shaft. Edging up his dick like sap in the Spring, he was on the borderline of a shattering, Enrico-enhanced orgasm himself. He pushed at Enrico in his head, and the woman's back rose as she came, first up onto her elbows, and then onto her hands. Her hair brushing Joey's chest like a summer wind.

"Joey!" the woman screamed.

"Enrico." Joey hissed through his lips.

"Mother?" said Te Amo from the doorway of the cabin. "Mother? What the fuck are you doing with Joey! Joey Diamonds! Get the *fuck* away from my mother!"

PRESENT DAY, AUGUST 1997

J oey had no idea what was going to come out of Te Amo's mouth as she started to speak from the stand.

The courtroom was hushed and expectant.

A surprise witness. A ratcheting up of tension. The Prosecutor looked like all his Christmases had turned up on the same day, tied up with a red silk ribbon.

Te Amo looked amazing, even Joey had to admit that to himself. Like Enrico, he hadn't seen her for a very long time, and the intervening months since she'd surprised him and her mother in the throes of rabid coupling, had if anything made her even more beautiful—and Joey thought with a totally unnecessary stirring in his pants, a lot more like her mother.

As he'd rolled off the Queen of Cocaine in the master bedroom of her yacht to see Te Amo in the doorway—gawping like a guppy caught in a surprise net—Te Amo's hand mechanically reached for the gun she kept in her purse, and her eyes blazed with all the fires of thirteen hells.

Joey had, for one of the only times in his life, been lost for words.

Sophia Reyes, Te Amo's mother had stood up from the bed,

naked, not trying to hide her frame. The juices from her pussy slathering her thighs, she held up her hand and said, "It's business darling. Nothing more."

"Business!?" Te Amo had screamed. Her voice had been so shrill and sharp, that Sophia's bodyguard Joao had bounded into the room, SIG-Saur drawn and ready to off anyone who got in his way. When Joao saw the tableaux of frozen bodies—two naked and one rigid with shock—he'd bent, as if it were the most natural thing in the world, and picked Sophia's robe from the cabin floor, handing it to his boss.

Sophia in turn had kept her eyes on her daughter with an unblinking stare as she put it on.

"I...I don't understand," Te Amo had eventually said, as the color returned to her face, and Joey had managed to pull a sheet across his sagging erection.

Joey had smiled at Te Amo, and shrugged. "Like she said, baby. Just...business."

Sophia hadn't admitted outright to Joey that she'd arranged the fake hit on him and Te Amo, but Joey didn't need her to any more. He'd gotten all the information he needed from Vinnie. But she had conceded that Te Amo had been feeding her information from the moment she'd snagged him at Seth's funeral. It had caused a momentary flash of anger in Joey as they'd sat on the deck of the yacht in the harbor, watching the sun go down over the ocean.

"So you know, I can say the word and Joao will afford you extra ventilation, Joey. You have balls of steel coming here, especially after the way you treated my daughter, but I suppose you wouldn't have made the trip just to get yourself killed."

Joey had raised the Courvoisier to his lips, the gentle spirit kissing his lips with illicit warmth. "I didn't come to be made dead, Sophia. I came to make a deal."

"What makes you think I want a deal? And especially one with you. You can take away the hiss, but you're still a snake."

Joey grinned. "Oh I still have my fangs. Look, we want a better supply of coke in New York. We want a better product, a better deal. We want to run a bigger operation here in your town, and I want it to happen with your blessing."

"You want a lot." Sophia lounged back on the deck sofa, crossing her long legs, kicking off her sandals.

"I do. But I offer a lot in return."

"Go on. I'm all ears."

"To the five families, L.A. is an open city. Any one of them can set up an operation there, and as long as we don't tread on another family's feet, all is good. But if you were to open up business there..."

"I know the rules, Joey. If I did that, there would be a certain amount of, shall we say, consumer resistance?"

"Yes. We'd crush you like a mosquito."

"And...so...?"

"Van Nuys."

Sophia arched an eyebrow.

"It's mine now. When I leave here later, it could be yours."

"On Sal's say so?"

"On mine. Sal has left our operations in L.A. to me. It is my gift to you, for the opportunity to work in and out of Miami in whatever way we choose."

Sophia considered.

She nodded, stood, and began unbuttoning her blouse.

"You don't want to just shake hands?"

Sophia shucked her shoulders out of the material, shook her head and held out her hand. "Where's the fun in only shaking hands?"

Joey stood too and smiled.

But now in the court room there was nothing like a smile crawling across his face. There was an unwelcome twist in his gut, which was being transmitted to his lips.

Te Amo knew where a lot of bodies were buried, and he guessed her turning up to testify meant that she no longer felt bound by whatever version of *Omerta* the Brazilian, Cuban, or Honduran gangs practiced. Maybe Joey fucking her momma's ass had taken a while to percolate; maybe the seed of hate he'd planted that day had grown into a thorny tree of hatred. It was a real shame, because making the deal to cut the Romano family a hefty slice of the cocaine business in and out of Miami—in return for a blind-eye to their relatively small operations and distribution networks in L.A. —would make both the Reyes' and the Romanos a tidy profit.

Te Amo had stalked from the boat without a word, when Joao had made it very clear that he would drop her if she pulled the gun from her purse, even just as a threat. And that had been the last Joey had seen of her.

Until today in the courtroom.

The deal *was* good, the emotional fallout not so much.

But Te Amo, according to Sophia, had left the country for Brazil, and would not be coming back any time soon. Joey didn't even know she was back the in the country until he'd seen her coming into the courtroom.

The Prosecutor approached the stand, he was smiling at Te Amo. Joey could see the smug bastard thought he had something really juicy in his pocket.

The last thing Joey wanted to do was show the world how scared he was now, how heavy the sword of truth that hung above his head, as he waited for Te Amo to cut the string and let it impale him.

"Perhaps, Miss Reyes, you'd like to explain to the court how you are connected to the accused, Mr. Diamanti."

Te Amo licked at her cherry red lips, and her eyes became the whole focus of the room. "Well I'm no longer connected to Joey, I mean Mr. Diamanti. But for some years we were lovers."

The was an audible intake of breath in the room, and even Judge Bartholomew leaned forward in his chair, so that he did not miss a single salacious detail. "Go on," said the Prosecutor.

"I assisted Mr. Diamanti with his business dealings, helped with investments, and provided secretarial support when appropriate."

"His legitimate business dealings?"

"Of course, Sir."

"You were aware that he was a member of the so-called Diamanti and latterly Romano crime families as well?"

"No sir, I was not aware of that at all."

The Prosecutor shifted uneasily on his feet. Joey got the sense that things were not going the way he had thought they were going to go.

"Miss Reyes, I'm afraid..." the Prosecutor began, his fingers working at the lapels of his jacket. But Te Amo was not for being stopped.

"I knew you wouldn't let me take the stand if I told you the truth out there. Not the *whole* truth..."

Judge Bartholomew rapped his gavel on the bench. "Miss Reyes you will answer only the questions you are asked!"

"I'm sorry, Your Honor, but I can't do that!"

Bartholomew banged at the desk again. "Miss Reyes you are in contempt of court!"

"Your Honor, I know that I am, but this court is in contempt of itself! Not only do I have evidence, incontrovertible evidence, that Joey Diamanti is innocent of murder, but that the Prosecutor—the Federal Prosecutor in this court—should not be standing where he is. In fact, I have evidence he should be in jail himself!"

Joey gripped Ray Rollins' arm as Te Amo stared first at the Judge, and then hard at the Prosecutor, who was stepping back as if he'd come across a dangerous dog in a dark alley.

Te Amo raised her finger and pointed at the Prosecutor, and spat her words at him, "The reason he should be in jail, is not only is he a member—a *secret* member, of the Diamanti crime family—but he is also Joey's Diamanti's half-brother!"

L onnie the Weasel had always been a weasel. That's how he got the nickname. He was a pissant little turd, who sucked up to the right people, and pissed on the guys he no longer thought could advance him in the Romano clan.

Sal only kept him around because he would do the dirty jobs. If someone was needed to go through garbage to get a gun that had been thrown after a hit, Lonnie would do it. If someone had to make sure that a body that was rotting in woodland had been dug up by animals, Lonnie would be tasked with making sure the stinking corpse was put back in the ground deeper and covered better.

Only a weasel would take on the dirty jobs, and Lonnie was that weasel. Joey had used him a couple of times out in L.A. to clean up after him, and Lonnie had done a fair job. But it was clear that Lonnie was developing a habit for booze, and his lips were loosening.

"I didn't say nuttin', Joey! On my life!"

Joey slapped Lonnie around the chops and the grey-haired man's head snapped back. Red fingermarks appeared in the pale skin of his cheek, the Miami skyline though the condo window blazed in the dying sun, the windows reflecting golden light. Cars moved thought the streets, as Joey could smell the salt in the air from the sea. Or was it Lonnie's sweat?

He didn't know, and he didn't care.

"Don't lie to me, Lonnie. You were overheard. You think when I called you down here, I wouldn't want to keep tabs on you?"

"Honestly, Joey! I swear. I didn't say nothing. This is all a mistake."

"The only mistake here was the one I made when I trusted you not to shoot your mouth off in a Miami bar about how you were some big shot down from New York to clean up Joey Diamonds' mess."

Joey could see the recognition in Lonnie's eyes, and his whole body seemed to collapse in on itself.

"We need someone who can take their liquor, Lonnie. Not weasels who are trying to impress women with their loose lips."

Lonnie had forgotten that Joey had tied his hands behind his back in the chair, sitting in the middle of the warehouse, because he moved his shoulders as if to raise his hands up and placate Joey.

"Joey, please. Someone spiked my drink. I didn't know what I was saying. The broad! It was her. She spiked my beer. I saw her, Joey. I saw her. After that I didn't know what I was saying!"

"The broad spiked your beer?"

Lonnie nodded vigorously, his bloodshot eyes rattling like slot machine cherries. "Yeah. I bet she works for that bitch Reyes. I bet she was trying to get dirt on you, Joey. Let me go, I'll find her. I'll bring her here. I'll get the truth out of her. You bet I will."

Joey shook his head. "You're pathetic, Lonnie."

"It's the truth!"

Joey punched Lonnie in his ample gut, sending the air rushing from his body like a punctured balloon. "It's not the truth, Lonnie. It's not even in the ballpark of truth. The girl you were with was Gail Rodriguez-Salento. She's on the payroll, Lonnie. I sent her to the bar to hit on you to see if the weasel would squeal."

Lonnie's bleary eyes looked up, what color there was in his skin had left completely now. He was translucent. See through. And Joey was seeing all the way through him.

"No one spiked your drink. You spiked yourself with the drink, and you spilled your guts all over the table. If Gail hadn't been one of ours, I'd hate to think what you may have given away, Lonnie."

Lonnie began to cry. His lips trembled and fat tears grew in bulbs on the end of his hooked nose.

"I...I..."

"You're a liability, Lonnie. You know that right?"

It took all of Lonnie to nod his own head.

"Enrico!" Joey shouted through the doorway into the bedroom.

Enrico appeared in the doorway with Gail. She was petite and raven-haired. She'd come to Joey's operation from Sophia's side of the deal, and she had proven to be a useful addition to his crew in Miami. She was trustworthy, hard-nosed, and knew how to get what she wanted from a man.

"Hello again, Lonnie," she said as she and Enrico approached the sobbing man on the single chair, beneath the single light in the ceiling.

Lonnie's crying was echoing off the walls. He knew it was the end, and he was going to face that end in exactly the way he'd lived his life. Like the weasel he was.

"Is there anything more pathetic than a crying man?" Gail asked as she and Enrico took positions on either side of Joey.

Joey shook his head. "So, who wants to get their hands dirty?"

Gail snorted, but Enrico said nothing. Exactly as Joey thought he would.

Joey turned to Enrico and looked at the man he thought he loved. He pulled a cold pistol from the shoulder holster inside his jacket. Joey held the silver weapon out in the palm of his hand. "Come on, Enrico. It's about time we blooded you, don'tcha think?"

Enrico's face was draining of color almost as fast as Lonnie's had. "I...I...thought...we..." he stammered.

"You thought we were just going to rough Lonnie up, give him a slapping and send him back to Sal?"

"Yeah...I mean...come on...we don't need to..."

"Don't we? But he's betrayed me, Enrico. He's said things to people out loud that he shouldn't have. I need men around me I can trust. If I don't have that trust around me, how can I operate? How can I make the life for myself and you that we want?"

Enrico took a step back, but Joey caught his hand and pulled him back. He put the weapon in Enrico's palm and closed his fingers gently around the grip. Then he lifted Enrico's hand so that the gun was pointing at Lonnie's head.

"Please..." Lonnie whined.

"I...can't...I...." Enrico said.

"Yes you can, my love. You can put a bullet through the weasel's skull and then, when you've done that, you'll be exactly the man I want you to be."

"But...but..." the gun was shaking in Enrico's hand. His face was white; there were tears in the corners of his eyes.

"Christ, not another crying guy," said Gail.

Enrico held the gun away from him like it was a venomous snake, which Joey thought was more than appropriate. "You see, what I'm seeing here is confusing me," Joey began, keeping his eyes tight on Enrico. "You're a Honduran bad boy. You ran guns for the Sandinistas, and you've taken to me like you didn't have a care in the world."

Enrico's hand was shaking so much that Joey was convinced the gun was going to fall from his fingers at any moment. Gail huffed like she was bored and Lonnie sobbed.

The sobbing was getting on Joey's nerves now. "And here you are, unwilling to off this weasel piece of shit. You know what? That makes me wonder why you've become squeamish all of a sudden, Enrico. Is there something you feel you oughta be telling me right now?"

Enrico let the gun slip from his fingers as the terror blossomed in his eyes.

A dark patch of urine appeared on the front of his pants as Joey called behind him. "Paul, you're welcome to come out whenever you want."

Paul—Enrico's Paul, who Joey knew as Mancuso Puglia, one of Sal's most trusted Cleveland Lieutenants—stepped out from a door that led to the condo's balcony.

He was calm and cool in his Armani suit, his shirt was unbuttoned halfway down his chest, and Joey admired the glimpse of a powerful physique behind the material. When they were finished here tonight, he planned to take Manny to his bed and get the bad taste of Enrico's betrayal out of his mouth.

Enrico sank to his knees.

"You wearing that wire now?" Joey asked, stepping forward to pick up the gun from where it lay on the dusty concrete.

Enrico didn't answer. He was already saying as many Hail Mary's as he could cram into his lying mouth.

Lonnie, picking up that things were getting to a climax, sobbed loudly now—not trying to suppress the sound, and so Joey shot the top of his head off.

Lonnie's body slumped in the chair, his brains drooling out of his destroyed skull and slipping past his ear. His eyes were moving, but they were sightless. His shoulders twitched, and his left foot shivered. Like an unwound clock running out of ticks, Lonnie's body eventually came to a stop, and the only sound in the room was the whisper of prayer coming from Enrico's mouth.

Joey went over to the man who had sold him out to the cops. He touched his face gently, and then ran fingers through his hair.

"Like Gail was for Lonnie, Paul was for you Enrico," Joey sighed. "I knew you were pissed about Bianca, but you should have worked harder to get over that. The rewards I would have given you eventually would have made anything else you agreed to with the Feds, pale into insignificance."

Joey looked up to the ceiling, still cradling Enrico's head. "You see, the cops you spoke to... They're my cops. They cost me a lot, but they're worth every penny to test out those of whom I am suspicious. I wanted to think you were a safe bet, Enrico, I really did. But, like Lonnie the Weasel there with his loose mouth, your loose balls have been your downfall. Right up to the end there, I wanted to believe that you wouldn't have really gone through with it. But there's no way you could commit murder, even if you weren't wearing that wire, huh? That's the one sure way of me finding out where your heart truly lies."

Enrico's whispered prayer ended, and he hissed a tearful "Amen."

Joey didn't look down as he broke Enrico's neck with one savage twist of his hands. The crack of neck bones shattering added a final and defining closure to the sounds in the room.

If Joey listened hard enough, he could hear the cars shushing by on the freeway as the night finally reached the city.

He could still smell the salt in the air.

PRESENT DAY, AUGUST 1997

T he case collapsed there and then.

Joey was freed from the court in a blur of camera flashes, yelling reporters, and dark looks from the court officials. The Prosecutor was hustled away by his team and the cops, as the watchers in the gallery—almost to a man and woman, supporters of Joey Diamonds—began cat-calling, laughing, and jeering. No amount of gavel bashing from the Judge could quiet them down. The uproar continued to ring in Joey's ears as he was propelled from the court into a waiting limo, where he bounced onto the leather seat, and settled, breathless next to the serene, smiling Te Amo.

The limo slid away from the courthouse like a shark, into the teeming waters of New York City traffic. Joey was still trying to put his thoughts in some order, as Te Amo passed him a flute of chilled champagne and lay back in her seat, laughing.

Joey drank the slow bubbling liquid, and enjoyed the feeling as the cold worked its way down into his belly. It didn't dampen the fire within, but it was an instructive portent of the cold revenge he would take on those who had put him in this position.

"He's my *brother*?" Joey knew saying that was going to take some getting used to.

Te Amo shook her head, "Half-Brother. The Prosecutor Steven Rein, is actually...to give him his full name, Leoluca Cardinale. He was the product of an affair your father had in Calamonaci, Sicily while your mother was nursing you in New York."

Joey blinked. "This makes no sense."

"It makes perfect sense. Leoluca was a secret, he was raised a secret. Your father paid for his education, and when the time was right, a new identity. He was brought to the U.S. and sent to the best schools—the best *law* schools—and he was kept entirely separate from the family. But, and this is the important thing, still close to your father. What better resource to have for one of the five families than a Prosecutor who would work for your best interests? He rose through the ranks, gained a reputation for taking down Mafia soldiers. If you look at his records, the majority of them were from rival families of the Diamantis. Of course your father would throw Rein a succession of low level goons to keep up appearances, but nothing that would affect the upward mobility of the Diamantis."

The rush from the courtroom to the limo was making all of this hard to take in. Joey's whole life had been a parallel to Leoluca's—where he had been schooled in the ways of the Mafia, its rituals, and workings, his half-brother had been guided through the legitimate world to an unparalleled position of influence.

The shock running through him was riding a wave of anger at his father's betrayal of his mother, as well as skimming across the relief of the court case collapsing in the most dramatic fashion imaginable. Joey was a stew of conflicting emotions, bubbling in every direction.

Te Amo must have seen the complex look of disbelief on his

face, because she took that moment to reach across the back seat and kiss him full on the mouth.

Immediately he could taste the tingle of cocaine on her lips, dusted into her lipstick. There was a thin crust of it on her tongue too that was mingling with his spit and the residue of champagne. The burst of it in his mouth lit up his head, and he kissed and pawed at her with all the hunger he could muster. She was grappling with the front of his trousers as their lips were crushed. Breath coming in snorts and grunts.

They were animals, bucking and crashing against each other on the white leather. As Te Amo unleashed Joey's dick, she hiked up her dress and straddled him without taking her lips from his.

He slid deep into her easily. She was ready, open, warm, and wet around him. She began her rise and fall, biting on his tongue and running her fingers through his hair—yanking on it, tearing her lips away, and forcing his face into her cleavage. He could smell Chanel and fresh perspiration, her hair falling about his ears, her hands pushing his head harder into her body.

Te Amo was back in his arms. Could this day have gotten any more bizarre? He hadn't seen her for years and thought that part of his life had been over for good after she'd found him with Sophia. But time heals as they say, and she felt good on his dick. Like she had been made for him.

He was lost in her now. All sense and sensibilities were gone in the moment. He could deal with his half-brother later. He could deal with his father later. He could deal with the fallout from the court case later.

Right now, all he wanted to do was deal with this.

"Te Amo," he said to her warm flesh and caressing hands, "I'm so glad you're back in my life, and I'm back in you."

Te Amo giggled, pushed down hard on his lap, and ground her hips from side to side.

Joey was close to the finish now. The sense that a cliff edge was approaching, one that he would willingly leap from and fill her pussy with his seed. He raked at her back with his fingernails, not caring if the material was ripped. He would buy her a dozen more, a thousand more.

It didn't matter. All that he cared about in that moment was the feeling of her around him, the weight of her body on his thighs and the taste of her body through the coke and the champagne.

It was a moment like no other he had every experienced. It was triumph incarnate. It was winning. It was...

Cold air rushed in the limo with a stink of garbage and a throaty growl of someone bodily exerting himself. A fist came out of nowhere and clattered into the side of Joey's skull, sending him crashing into the door pillar on the other side of the limo.

Rough hands gripped Joey and yanked him out from under Te Amo.

"Hey!" was all he could manage to say before he was dragged from the vehicle and thrown onto the damp concrete. The place was cold, and in the hot August of New York, a shock to Joey's body. It wasn't the welcome chill of air conditioning; it was dank and rancid, like they were underground in a place vagrants might use as a toilet. The concrete beneath him reeked of dirt and piss. There was a sheen across the surface of the thin coating of mud that could have been oil. Whatever it was, it was going to ruin his suit, but Joey had more pressing things to worry about as a boot flashed out of nowhere and caught him in the guts.

The pain was a starburst of agony that rolled him into a ball, expecting another blow that didn't come. Joey breathed shallowly, holding his arms across his stomach, not daring to look up.

How could he have been so lax?

He couldn't even remember who had propelled him towards the limo down the steps of the courthouse. His thoughts were so jumbled and incoherent after Te Amo's revelations and the eruption in the court.

He hadn't taken in who was driving the limo, his eyes were completely locked on Te Amo on the back seat. And when she'd filled his mouth with cocaine and champagne, he'd lost all sense of where the limo was headed.

With Te Amo across his thighs—pulling his head into her breasts, forcing his eyes against her skin—he didn't have any sense of the limo coming here, to a place that out of the heat of the day, must have been an underground garage. The echoes of footsteps around him, told him the place was large, but almost entirely empty.

"Open your eyes, you pig."

It was Te Amo.

Joey opened his eyes, looking up at the woman who just moments before he'd been fucking like a bitch in heat. She'd pulled her dress down, and was pulling her hair back to tie with a band as she looked down on him with utter contempt.

"For a bright boy you can be so stupid sometimes," she said, letting her hands fall from her hair to fold over her breasts.

Te Amo was so close, Joey could have reached out and touched her, but he dare not. Standing next to her like a wall that had grown legs and stretched a suit across its bricks was Joao. Joao was the bodyguard who had come thumping down the stairs in the yacht when he'd heard the commotion of Te Amo screaming at the sight of Sophia's ass being pummeled by Joey.

Joao wasn't armed, but his jacket was off, the sleeves of his white shirt were rolled up, and the top two neck buttons were undone. His fists were bunched and ready.

"Make one move to get up and I will put you down again,"

Joao spat, muscles in his forearms working and pulsing as he bunched his fists.

Joey was in no position to move. His guts were on fire, his head was swimming from where he hit the limo's door pillar.

"I've waited a long time to see you groveling in the dirt."

A different voice. A woman, her voice smoky and rich. Dripping with hate.

Sophia Reyes.

Te Amo's mother walked around from behind Joey, all red heels, red dress, and wild hair. Unlike Joao she was armed. A gold-plated Desert Eagle hung in her right hand, her finger in the trigger guard.

"It took us three months to find his body! Three months!"

There have been so many bodies, it took Joey a few moments to flick though his mind's rolodex to settle on who Sophia must have been talking about. It was obvious once he'd settled on the name.

Enrico.

Joey, Gail, and two soldiers had taken Enrico and Lonnie's bodies from the condo and buried them in a densely wooded area in A.D. Barnes Park—a sixty-five acre tropical city park in central Miami. They didn't have time for anything else. Joey needed to be elsewhere fast.

Either Gail or the soldiers had spilled the location of the body. Perhaps through torture, perhaps through traitors. Joey wished he'd put a bullet in all their heads as insurance, but it was too late to worry about that now.

A thick gob of spit hit Joey full in the face from out of the darkness. O'Ryan stepped forward into the pool of light cast by the ceiling fluorescents in the underground garage.

O'Ryan had happily testified to the Prosecutor, and Joey could smell the stink of a grudge about him. Perhaps carelessness on Joey's part had cost the cop his job and his honor.

Perhaps not. But he was here now, and his opening gambit had been to spit in Joey's eye.

"Turning into a regular get together," Joey said, looking at the people who hated him.

Joao kicked him in the guts again.

Joey rolled in the dirt. Gritting his teeth.

"One thing I don't get," he said as he caught his breath and blinked the tears of agony from his eyes, "How did you find out about Leoluca? The Prosecutor? If his real identity and position was such a tight secret...who knew to blab?"

Joey knew he had to play for time. If he was going to get out of this alive—and it was looking increasingly like he wouldn't —then he had to delay whatever they had planned for him long enough to at least get enough strength to make a fight of it.

There was only one gun—that he could see—and Sophia was holding that. If she came close enough to kick it out of her hand...maybe...maybe there was...

"Frocio!"

Another voice from behind him. A voice he'd known his whole life.

Vincenzo. His father.

Vincenzo Diamanti, dressed in the chauffeur uniform he'd worn to drive Joey and Te Amo into this concrete kill zone, stepped around Joey's frozen form.

"Not only are you a fuckin' *Frocio* but you sold out your family to Sal fuckin' Romano. I curse the day my wife spat you out of her cunt. You have soiled my name, my reputation, and my family."

Joey couldn't find words. His throat was stilled with shock now.

"Leoluca couldn't be more different than you Joey, except in one important respect: he's as greedy as you," Vincenzo explained. Pulling a small Beretta from a hip holster, he checked it, snapping the mag out and back in, and flicking off the safety with his thumb. "He went to Sal Romano and offered him the same deal for their family, as he had with his own. Like you he'd gotten too big for his boots, Joey. Must run in my genes, eh? I'm sure he'll survive six maybe seven months in jail. We'll just give him the idea that he's not gonna be whacked and then...kaboom."

Vincenzo winced as he knelt down beside Joey, his steely eyes still those of a young buck full of spunk and raw power. The craggy face around those eyes may have given away his true age, but Joey could see in his father the thrill of the approaching kill. His lips were parted so his quickening breath could move freely, a pulse throbbed in his neck showing how his heart rate was up.

Joey knew these feelings all too well. He was his father's son.

"And so, like you, Leoluca had to be dealt with. Sure it's going to put the heat on the Diamanti name for a while, but I've spent the last five years making contingencies for today, Joey. You won't see the day out, but the family you've dragged through the dirt will. The Reyes too. They're here for retribution and revenge as well. Sophia's daughter, disrespected in the most appalling fashion, and Enrico—who was like a son to Sophia—killed by your own hand. You've stacked up more enemies than a man could reasonably expect to outrun, son. And today is the day we've decided to catch up with *you*."

Vincenzo lifted the Beretta and placed it against Joey's forehead.

"Pop...please."

Vincenzo shook his head. "Don't beg, Joey, be a man. Do something right for me. Just one thing. Be a man. It's your very last chance."

Joey looked into his father's eyes. The eyes of the man who

was about to end his life. It was like looking into the face of God.

And so he began to pray.